KINGDOM

OF

FAEWOOD

KRISTA STREET'S
SUPERNATURAL WORLD

Fae of Woodlands & Wild

Kingdom of Faewood
Veil of Shadows
Queen of Fate

Fae of Snow & Ice

Court of Winter
Thorns of Frost
Wings of Snow
Crowns of Ice

Supernatural Standalones

Beast of Shadows

Supernatural Curse

Wolf of Fire
Bound of Blood
Cursed of Moon
Forged of Bone

Supernatural Institute

Fated by Starlight
Born by Moonlight
Hunted by Firelight
Kissed by Shadowlight

Supernatural Community

Magic in Light
Power in Darkness
Dragons in Fire
Angel in Embers

Links to all of Krista's books may be found on her website:

www.kristastreet.com

Kingdom of Faewood

OF

Faewood

FAE OF WOODLANDS & WILD

BOOK 1

KRISTA STREET

WELCOME TO THE FAE LANDS

Kingdom of Faewood is book one in the *Fae of Woodlands & Wild* trilogy, which is a slow-burn, fae fantasy romance.

This book takes place in the fae lands of Krista Street's *Supernatural World*. Although Krista's other fantasy and paranormal romance books also feature the fae lands, the *Fae of Woodlands & Wild* series is entirely separate so may be read before or after her previous series.

N

S

THE

SILTEN

Nelive Sea CONTINENT

GLOSSARY

Kingdoms of the Silten Continent

Faewood – southeast kingdom, colors are turquoise, white, and dark brown. Elowen's kingdom. Magic is elemental.

Ironcrest – southwest kingdom, colors are silver, magenta, and dark orange. Magic is sensory.

Mistvale – northwest kingdom, colors are bright yellow, dark purple, and deep red. Magic is mental.

Stonewild – northeast kingdom, colors are forest green, gold, and sapphire blue. Jax's kingdom. Magic is shifting.

Seas of the fae lands

Adriastic Sea – the ocean to the west of the Nolus continent and to the east of the Silten continent.

Brashier Sea – the most northern ocean in the fae lands, large icebergs often present.

Nelive Sea – the ocean to the west of the Silten continent.

Tala Sea – the ocean to the south of the Solis continent.

Fae races

Silten fae – the Silten fae reside on a continent surrounded by ocean. Silten fae have numerous subspecies. The Silten species that is considered most powerful are the *siltenites*. Siltenites have bodies like humans, pointed ears, and varying skin and hair shades. The other Silten fae subspecies are called *wildlings*. Wildlings have primitive Old Wood magic, which connects them to aspects in nature. Wildlings typically have animalistic features: horns, scales, hooves, and tails, yet are often as intelligent as siltenites. Wildlings that don't reside in cities, usually live in underground dens, hollow logs, or wooded forests. Silten fae ages vary based upon their subspecies, but siltenites live thousands of years.

Solis fae – the Solis fae reside on the icy, most northern continent of the fae lands planet. Solis fae have silvery white hair, crystalline blue eyes, and wings. They typically live for thousands of years.

Nolus fae – the Nolus fae reside on the central continent. They often have various shades of colorful hair, pointy teeth, glowing skin, and otherworldly strength. They typically live two to three hundred years, but royal Nolus fae live for thousands of years.

Lochen fae – the Lochen fae reside on a southern continent, islands, and in the seas throughout the fae lands. They can morph into fish-like creatures, similar to mermaids, but they can also walk on two legs and live on land. There are subspecies of Lochen fae who live in fresh-water rivers, lakes, and ponds. The Lochen fae typically have green eyes and varying skin shades and hair colors.

<u>Silten Fae Wildling Species</u>

Beemi – a small wildling fae with yellow eyes that lives in the Wood. More animal than fae, with less intelligence than other wildlings.

Cerlikan – a small wildling with large eyes and a furry body. Highly intelligent and capable of language. They live in dens in the Wood and have an intricate community in which their chatter often fills the Wood with sound.

Fusterill – a huge monstrous wildling fae, with the strength of a giant.

Grundle – a wildling fae species who commonly works in serving jobs if they live in cities. They have hard scales on the backs of their body, furry eyebrows, and stubby fingers tipped in claws. They also molt like reptiles.

Half-breed – half-breeds are Silten fae of siltenite and wildling descent. They are able to procreate at a faster rate than siltenites, and some half-breeds are magically powerful. Because of this, procreating among siltenites and wildlings is against the law. Half-breeds that do come into existence are shunned in the Silten culture.

Iloseep – a wildling similar to a large rat with an excellent sense of smell.

Ramifin – a wildling fae with hooves who walks on two legs. Has a snout like a horse, but is able to speak and has high intelligence.

Siltenite – Elowen's species, considered the superior species among the Silten fae due to their appearance being most similar to the Nolus, Solis, and Lochen fae, and their ability to harbor and wield powerful magic. The siltenites have human-like bodies and a varied range of hair, eye, and skin color. They usually live thousands of years.

Wildling fae – fae of the Silten continent who aren't siltenites. Each wildling species has some animalistic trait or feature. Intelligence along with language abilities vary among the wildlings.

Yewen – a wildling with a long trunk that they often use to play music. Most yewens are musically adept.

Fae Terms

Calling – the term used when Elowen travels to the Veiled Between to interact with the semelees on another's behalf.

Full season – equivalent of one year.

Kingsfae – the law of the land in the four kingdoms, similar to police, and commanded by the kings.

Lady – a noble title for a female fairy.

Lorafin – a female siltenite who possesses rare magic. Lorafins can venture to the Veiled Between. This is where the semelees reside.

Lordling – a noble title for a male fairy.

Salopas – a fairy version of a bar with no serving staff. There is a bartender and magically enchanted trays that serve patrons.

Semelees – all-knowing shadow creatures that live in the Veiled Between. They are neither dead nor alive, yet they are able to be commanded by lorafins.

Veiled Between – a plane of space between universes that is neither a realm of the living or the dead but rather an alternate reality in between.

Fae plants and food

Babbo tree – a tree with a very wide base and thick branches. It's a common tree on the Silten continent.

Barnbrambles – a thorny bush with spikes as sharp as needles.

Bolum – a creature that's part animal and part rock that lives in the Shadow Valley of Stonewild. If fae fall into them, they're often eaten, although it takes the bolum weeks to digest them.

Cottonum – a plant similar to cotton.

Femeral bush – a bush in the Wood, with wide velvety leaves that hold a pungent scent.

Goldling tree – a magical tree whose golden leaves can create priceless metals and gems from simple rocks or bricks.

Leminai – a bright-green alcoholic drink common throughout the fae lands.

Saggerwire – a common shrub in the Stonewild desert. The center of its leaves holds water.

Wintercrisp fern – a plant on Stonewild's royal crest and a leaf that symbolizes trust and strength.

Fae animals

Brommel stag – a stag or deer-like creature that can run so swiftly hardly any fae can hunt them.

Colantha – a large cat that resides in jungles.

Dillemsill – a messenger bird whose magic allows it to travel instantaneously throughout the realm.

Domal – an animal similar to a horse but more intelligent.

Ice bear – a large bear with six-inch claws and a naturally white furry coat, which stands eight feet tall on two legs. An ice bear's coat can change color to match its surroundings.

Ustorill – a wild animal that lives in the forest, similar to a boar.

PRONUNCIATION GUIDE

Names

Elowen – Ell-oh-when

Jax – Jacks

Alleron – Al-err-on

Lillivel – Lill-ih-vell

King Paevin – Pay-vin

Mushil – Moo-sheel

Esopeel – S-oh-peel

Messepire – Mess-eh-pyre

Himil – Him-ill

Serinity – Ser-en-it-ee

Phillen – Fill-enn

Trivan – Triv-en

Lars - Larz

Bowan – Boe-en

Lander – Land-err

Malimus – Mal-ih-muss

Valorus – Val-or-us

Saramel – Sarr-uh-mell

<u>Fae Races</u>

Solis – Saw-liss

Nolus – Naw-luss

Lochen – Lock-uhn

Silten – Sill-tun

KINGDOM
OF
FAEWOOD

CHAPTER 1

My calendar hung on the wall of my bed chambers, and I tallied the remaining days and months until I was free.

Only one full season, eight months, and eleven days until my freedom is won.

A small smile spread across my lips, and a sense of determination slid through me. The *calling* this afternoon would be exhausting, but I'd likely fall into a deep sleep afterward, which meant the day would pass even faster. Then, I would be one day closer to the day that marked my freedom—the day my collar was removed and the supernatural courts deemed me safe to decide my own fate, making me a slave no more.

"Look at all this fuss," my lady's attendant called from across the room. She stood at the window, watching the activity across the valley as the curtain swirled around her.

My grin grew as humid air and a warm breeze brushed

across my cheeks. I slashed a mark through the previous day on my calendar, then joined her at the window.

Across the valley, atop the largest hill, the palace waited. The soaring white stone walls of the king's residence shone like ivory in the sun, and beyond that, the distant buildings from the capital shimmered near the Wood's edge.

But my attention focused on the land near the palace grounds. A huge section of the Wood had been cleared for the Centennial Matches. Fences stood half-erected. Partly constructed mazes resembled piles of firewood. Circular arena floors waited for sand to fill them. Most fae in our kingdom were eagerly anticipating the Matches.

"Have you watched any of this today, Elowen?" Claws tipped each of Lillivel's fingers, and they flashed in the morning sunlight when she clasped her hands behind her back. "They're nearly done with all of the construction for the Matches, from the looks of it. It's hard to believe in only a month they'll begin."

"I've watched a bit. It's hard not to when they wake me up each morning." I gazed out the window at her side. "Looks like the stadium is finally complete, but those buckets of sand look heavy."

"The poor dears." Lillivel sighed. "Such a struggle."

I winced. "I have to say I agree." The monstrous stadium being erected was constructed of wood and stone, and it would be a miracle if the wildling fae hauled all of the sand inside before the Centennial Matches' Final selection process began next week. "That looks near impossible to finish."

Lillivel released another sigh. "If only King Paevin would call in a siltenite from Mistvale Kingdom, then all of the work could be done so quickly with telekinetic magic." Lillivel frowned, her furry brows drawing together.

I snorted quietly. "I doubt King Paevin's ego would allow him to request help from another kingdom."

The king had hired wildling fae to construct all of the equipment and buildings needed for the Centennial Matches, but their kind only harbored Old Wood magic, which was primitive at best and varied in strength depending upon their wildling subspecies. But no wildling fae were like siltenite fae —my kind—which were entirely magical.

I gave the far-away wildlings a sympathetic look, and unconsciously, my fingers strayed to the collar encircling my throat. Like the wildlings, I was also in a position of service. I ran a fingertip along the cool metal, and a hum of magic washed along my skin before I dropped my wandering hands to my sides. "I hear the competitors are all arriving in the coming week for the Finals." I angled my head toward Lillivel, having to look down since she barely came to my elbows.

She hummed low in her throat. "I heard the same. It would be most rewarding to watch the Finals. They're not nearly as crowded as the actual Matches once the true competitions begin, and from what I remember of the last Centennial

Matches a hundred summers ago, the strongest fae in our kingdom came to compete. How magnificent to be a spectator."

My eyebrows shot up. "You got to watch the last Matches?"

"Oh, no, no. Nothing like that. Even though I was alive at the last one, it was in Ironcrest, and the journey was too great. I missed the traditional Ironcrest Ball as well." When I cocked my head at her, she added, "The Ironcrest Ball is held after the Centennial Matches conclude. All fae throughout the kingdoms are invited to the grand party. It's a huge outdoor event and lasts for three days. But I missed that in addition to the Matches. Such a pity." Her expression turned wistful. "But attending a Match this time around would be an entertaining sight to behold. That is for certain."

"Then you should go. This one is so close. You can't pass up the opportunity, even if we don't make it to the ball afterward. Surely, Guardian Alleron will be fine with it."

Her lips curved, parting her snout. "I suppose I should, and *you* should too. There's no reason we both can't venture to a Match on a day off. But enough of that. We best get to work. Come, Elowen, your hair needs to be done before you leave." Lillivel bustled to my vanity and patted the stool. "Have a seat. Guardian Alleron wants to leave within the hour since the king's expecting you by high noon. We best stop procrastinating."

At the mention of my upcoming calling, a stirring of my

lorafin magic roiled within me, cooling my blood. But just as fast, a hum along my collar rushed over my skin, dousing the internal shadows that wanted to rise. The momentary war of power between my inner magic and wrestling collar halted my steps.

"Elowen?" Lillivel called again.

I lurched forward. "Sorry. Coming." I went to the stool and hastily sat.

Lillivel's face scrunched up in concentration while she worked through my long chestnut-brown hair with a barrage of pins and clips.

Sunshine streamed through the windows lining my chamber's eastern wall and shone on the hard scales covering the backs of her hands. Her scales shimmered in color, changing from rustic beige to burnt orange and then pearly white, depending upon which angle the light hit them.

Unlike Lillivel, I hadn't been born with scaled skin, a snout, or furry eyebrows, not as all *grundles* were. Nor did I sport horns, a tail, talons, or any other feature the wildling fae species had.

But a part of me yearned to know the realm as the wildlings did. Despite their animalistic traits, they had higher rates of fertility. Lillivel had a dozen children and just as many siblings.

But I only had my guardian. My blood family was long gone.

My heart squeezed, the feel of an arrow striking it. I'd

never learned who my blood family was or why they'd left me, and a fresh rush of hurt washed through me, just as it always did every time I thought of them.

Maybe they had a good reason for abandoning you, Elowen. Maybe they died, and that's why you were found alone as a babe in the Wood.

Frowning, I gazed at my reflection, not for the first time wondering if my mother had looked like me.

Pale skin, bright-green eyes, and siltenite fae-tipped ears stared back at me in the mirror. Already half of my sun-kissed brown hair was pinned up.

I ran a hand over my lower stomach, right where I bore my shadow mark—the mark that signified I was a lorafin. According to Guardian Alleron, *that* was the reason my family had abandoned me.

I sighed with impatience. *If only I could ask the semelees, then I would know the truth.* I took a deep breath. *You can soon. In one full season, eight months, and eleven days, you can ask them after you've gained your freedom and your collar's removed. Everything you've ever wanted to know will be revealed.*

My fingers curled into my palms as I thought of that day. Without my collar, I would be able to access all of my magic and perform a calling for *me* since the collar would no longer be suppressing my lorafin abilities. But before being allowed to do that, I would have to prove to the courts that I wouldn't be a danger to others.

Stars Above, I hope I can do that.

"There we are." Lillivel patted my shoulders. "All done."

I angled my head to take in the design. All of my hair was artfully coiled around my head, leaving my throat exposed and drawing one's attention to the gold collar locked upon my neck. At its center, a purple stone—a gem mined in a foreign land—sparkled in the sunlight.

A long, sleeveless cobalt-blue ball gown hugged my frame. It was one of my finer gowns, with its endless silk and tiny stitching barely visible, yet nothing less was expected when meeting with the king. Guardian Alleron had it crafted for such an occasion, and the Goddess knew he always strived to impress royalty.

I angled my head more. "You make me look much more beautiful than I ought to." And I meant every word of that. Lillivel had learned in school how to arrange hair and apply makeup, which ultimately had landed her the position as my attendant.

Lillivel dipped her head. "You do flatter me, Elowen, but it's easy when you've been blessed with such beauty."

"Hardly. Any beauty I have is due to my lorafin magic and you being *very* good at your job." I stood, then spared one last glance out the window.

Banners now hung from the stadium spires, proudly displaying our kingdom's colors. Flashes of turquoise, brilliant white, and deep brown waved in the sun as the wildlings scurried around the structure. Trees, vines, and colorful fluttering leaves of the Wood filled the rolling hillside just beyond it.

"Good luck, Elowen," Lillivel added as I reached my chamber's door. "I'll see you tonight when you return. I'll have your bath ready."

"Thank you." I bobbed my head before heading into the hall. "Bye, Lil."

THE TWO GUARDS who Guardian Alleron insisted accompany me wherever I went followed me down the stone corridor of my guardian's massive estate. Even though we were inside, my guardian still didn't let me wander freely. Guardian Alleron always prepared for the worst, and considering many lordlings would love to steal me away and claim ownership of me, I couldn't blame him.

But a small smile tilted my lips because I also suspected his protectiveness was due to the fact that he loved me and couldn't bear to part with me . . . even if he never admitted to that.

My slippers barely made a sound as I glided down the halls. Paintings and tapestries hung on the walls, and open windows allowed the summer's warmth to flow through the multitude of corridors.

"Did you hear the Dark Raider was sighted in Faewood

yesterday?" Zale called over my head to Mushil, the guard on my other side.

"I heard." The older guard shrugged, looking unimpressed. "Our wards won't allow him in. Let him come."

"I heard whisperings yesterday as well that the Dark Raider had been spotted," I chimed in.

Zale scoffed, then curled his lip. "It's the first time anyone's seen him in months. I thought perhaps the bastard finally met the end he deserves."

I made a noncommittal noise, but secretly, I hoped the Dark Raider was able to bypass whatever wards he encountered. Taking from the rich and giving to the poor seemed like a noble action to me, especially if he only took from the rich lordlings rumored in our kingdoms to be the most despicable and abhorrent of them all.

"Did you get enough rest last night, Elowen?" Mushil asked as I mentally counted the halls, looking for the one I needed. "Sounds like you're going to have a busy afternoon."

Busy afternoon? I eyed him curiously, only to find the older guard frowning. Uneasiness slithered through me, but I replied, "I got enough. I'll be fine."

Zale smirked. "If you say so."

I glared at him, the usual annoyance I felt around my younger guard surfacing, but I entwined my fingers together and forced myself to ignore the coiling in my stomach.

Returning my focus to the hallways, I swerved tightly

when I finally reached the correct one, which caused me to inadvertently bump into Mushil.

"Sheesh, Elowen. You nearly knocked me to the ground," he grumbled, but a teasing smile lifted his lips.

"Sorry." I laid a hand on his forearm. Unlike Zale, Mushil never exerted his strength over me or seemed to take enjoyment in exacting his control.

He patted my hand. "'Tis all right."

I smiled brightly at him. "One of these days, I'll know my way around entirely and will stop bumping into you."

He chuckled. "As we all will."

Zale puffed his chest up. "I already know every hall and chamber, unlike you slow-learning lot."

Mushil sighed, not commenting, but I didn't even bother trying to hide my eye roll. Guardian Alleron had only moved all of us into Emerson Estate two weeks ago, after we'd been living in a temporary home the months prior to his estate being constructed. All of us were still getting used to the monstrosity of this place, even if Zale was too prideful to admit it.

"Ah, there it is!" I finally spotted my destination ahead and proceeded down the stairs to the large and grand entryway. On the first floor, just off the foyer, my guardian's study door was open.

I heard him before I saw him, and I hastily checked my hair and smoothed my gown before I presented myself to the male I considered my father.

Head held high, I followed the sound of Guardian

Alleron's silky tone. It carried from his private quarters into the massive foyer. "Yes, we shall be there shortly, Your Majesty."

"And she can do three callings today? You're sure of it?" King Paevin asked in a demanding tone.

My footsteps froze.

Zale chuckled and leaned down. "Told you that you'd need to be rested," he whisper-hissed into my ear.

I flared my nostrils at him but stayed rooted to the spot and listened. *Three callings?* Goddess Above. I hoped I'd misheard my guardian. Surely, he wouldn't ask that of me. He knew how impossible that was.

"She's never done that many at once before," Guardian Alleron replied, and some of the nerves in my stomach calmed until he added, "but I have no doubt she'll be able to."

Stars! He's serious. He actually just promised that.

"Hmm, so this shall be an experiment in a way?" the king replied in an unimpressed tone. "I do hope she'll be able to perform. Lordlings Messepire and Himil both agreed to my terms on the Osterland Exchange with the understanding they'd each be given a calling. They're counting on your lorafin being able to venture to the Veiled Between for them. Not to mention, I would like my own calling as well, now that the necessary time has passed since the last one."

"Of course, Your Majesty. Elowen will be able to perform. I'll make sure of it."

My magic swelled, but a sting of warning from my collar

rushed over my body like a coating of armor, quelling whatever power tried to rise from my emotional response. Apparently, I was to do three callings today after all—I hadn't misheard—and for two lordlings I'd never met before on top of that.

I froze as a memory of a calling with a lordling I never wanted to see again stirred in my mind. Lordling Neeble's calling had been thrust upon me as well, and he'd—

"You know, I never asked you . . ." The king's tone turned curious. "How long have you had her? If I'd known a lorafin had been born within my kingdom, I would have sought her out myself."

My guardian laughed lightly. "If it appeases you, I didn't find Elowen here. I was in Ironcrest Kingdom when I happened upon her many summers ago. She was just a babe when I found her in the Wood. She'd been abandoned, only a thin blanket covering her. My guess is as soon as her mother saw her mark, she fled, not wanting the responsibility that comes with raising such a creature."

My entire body tensed, causing my collar to electrify again.

Zale hissed when a zap jumped to him. Rubbing his arm, he growled, "Onward, Elowen. Quit stalling. He's waiting." As if to make his point, he shoved me.

I lurched forward, tripping on my gown, and I would have fallen if Mushil hadn't grabbed me in time to stop my forward movement.

"Zale," Mushil hissed. The older guard loosened his hand

and let go of me completely once my balance had righted. "Don't push her around. You know how I feel about that."

But instead of apologizing, my younger guard just shrugged. "She's always trying to delay her callings. I'm sick of it."

Trembling from my near fall, I smoothed my gown and gave Mushil a nod of thanks, but I completely ignored Zale. The bastard loved to torment me, and when I verbally reacted to his physical shoves or slaps, he seemed to delight in it, so I'd learned summers ago not to.

Holding my head high once more, I clasped my shaking hands and finally stepped into my guardian's view.

Guardian Alleron sat at his wide desk. Rows of books lined the shelves behind him, and a globe of our realm, showing the four large continents and the multitude of islands in the seas, sat on his desk's corner.

In his hand, my guardian held a mirror-like object, and I zeroed in on it. Guardian Alleron glanced up from the looking glass, which showed the king within its oval frame. But even though the king was miles away in his castle, his voice and image were perfectly clear, thanks to the looking glass's magic.

"If there's nothing else, Your Majesty, my lorafin has arrived, which means we shall be on our way." My guardian's eyes met mine over the mirror, and he gave me an approving nod when he took in my gown and hair.

A relieved smile bloomed across my face.

In the looking glass, the king straightened his lapels. "Yes, please do, and make haste. I have several things on my agenda this afternoon, so I can't be running late."

With a charming smile, my guardian replied, "Of course, Your Majesty. We'll be there shortly."

WIND WHIPPED through my hair as we zoomed along the road through the Wood toward the palace. Guardian Alleron had his enchanted carpet moving at full speed, and I loved the fresh air brushing across my face.

Trees towered over us, their thick canopy blocking most of the sun. Every now and then, a set of eyes appeared at the road's edge, through the brush as the wildling fae watched us pass. Most of the time, we were moving too quickly for me to see which creatures observed us, but when we careened around a corner, the carpet slowed enough for me to see a pair of familiar eyes.

Esopeel watched us from under the brush. The small female *cerlikan* waved to me in greeting, and I had just enough time to subtly wave in return before we flew past her.

Our hurried pace continued as we glided over streams and caressed the tips of low-lying shrubs that brushed the side of the Wood's road. I tried to spot more of my wildling friends, but our speed made that difficult. It was probably for the best, though. Guardian Alleron had no idea how many wildlings I'd befriended in the time since we'd settled here, waiting for his estate to be built, and he would likely put a stop to it if he knew.

A ray of sunshine warmed my cheeks when we reached a small clearing, and just above the trees, one of the palace's spires appeared. I quickly checked my hair, but despite our rushed flight, the hairstyle Lillivel had chosen for me kept my long locks in place. Only a few strands had slipped free from one of my braids. I tamed them as best as I could, but my fingers trembled even though I tried to steady them.

We flew past the Centennial Matches' activity on the land bordering the palace, and finally arriving at our destination, our carpet glided to a stop right in front of the palace doors. Wide stone steps lined with blooming manicured gardens led to the opulent palace entrance.

"Wait here," my guardian instructed the four guards who accompanied us.

They all dipped their heads at Guardian Alleron and stood stoically. But two of them cast their attention to Leafton, Faewood Kingdom's vibrant capital, visible in the distance. Most of the guards employed at Emerson Estate were quite familiar with the capital's many *salopas*, and I couldn't help but wonder if they were imagining their next night off.

Guardian Alleron jumped from the carpet, his solid frame landing lightly. He stood tall, his lithe yet powerful figure filling out his tapered jacket perfectly. White teeth flashed when he smiled, and his tanned skin looked made for the bright sun streaming upon us.

Several wildling fae employed to tend to the palace grounds stopped to watch him, and Guardian Alleron made a show of holding his hand out to assist me down.

I took his outstretched palm, knowing it would please him, and the familiar feel of his large hand closed over mine. Automatically, I fell into the role of his dutiful lorafin about to be sold off to the wealthy for a calling.

Smiling up at him, I nodded my thanks when I finally stood back on solid ground.

A flare of approval radiated from him. "You're doing wonderfully," he whispered so quietly that I knew only my ears had heard him.

My heart soared.

Ahead, at the massive stone entry doors, the palace staff stood at attendance, all wildlings. A male *ramifin* took charge, one I hadn't dealt with before.

"Welcome!" he called. "If you would please follow me."

In no time, my guardian and I were inside the palace and being ushered down numerous hallways and corridors.

"The king and his guests are in his favorite sitting room." The ramifin's hooves clopped on the stone floor with each step he took. He wore the same attire as all of the serving staff we passed—dark-brown slacks and an aqua top with pearly buttons up its center. "It's just this way. Almost there."

I kept my head held high as we followed, but I was thankful for my guardian's firm grip on my elbow. I was to perform three callings today. *Three.* Stars and galaxy, I hoped I could.

My silky, flat shoes slipped softly over the polished flooring, barely making a sound while the wooden heels on my guardian's shoes clicked loudly. Their footsteps were the only sound in the monstrous palace save for voices that could be heard drifting to us from farther ahead.

"Just a few more turns," the ramifin called over his shoulder as a few snippets of conversation reached me from ahead.

" . . . a noble spotted him last night in the Wood. I have a feeling he's after my shipment that's on its way to Ampum."

"What makes you think that? I thought you've kept that stash hushed? How could he possibly know about it?" another male asked.

"I have kept it quiet," the first replied, "but anyone would crave the wealth of gold bars I acquired from the mines in Mistvale. It's possible I have a traitor in my midst, or maybe one of my staff slipped up and spoke about it."

A female gasped. "But how do they know it was actually the Dark Raider that's been spotted?"

"His black mask and head scarf." A third male replied, and the sound of *his* voice nearly made me stop cold, but I quickly righted myself, and my blunder only got a small, disapproving frown from my guardian. However, my skin crawled as Lordling Neeble continued. "His telltale attire gave him away, but the noble could have been wrong. When he looked again, he said nobody was there."

"And have the kingsfae been sent to search for him?" another female asked indignantly.

Lordling Neeble replied again, and memories of what he'd done to me sprang forth in my mind, but I quickly shoved them down. "Of course, they were. What do you take us for? Fools?"

A smattering of laughs and whispered comments followed, and somehow, I managed to keep following the servant, but when we passed the large receiving room that held several nobles from the ten Houses, it took everything in me to ignore them.

Lordling Neeble was in there, and just being near him made my blood turn to ice.

My legs were shaking so badly by the time we made the final turn to the king's sitting room that I worried I would tip right over, but I didn't have time for any nerves. The second I appeared in the king's line of sight, his eyes flashed with eagerness.

"Ah, here she is!" The Faewood Kingdom ruler hooked both hands on the lapels of his turquoise coat. The shimmering color flowed around his large, solid frame, highlighting his protruding belly and thick legs. He wore tan slacks and had a stark white top underneath the grand coat. All of his clothing looked spun from the finest cottonum, airy yet regal, and was suited to our warm climate. "Do come. I have some visitors who are dying to meet you."

King Paevin's boisterous and booming voice clouded around me. The ramifin servant bowed at the king, then closed the door behind us just after Guardian Alleron ushered me inside the sitting room. My voluminous dress swished around my legs, and I internally cursed its hindrance, but then I reminded myself that my guardian loved when I dressed so finely, and some of my annoyance dimmed.

"You certainly did make haste," the king said to my guardian. "We couldn't have been talking more than ten minutes ago."

Guardian Alleron bowed. "I do aim to please, Your Majesty. When you said you had a full agenda, I wanted to ensure we didn't impede anything."

The king chuckled. "You always are so accommodating. I do hope you'll stay in that new estate of yours since it makes it so easy for you to bring your lorafin by."

My guardian's smile grew. "Of course, Your Majesty. As always, it's my highest honor to serve you."

The king waved his hand, yet his lips spread even more. He always pretended not to care for flattery even though it was obvious he loved it.

My guardian and the king murmured a few more pleasantries to each other. The entire time I stood dutifully at Guardian Alleron's side, but it was impossible to keep my gaze from sliding to the two male siltenites behind the king. They had to be lordlings. Their clothing reeked of wealth.

I forced my expression to stay serene and aloof, the portrait of a patient lorafin—the expression my guardian preferred I wore when I performed callings—but inside, my stomach was churning. Trying to distract myself, I instead focused on a map of the Solis continent above the fireplace. Encased within an intricate golden frame, it showed all of the territories of our realm's icy northern continent.

I frowned and couldn't help but wonder why the king would have a map of a foreign continent in his favorite room and not a map of the Silten continent. Or even to have portraits of his children, the prince and princess of Faewood, would seem more fitting versus showcasing a far geographical location that we didn't often interact with.

"Alas, do you want to see her?" the king asked the two males behind him, which snapped my attention back to them. "Lordlings Messepire and Himil, have a look and see what your signatures bought." The king's expression morphed into anticipation when he waved dramatically at me. "She's always so beautiful. Every time I've seen her, she's this stunning. Look at her curves and how she fills out that gown." He made a satisfied sound in his throat, then addressed the lordlings again. "The ancient texts always speak of the lorafins and how breathtaking they are. It seems that time hasn't diminished that in the slightest."

Guardian Alleron pushed me forward, his grip tightening

on my elbow in a reminder to do whatever they asked before he let go.

I plastered a smile on my face, but with each step I took toward the king, the magic inside me crackled and clouded, nearly triggering my collar. Somehow, I managed to continue my deep breaths, but I had to curl my fingers into my palms and dig my nails into my skin to keep my magic from reacting more.

"Well, Lordling Messepire, what do you think?" the king asked the male to his left.

The shorter lordling with stocky thighs and midnight black hair that matched the color of his eyes grinned. "How fascinating. She's certainly stunning and is just as ravishing as you'd claimed she'd be." His brown skin glimmered in the sunlight when he clasped his hands behind his back, but while his posture was unthreatening, his gaze wasn't. He turned his sharp eyes on my guardian. "How do you resist her?"

Guardian Alleron shrugged. "She's been with me since she was a babe, so she's like a daughter to me. I've grown immune to my lorafin's supreme features and figure."

"You're a stronger male than I," Lordling Himil, the other one, quipped. He was tall with rust-colored hair and a smattering of freckles across his nose. Startling blue eyes raked over my body when he assessed me, then halted momentarily on my cleavage. "Mouthwatering indeed." Lordling Himil licked his lips.

My skin crawled just as Lordling Messepire asked my guardian, "Is it true that you have a device to control her?"

"Oh, do show them!" the king said with a booming laugh. "Its magic is absolutely fascinating. I've never seen the likes of it."

"I would be happy to, Your Majesty." My guardian withdrew the adaptor from his pocket and held it forward for them to see. The gem on its tip—matching the gem in my collar—flashed in the sunlight streaming into the room. With every wave of his arm as he showed it off to the king and lordlings, the gemstone sparkled, the light refracting from it and trying to connect with my collar.

My breath sucked in, my entire body going as still as stone.

My guardian did those movements so carelessly. He was obviously too distracted with impressing the males to consider what an involuntary trigger of his adaptor could do to me.

Sweat beaded at the small of my back as I stood ramrod straight. I kept my lips pressed together and focused on my breathing. *This will all be over by tonight, then you can return home and soak in that luxurious bath that Lillivel will have waiting for you.*

All three males studied the adaptor, their attention sliding from it, to my collar, then to my expression as my guardian explained how the device worked.

I smiled serenely, pretending to be unbothered, but at least their interest in the adaptor allowed me a second to assess their auras and try to determine what their magic was going to do to me. Lordling Himil wore colors of my kingdom—dark brown, turquoise, and white—so he likely had an elemental power, and given his pounding aura, his magic was strong.

Lordling Messepire, however, wore Mistvale Kingdom colors: bright yellow, dark purple, and deep red.

My stomach churned. Mistvale magic was always a wild-card during callings. And who was to say if these two only harbored magic of their kingdoms. It was possible they'd been blessed with the unusual ability to wield magic from more than one kingdom.

But other than their kingdom colors hinting at their magic, I had no idea what was in store for me since the two lordlings appeared as all siltenite fae did. Smooth skin, fae-tipped ears, and no animalistic features. They looked like any other high fae of the realm.

Yet Lordlings Messepire and Himil undoubtedly harbored some kind of extreme magic if they were important enough to be needed for document signing. Most likely, they each led one of the ten noble Houses of their kingdoms.

I really need to learn who all the House leaders are, I thought for the umpteenth time. But House nobles changed like the wind at a king's discretion, and we'd been so busy over the past season as Guardian Alleron clamored for funds in order to build his beloved estate that I hadn't looked at the House lists in ages.

At least I knew what to expect from the king's calling. King Paevin had an air elemental power. At the end of his calling, I would feel like I was floating. Air was always an easy one to deal with, but as for the other two males . . .

I pumped my hands into fists. *Regardless, it will all be over by tonight.*

Activity from outside shone through the window, and I welcomed the distraction of the wildlings working just past the palace's land. The same scenes that had filled my windows graced the king's sitting room as well.

But none of the males here seemed to care about the Centennial Matches. Instead, they all continued to assess me—avidly, hungrily—as they asked their rabid questions.

A shiver of dread danced down my spine, but I did my best not to let fear shine upon my face, then reminded myself that once I did my duty, my guardian would allow me to leave.

It would be the same as it'd always been.

"Right over here, girl." The king indicated a settee by the cold fireplace.

His command startled me, and awareness hit me that in the time I'd been watching the wildlings outside, all four males had stopped talking.

"As you wish, Your Majesty." I curtsied and kicked myself into action, but irritation prickled my skin at being called *girl*. I'd known the king for months now, yet he still treated me like a nameless, brainless young thing even though I was highly educated and twenty-eight summers old, making me a fully matured adult.

My swirling gown brushed against the furniture on my

way to the settee. Since the lounge chair was positioned right next to Lordling Himil, I had no choice but to pass closely to him.

When I did, his finger subtly reached out and ran along my skin. It left a tremor of coldness in his wake.

When the frost from his fingertip melted away, some of my anxiety calmed. *So he wields a water element, not fire. Thank the stars and galaxy.* At best, I would be freezing when I awoke from his calling. At worst, it would feel like I was drowning. Coldness I could live with. My upcoming hot bath would eventually cure that. As for drowning, well, the sensation was scary but would eventually pass. But fire . . . I shuddered. The pain from fire was always unbearable.

I lowered myself to the settee and lay back. The ridiculous gown I wore fluffed like a cloud around my legs, and the tight corset dug painfully into my ribs. My guardian gave me a sharp look, and I quickly smoothed whatever expression I'd been wearing.

The king and his two lordlings gathered closer, hovering above me. Their eyes practically glowed with anticipation.

Guardian Alleron's handsome features carved into the expression he usually wore during my callings—patient appeasement. "She needs to be touched by whomever would like their calling done first. Who would like to start?"

Lordling Himil lifted a hand immediately. "I'll go."

Guardian Alleron inclined his head. "And what is it you wish Elowen to discover in the Veiled Between?"

Lordling Himil's throat bobbed, and for the briefest moment, his anticipation faltered. He blinked rapidly. "I'd like to contact my daughter, Serinity."

Guardian Alleron's voice dropped in sympathy. "Of course, please grasp Elowen's hand."

I closed my eyes when the lordling's dry fingers tightened painfully around mine, then sent a silent prayer to all of the gods and goddesses that I wouldn't be broken upon waking.

My guardian waved his adaptor and tapped the wand in a series of connected beats. A powerful well of magic vibrated around my collar, unlocking it, and then . . .

My magic unleashed.

CHAPTER 2

What do you seek, Daughter of Darkness? The semelee swirled around me, its scaled black serpentine body an inky shadow in the Veiled Between.

I floated in its midst, a commanding presence that the semelee was intrinsically drawn to. *I need you to find this female. She's crossed to the afterlife.* I pulled on Lordling Himil's magic in the fae lands, just enough to show the semelee an image of the lordling's daughter.

Serinity had been an adult, but still young when she'd died, not older than a hundred summers. I studied the image at the same time the semelee did. Long blond hair. A radiant expression. Dazzling light-brown eyes.

I had no idea what had befallen her or why the gods had decided to take her so young, but she was gone from our realm forever, now only a memory of those who loved her.

The semelee studied the image more as others crept from

the darkness to slither around me. A shiver of pleasure wracked my ghostly form with each fleeting touch of their shadows. Sheer power vibrated from them, and I caressed each scaled back that slid and slithered by my sides.

Find her. Now, I commanded in a forceful tone.

The semelee hesitated briefly before spinning away into the darkness, and its hesitance was enough of a reminder that I didn't control them completely. And possibly never would.

A hum vibrated along my collar, connecting me mentally to the fae lands once more. That damned connection was why I wasn't fully in control of them, but then I reminded myself that I couldn't blame my collar for everything. I needed to be more forceful when I spoke to them. More powerful. It was the best I could do since my collar kept me somewhat contained, even when my guardian relaxed its magic.

She's here. The semelee reappeared abruptly, and at its side, I sensed another presence. Softer. More fragile. Frightened.

Where am I? Serinity Himil called out, her voice quiet and timid.

You're in the Veiled Between, I replied in as soothing of a tone as I could muster. *Your father has asked me to summon you. My name is Elowen, and I'm a lorafin who resides on the Silten continent. I've called you from the afterlife today because your father wishes to know how you fare.*

My father? Her voice grew more animated.

Yes, let me speak with him briefly so I can help you two

communicate. I squeezed my eyes shut and concentrated on the lordling's physical hold on me in my realm. I called upon more of his magic and asked his first question for his daughter.

Serinity? Is that you?

Da! Oh, my dear da, how I miss you!

A choked response came from him, and then he asked her things rapid-fire. It was a struggle to keep up, but he started the way most fae did. He asked her personal things. Identifying questions that only she could answer.

It was a test—a hesitance on his part to accept that I truly was a lorafin.

Minutes passed, but Serinity answered everything immediately, and my whispered replies to him in the fae lands eventually seemed to convince him that I truly was in the Veiled Between.

Once Lordling Himil realized that, their conversation became excited and joyful. It continued long enough that I eventually had to put a stop to it. I had to remember that I had two more callings today and needed to conserve my energy and not dispel all of my magic on the first.

I must let her go, I whispered to the noble.

A little longer, the lordling replied in an irritated tone when I began to release my hold on him.

I can't. I'm sorry.

Da! Serinity cried.

Damn you, let me talk to her longer.

I'm sorry. I have to let her go. I summoned the semelee again before either could argue further. *Take her away.*

Serinity screamed when the semelee whisked her back to the afterlife, sucking her soul away to the realm that I could not see, the realm we all passed to when death came for us.

Another curse spewed from the noble, but I released his magic just as the effects of his calling raged through me.

A shiver wracked my ghostly form, coldness seeping into my bloodstream from the lordling's elemental magic. Icy waves of torture crept along my limbs, making me feel like I'd been doused in the Brashier Sea with its floating icebergs and frigid waves. But a moment of relief passed through me too. It didn't feel like I was drowning. Coldness I could live with. It was much less scary.

Next? I called in a tired voice in the fae lands. *Two more. I have two more of these. Conserve your strength, Elowen,* I thought to myself.

A new hand clasped mine in the fae lands. Dark, snapping magic instantly clouded around my thoughts, like jagged knives of slashing death.

A wave of horror washed over me as Lordling Messepire's magic engulfed me. Breathing heavily in my physical body, I had to force myself not to recoil. Yet despite my terrified reaction to his monstrous magic, I could have sworn that Lordling Messepire smiled.

I LAY on the enchanted carpet, zooming back to my guardian's estate. Zale, Mushil, and the two other guards who'd accompanied us stood at each corner of the carpet, studiously watching our surroundings.

Above, the galaxy's stars twinkled like sparks of glittering sand.

Guardian Alleron sat beside me in the center of the carpet, counting the rulibs in the velvet sack the king had given him. The coins' heavy weight clinked together. It was the only sound besides the howling wind and wildling chatter from the Wood.

"Are you doing all right, Elowen?" my guardian finally asked after he finished his accounting.

Another shiver wracked my frame. "I'm fine, just cold. The king's and Lordling Messepire's magic have thankfully worn off."

Guardian Alleron's voice dropped in sympathy as he pocketed his coins. "Nightmare magic is quite terrifying, but it was all an illusion. Messepire's magic couldn't actually hurt you."

"I know, but the images that I was seeing were horrifying, and the hallucinations—"

"You're fine now, are you not?" he asked, his tone a bit sharper.

I pressed my lips together. "Well, yes, but—"

"Then there's no need to carry on about it."

My brow furrowed. *Am I carrying on again?* I contemplated that. I didn't think I'd been, but I was tired, and time always seemed to pass at a slower rate when I was dealing with the side effects from a calling. Perhaps he was right, and I'd been complaining more than I'd realized.

Nodding, I pressed my lips together once more and also reminded myself that my guardian hadn't once scolded me for struggling to fulfill all three callings today. I should be grateful for that even if I'd done what he demanded to the best of my ability.

After all, I'd been successful to some degree on all three callings. I'd found Lordling Himil's daughter, I'd provided Lordling Messepire with the location of a missing heirloom, and during the king's calling, I'd revealed answers about the future. All with the help of the semelees.

I'd done what'd been demanded of me even if it'd hurt me in the process and even if I'd grown so fatigued I'd been put in harm's way.

A memory of the largest semelee that I'd interacted with during the king's calling brushed against my mind like fluttering wings. The semelee had called to me, lulling me with its siren song. I'd been so tired I'd almost detached from the fae lands entirely. It was only the activation of my guardian's device on my collar that had stunned me from the semelee's grip.

"Elowen?" my guardian said, his tone a bit less sharp. "You're all right, aren't you?"

Shuddering, I shoved that fearful memory aside and

locked my gaze upward as the carpet swayed and billowed beneath me. "Yes, Guardian. I'm fine."

He hummed in satisfaction and settled back for the remainder of the ride.

Light from the three moons barely penetrated the canopy when the Wood grew dense again, but in the open areas, the shimmering array of constellations and the plethora of stars held my attention.

I concentrated on our realm's natural beauty, anything to keep my mind off the numbing coldness that continually made my entire body shudder. But, as my guardian had pointed out, at least the king's elemental magic and Lordling Messepire's psychic power had finally abated. At the moment, I was only dealing with Lordling Himil's water elemental side effect.

Shivering, I forced myself to once again gaze at the stars for a distraction. The Alonidrus constellation blazed brightly above, and it was easy to locate the three planets visible tonight in our solar system—Jeulic, Merimum, and Titun. The planets shone brighter than any star, and they pulsed in colorful waves that shimmered around them like a halo. Each planet's magic formed a protective cloud, like an aura, and not for the first time, I wondered what color our planet emitted.

I doubted I would ever know, but at least the beauty of the skies helped numb the terror of my work today.

My teeth began to chatter when we careened over a bubbling stream, and the wind picked up on our final stretch through the Wood.

"We're almost back, Elowen, and then I shall reward you with three full days of rest. You did well tonight even though you once again couldn't twist fate." Guardian Alleron's tone cut through the wind whistling through my ears.

"But . . . twisting fate is illegal, Guardian. Even though King Paevin would like me to, I don't think it's wise to try."

He shrugged. "Is it truly illegal if a king demands it?"

Frowning, I clamped my mouth shut. Twisting fate was the ultimate power of a lorafin, yet I wasn't even close to having enough control over my magic to do so. And despite what my guardian claimed, it *was* against the law. I could be brought before the supernatural courts for twisting fate, even if a king demanded it. So while King Paevin may not be reprimanded, I certainly would be.

My guardian carried on, oblivious to my discomfort. "The king was still pleased, however. Thanks to what the semelees revealed, he now knows how many spectators will show for the Matches. He shall have the staff prepare. Yet, he also told me that he wants you to keep trying to master your magic completely. One day, if the semelees are agreeable, he would like you to twist fate for him."

I squirmed, not liking where the king's interest was going at all. "I'm sorry, Guardian. I still can't access that part of my magic . . ."

"I know, which is why you won't be punished. However, the king has requested your presence again in two weeks' time with only him in attendance. Of course, for that much rare continued access to you, I shall have to raise the price. Even a king has to pay if he wants to use my lorafin."

My lorafin.

It was often what Guardian Alleron called me. Sometimes hearing that warmed my heart and made me feel special and loved, but tonight . . .

My brow furrowed as confusing, conflicting responses rose up in me as they sometimes did following a calling. Tonight, I felt tired, unbearably cold, and hearing him calling me *his* lorafin . . . It didn't make me feel loved. It made me feel owned.

Although technically, I *was* my guardian's lorafin, but if not for my unique and powerful magic, I wouldn't be his prized trinket. Slavery was outlawed in the four kingdoms, yet due to the inherent nature of those like me, which could be destructive beyond imagination if I commanded the semelees fully, a treaty had been signed centuries ago.

Any lorafin could now be kept caged and owned if her guardian proved she was a danger to others. And the Goddess knew when I'd been five summers old, I'd proven just that.

Yet Guardian Alleron had also worked with me on controlling my magic with the help of the collar. I was older now, more mature, and if the gods and goddesses deemed me worthy, perhaps they would bless me and help me stay innocent of any wrongdoings. Then once I turned thirty and my guardian removed my collar, I could go to the supernatural courts, plead my case, and with any luck, be granted my freedom. Then I wouldn't be owned by my guardian anymore. I would simply be his daughter and nothing more.

"Isn't Emerson Estate the most magnificent home we've ever lived in, Elowen?" my guardian asked, drawing my attention back to him.

Another shiver hit me, but I nodded. "It certainly is. It's quite grand."

"And you have your own suite now. Not to mention, you have Lillivel at your side to help with anything you may need. You're a very lucky female, I must say."

A moment of guilt hit me. I had so much, and I shouldn't complain. "You're right, Guardian. I'm very grateful for that."

"It's lovely, isn't it, that after seasons of traveling throughout the kingdoms, we've finally settled down."

I *hmmed* in response, too tired to comment further. But, again, he was right. It *was* nice to finally have a place to call home. My entire life, my guardian had used my magic to amass his rulibs from the wealthiest lordlings in each city we traveled through, and he'd finally collected a large enough fortune to build the estate in his home kingdom he'd coveted since childhood.

Guardian Alleron now lived like a king—the irony that the king was our neighbor wasn't lost on me—and he was hoping to eventually be made a noble and be appointed as one of the ten Houses of Faewood. Of course, for that to happen, one of the noble families would need to be removed, but that didn't faze Guardian Alleron. Ambition had never been lacking in him.

Ahead, lights from Guardian Alleron's estate filtered faintly through the Wood. Anticipation of a hot bath and a soft bed infused energy into me, and I was about to force myself into a sitting position when something pricked my attention.

Absolute silence had descended. The wildlings of the Wood had grown entirely quiet, and the ever-present chirps and hums from the insects and beetles had stopped.

Yet the Wood never grew quiet. Ever.

Frowning, I peered around. "Mushil? Do you—"

An arrow whizzed through the air, and its sickening, slick punch penetrated my guardian right in his shoulder.

My guardian groaned, his hand going to the arrow.

I shrieked. "Guardian!" I tried to cross the distance between us, but a smattering of hooves pounded along the ground, and one of the guards shoved me down.

"Hold!" Zale shouted, and all four guards raised their crossbows. "Formations now!"

The four guards formed a protective wall around us.

Before I could take another breath, the enchanted carpet careened around a tree, its magic propelling it onward to our destination despite the fact that my guardian was now doubled over, clutching his shoulder as his four guards all shot their weapons from their protective stances.

My heart lurched, yet more attacking arrows flew. They came at us from all angles, sailing silently through the night like deadly shadows.

A whizzing sound rushed by my ear, and four arrows

simultaneously struck true, each hitting a guard dead center in his chest.

I screamed just as all four guards tumbled off the carpet. When Zale's body landed with a fleshy thump, his lifeless eyes gazed skyward, and a brief moment of clarity hit me.

He'll never hit me or order me around again. But just as quickly, my heart lurched when I beheld Mushil's unmoving form.

"No!" I wailed. "Mushil!"

But my guard didn't respond. He'd likely already passed to the afterlife.

Agony ripped through me, and I whipped around, searching for our attackers, but I saw no one.

Yet galloping hooves on the Wood's floor grew closer, even though everything else in the Wood remained silent. Even the wind seemed diminished in the presence of whatever was approaching.

"Elowen, get down . . . *please!*" Wheezing, Guardian Alleron reached for me.

A survival instinct kicked in, and I shoved my face to the carpet, the fibers scratching my cheeks as I lay as flat as possible. Wheezing from my guardian grew, and a moment of hysteria made me want to sob. If my guardian died, my freedom would come early, but then the only father I'd ever known would be gone. I would be entirely alone in the realm without Guardian Alleron. Abandoned again.

My fingers crept along the carpet in search of my

guardian's hand. The power inside me sang, rising and careening through my limbs until my collar activated. I cried out when magic shot like lightning along my limbs, igniting coldness and slashing pain with it. The momentary reprieve I'd had from Lordling Himil's magic faded, and shocking agony reverberated through me anew as a fresh flow of ice slid along my limbs.

I bit my lip to keep from screaming, and the metallic taste of blood filled my mouth.

Wind continued flowing against my back, but I stayed plastered to the carpet. My guardian's estate grew closer. Closer. *Closer.*

If we could just reach it, his protective wards would enclose us and stop whomever pursued us.

"Elowen!" Guardian Alleron bellowed.

Before I could process his fearful call, hoofbeats were suddenly right beside us. Just as fast, an arm wrapped around my waist and whipped me off the carpet so quickly that my head spun, and blackness coated my vision.

Someone tilted me upright, settling my rump against something hard that moved in a rocking motion. The moment I was righted, my vision returned, but the realm around me had turned into an impossibly dark blur, and the wind whipping against my face was so fierce that I couldn't keep my eyes open.

My heart thundered, nearly jumping out of my chest. Whoever carried me cradled me to them in a tight embrace. It was as though a phantom had snatched me from the enchanted carpet and was carrying me to the netherworld. But phantoms didn't carry a scent. They didn't smell of fresh pine and a hint of spice. And they certainly didn't have solid bodies and arms like steel.

Yet phantoms did move like the wind, and whoever had just taken me flew so fast through the Wood that everything around me blended together.

Wits finally returning, I punched at whomever held me and tried to wiggle out of his solid hold. But his arm tightened, making my breaths shallow. Still, I fought, but the three callings had rendered me so weak, just a shell of the female I had the potential to be, and when a momentous *zap* from my collar activated, I seized, my mind going numb.

Everything inside me shut down . . . down, *down*, until nothing was left but the solid arm around me, the harsh feel of the wind across my cheeks, and then . . . nothing.

CHAPTER 3

Hazy sunlight brushed against my closed eyelids. A pounding headache came next. Groaning, I shifted beneath heavy blankets, then immediately stopped. An ache, so deep it penetrated me all the way to my bones, took my breath away.

"Lillivel?" I croaked.

Someone shifted beside me, and a commanding aura pounded around them. It was someone big and powerful.

Not Lillivel.

My eyes flew open, and my magic immediately flared.

A male dressed entirely in black, including a black mask on his face and a black bandana over his hair, stared down at me. Only his blue eyes and a slit of tanned skin were visible.

For a brief moment, shock rendered me immobile, but the second that wore off, I scrambled away from him. Or tried to. The pile of furs and blankets covering me was so thick, and my gown was so bulky that I could barely get out from under them. Zaps from my collar started just as fast, zinging along my nerves.

The male stared at me, unmoving. His gaze was intent, yet his eyes revealed nothing.

Oh Goddess. Oh, stars and galaxy above. It all came crashing back. Meeting the king. The three callings. Traveling back to my guardian's estate. My abduction.

And the whisperings yesterday of who'd been spotted in the kingdom.

My captor sat beside me on a log, right next to my makeshift bed. A tent billowed around us, and the soft light penetrating the canvas flaps hinted that it was morning.

Panting, I scurried away and pressed myself against the tent's far wall, which only put me an arm's length away from him, but it was better than nothing. The material sagged against my back, but the structure held, not allowing me to roll underneath it and escape.

"Did you sleep all right?" the male finally said, his voice deep yet calm.

Did he seriously just ask how I slept? My heart pounded so hard it hurt, and my magic rattled painfully inside me. I tried to slow my breathing. Tried not to panic until I was a mindless mess, but Goddess, I'd been *taken.*

"Who are you?" My chest heaved, but I managed to suck in a deep breath and calm my collar slightly.

The male cocked his head. Irises, so blue they resembled the Adriastic Sea, glittered in the dim sunlight as he continued to assess me. "I'm someone in need of your services."

"In need of me?" I recoiled and quickly assessed my clothes. I was still dressed. Not ravished. At least, I didn't think I'd been. Nothing between my legs felt sore.

A rising pulse from his aura filled the tent. "Not *those* kinds of services. I'm not going to hurt you."

I scoffed and replied in a trembling tone, "Says the male who took me against my will and drugged me to sleep."

His ebony eyebrows slanted together, and it hit me that since I could see his eyebrows, I knew he had black hair. "I never drugged you. You passed out."

I sat rigidly, and my collar vibrated repeatedly at my throat. My entire body began to shake. Shivers racked up and down my limbs. I was losing it. About to panic.

He held his hands up, and his tone turned slow and cautious. "Again . . . I'm *not* going to hurt you."

But my lorafin magic coiled and writhed more, threatening to rise and come to my bidding, yet if I didn't get myself under some semblance of control, I wouldn't have just this male to contend with. I would have the pain of the collar's full dousing effects as well.

Inhaling more deep breaths, I endeavored to steady my nerves. "Tell me *who* you are, not your reason for taking me."

He quirked an ebony eyebrow. "All right, my name's Jax."

Jax? Breaths still coming too fast, I studied him. He wore all black, from head to toe. *Black, black, and more black.* The perfect color for a nighttime raid. And the reason he'd been named the Dark Raider by the kingdoms.

But he'd just called himself Jax, not the Dark Raider. This male could be an imposter pretending to be the Dark Raider.

I forced myself to take another deep breath and asked as calmly as I could, "What do you need my magic for?"

"You're a lorafin, are you not? I need you to find someone for me."

"Then why didn't you just request that of my guardian? Guardian Alleron would be more than happy to lend my services if you paid him."

He growled, the low sound filling the tent. "I don't pay slave guardians."

I scoffed. "So, you abduct females instead?"

"Not usually."

The slight twinge of amusement in his words made me pause. I studied him again, waiting for something—I didn't know what. But despite his wry tone, I was convinced something horrible was about to happen. Him lunging at me or perhaps striking me. This male had attacked us after all.

My heart twisted when I recalled the events of last night. Mushil was dead because of this male. Perhaps my guardian was too. Another rattle came from my collar, and I sucked in a hasty breath.

No, Guardian Alleron's fine. He's not dead. It was just a flesh wound. He'll be fine, and I'll find my way back to him.

But Mushil had definitely passed to the afterlife. Sweet,

uncomplicated Mushil. He'd never been anything but kind to me. Pain at that loss rose up in me so sharply that a small mewling sound emitted from my lips.

Jax cocked his head again, his brow furrowing.

Pulse leaping more, a moment of fear hit me as we stared at each other. This male didn't know that I couldn't do what he wanted. I had no way of finding whomever he sought, not with the collar in place. Because without my guardian's adaptor to loosen it, I couldn't access my abilities. And perhaps because of that, Jax would dispose of me as easily as he'd done Mushil.

Or maybe he'll let me go if he knows.

Hope surged through me, and I opened my mouth to tell him about my restrictive collar, but a noise outside the tent stopped me.

Footsteps.

They were soft, barely detectable, but since they were right behind me on the other side of the tent, I heard them faintly.

Tensing, my limbs locked in place when whoever was circling our tent went round to the other side and flapped open the tent's canvas.

Another huge male entered.

My eyes bulged. The new male was dressed the same as my captor. All-black attire and a concealing mask and scarf. My belief that my abductor could be an imposter impersonating the Dark Raider slipped down a notch.

"Ah, she's awake." The second male lumbered into the

tent, taking a seat beside Jax. "Did you have a nice snooze, lovely?"

I recoiled. "Who are *you?*"

The newest male laughed, the sound low and deep. Unlike Jax, he didn't have blue eyes or black hair. From the looks of it, his hair was auburn, given the color of his eyebrows and his eyes were brown. "A new friend."

I wrapped my arms around myself and tried to edge farther away from both of them.

Jax raised a hand. He had a large palm, long fingers. Working hands. This male didn't sit on his arse for a living, that was for certain. "Phillen, if you would give us a minute?"

Phillen slapped his knees and rose. "Apologies, Jax. Just thought it would be best to get moving, and when I heard her talking, I thought I'd come remind you of that."

Jax sighed, and an edge of irritation slipped into his tone. "I'm aware. A minute, if you would."

"I'll ready the camp." Phillen ducked out of the tent without another word.

My heart began to pound again. *Camp?* He'd said *camp*, which indicated that there was more than one tent erected, which could only mean there were other fae in this group. I listened again through the tent's material, but other than Phillen's retreating footsteps, which grew silent surprisingly quickly for such a large male, I didn't hear anything other than the normal buzzing, chirping, and trills of the Wood.

Which left me to believe that these males were no

strangers to prowling around unbeknownst to others. Not good.

I wrapped my arms even tighter around myself. "So, Jax . . . who exactly are you?"

My captor placed his bent elbows on his knees and leaned forward. His shirt stretched across his shoulders, and a wave of his aura brushed against me, heaving and probing. I shivered. This male held power. *Immense* power from the feel of it. "Since you're already aware of my name, you may keep calling me Jax, or if you prefer, you could call me the Dark Raider."

My heart jumped into my throat. Rapid breaths made my chest heave, and my power swelled, getting a vibration from my collar.

Eyes wide, I studied him again, looking beyond his black attire. *Silent attacks. Flies like the wind. Brutally violent raids that are practically unseen.* Every whispering I'd heard throughout the kingdoms about this male came careening back to me.

And they perfectly described my abduction.

It *was* him.

"Given the panic on your face, it looks like you've heard of me?"

"Everyone's heard of you." I couldn't say more. My mouth had gone dry, and my pulse throbbed in my temples. All the kingdoms knew of the Dark Raider—the vigilante who ruthlessly stole riches from noble or rich fae that were taking more than they should, and giving those riches to the poor. Murder wasn't above him. Gruesome murder if the stories were to be believed. And given what he'd done to Mushil, those stories were true.

Despite that, the poor saw him as a savior. So many underprivileged rooted for him even if the rich saw him as a nuisance who needed to be captured and executed.

I scoffed. And to think just yesterday, I'd been silently cheering for him. *So foolish.*

"Are you going to kill me?" My voice sounded breathless, thready, but it felt as though I was gasping for air. Another vibrating warning came from my collar.

He sighed. "No, Elowen, I'm not going to kill you or hurt you. I simply need your magic."

My spine snapped into a rigid line. "How do you know my name?"

"I know many things about you."

For a moment, I sat dumbstruck. *The Dark Raider knows me?* I tried to comprehend that, but my damned collar kept rattling. I concentrated on taking more deep, steady breaths and managed to get out, "You truly only want me to find someone for you? That's it? That's the only reason you took me?"

A flare of magic simmered around him, almost as though he was irritated by my fear. "Yes."

Another rush of dizziness swept through me, except this time, it was one of relief, even if I was a fool to believe him.

I released a breath and licked my lips. Stars, my head was

pounding, but if he truly wasn't going to hurt me, then it was best he knew now that I couldn't help him. He might just let me go. "I'm sorry, but I can't help you. You've taken me for naught. You might as well release me to Guardian Alleron now and find another lorafin."

He snorted. "You act as if your kind are easy to come by."

"Surely, there's another somewhere in the kingdoms."

"On the contrary, I believe at the moment you're the only one."

I am? For a moment, I couldn't reply. I knew my kind were rare, but I'd never known an actual count had been done on how many of us were currently alive. Despite Jax's admission, I drew myself up more. "Regardless, I can't help you."

"I doubt that. You just don't want to."

"It's true." I pointed to my collar. "You would have to remove *this* for my magic to work, and you can't do that."

Jax's eyes narrowed, and he leaned closer. A hint of his scent, a spicy fragrance that reminded me of night, pine trees, and darkness, rolled into fire, billowed against my senses. Strangely, his scent was incredibly appealing.

The Dark Raider reached out and ran a fingertip along my collar's edge. A pulse of magic tingled against my skin, and I knew it hummed along his as well.

His eyes narrowed more. "What is this?"

"It's how my guardian controls me. But without his adaptor loosening the collar's ability to suppress my magic, I can't access my lorafin powers enough to help you. Truly, I can't do a calling for you and find whom you seek."

"You're telling me this isn't simply a necklace?"

"No, it's not. The collar's magic keeps me caged. Only my guardian's adaptor can release its hold on me."

His finger dropped, and his eyebrows drew sharply together. "Where's the adaptor?"

"My guardian has it. He never parts with it."

Jax fingered my collar again, running both hands along the top of the smooth metal, then around to the back. His skin felt like fire on mine. Heat emitted from his hands, and my cool skin greedily soaked up his warmth despite also wanting to recoil.

He finally leaned back, taking his blessed warmth with him. "If I cut this off, could you access your magic?"

"Cut it off?" My eyes flashed wide. "You can't do that. The collar's magic won't allow it, and I would need time to prepare for such an event even if you could." I shuddered, thinking of what I'd done as a child. "It's not to come off until I'm thirty summers old. And when that day comes, I'll need to be fully prepared for my magic being entirely loose."

Jax eyed me again, his carefully assessing gaze growing so intent it was hard to maintain eye contact. "When was the last time your guardian removed this collar from you?"

"It's never off me."

"Ever?"

I shook my head, thinking back to my childhood, to the act

that had taken place before this collar had been locked on me. "No. Never. I've worn it since I was very young."

"If your guardian were to remove it now, how would he do so?"

I shrugged. "I don't know. Truly, I don't. He's never taken it off or tried to remove it from me before. I'm telling you. I can't stress enough that I'm of no use to you. Please, just let me go."

"I disagree. This is simply a hurdle I didn't foresee." The Dark Raider abruptly stood and peered down at me, his azure eyes piercing.

I tilted my head back and back. He was tall, taller than Guardian Alleron and probably taller than his friend, Phillen. Broad shoulders stretched his shirt. Strong thighs filled out his black pants. Yet he was lean, his waist toned. Everything about him preceded his reputation. He looked like a killing weapon harnessed in fae form.

He tapped a finger on his hip. "We'll ride for the day, and I'll sort out this slight problem in the interim while you rest and prepare for my calling."

I cocked my head. "You know that I need to prepare?"

"Of course. You just did three callings yesterday, which means you'll need several days to recover before you can do one again. Am I wrong?"

Startled, all I could do was stare, but after a moment I shook my head. "Um, no, you're correct."

"Then in the meantime, we'll ride now that word's no doubt reached your king that I've taken you."

I pushed to a stand, wincing when my entire body ached. But that was the least of my concerns since it didn't appear he was going to let me go after all. "Where are we going?" I winced again when another slash of pain from yesterday's callings cut through me.

A groove appeared between his eyes, and he looked me up and down. "Are you hurt?"

I shook my head and forced my limbs to relax.

When I didn't say anything further, he added, "There's food outside. You'll eat, do whatever other business is needed before we mount, and then we go."

I took a step toward him just as he reached the tent's door. "But go where?"

Instead of answering, he slipped out of the tent, the early morning sun shining upon his back, and reality hit me that I wouldn't be returning to Emerson Estate anytime soon.

If I ever did.

CHAPTER 4

The camp that the auburn-haired male had spoken of was indeed a camp, albeit a small one. There were two other tents and four other siltenite fae males in addition to Jax and Phillen, making six males total. None of the other four spoke to me, but all of them gave me side-eyes when I finally emerged to join them.

Squinting in the brightening eastern sunlight, I studied them covertly. Jax was the tallest of the six, and that was saying something since none of them appeared under six feet.

Phillen was the brawniest, with arms like logs and legs like tree trunks. He also had a pale complexion, given the slit of skin his mask revealed. As I watched him, he hefted his tent clear off the Wood's floor and shook it out before folding the canvas and stacking its wooden poles.

Two other males worked beside Phillen. One had an

earring through his left ear, and he appeared to have short brown hair and light-brown skin.

The other was the shortest of the bunch at maybe six-one. He had blond hair, tanned skin, and long legs. He looked lean and quick and could probably draw the blade in his boot faster than I could blink.

The remaining two worked behind Phillen, but since they were farther away, and they were all masked and wore identical ebony clothing, it was harder to discern their features and coloring.

But all of them wore black and were masked, concealing their identities, and all were siltenite fae. No wildling fae were among them, which wasn't overly surprising since siltenites were more magically powerful than wildlings.

The dipping and twisting in my stomach continued, and I went in search of a bush to relieve myself.

"Don't go far, lovely!" Phillen called from behind me. "I would hate to hunt you down in the Wood."

I glanced warily over my shoulder. The blond male beside Phillen made a snickering sound. At least, I thought it was the blond, but since I couldn't see his eyebrows, given the angle he stood, I wasn't entirely sure. But he was the leanest one, so I was pretty sure it was the blond.

Heart beating rapidly, I tracked my way through the trees even though my muscles protested the quick movement. My gown caught on every branch, but I didn't stop until I found some semblance of privacy and ducked behind a tree.

The sound of the Wood filled the air, and the constant chirps and buzzing snagged my attention as I made quick work of my needs. When finished, I let just enough magic rise to cleanse my entire body along with scrubbing my teeth and freshening my breath. Thankfully self-cleansing had never been an issue with my collar, but it wouldn't help my clothing.

My gown was entirely wrinkled, had several dirt stains, and was ripped in multiple places. Not to mention, it was tight, constricting around the ribs, and entirely uncomfortable. This dress had been crafted to impress the king, not to garb a female who'd been abducted and was traipsing through the Wood with the Dark Raider.

A moment of hysteria hit me, and I slapped a hand over my mouth before a maniacal laugh could escape me. I was in the Wood. With the Dark Raider. And I was worried about the annoyance of my gown.

Seriously, Elowen? That should be the least of your concerns . . .

Trying to think more clearly, I stayed where I was. Hard bark from the tree pressed into my back, scratching my bare skin above the gown's silk, which pulled some of my attention away from my aching muscles.

A quick glance at the sky told me it was still early morning, but even though it'd been hours since I was taken, I knew my guardian would be in pursuit of me. Or if he wasn't yet, he would be so soon.

Thankfully, from what I'd seen of my guardian's wound,

it'd been a flesh wound, and if there was one thing I knew of my guardian, only crossing to the afterlife would stop him from finding me. He loved me, just as I loved him. I knew he did even if he never voiced it.

Nibbling on my lip, I contemplated my situation. Jax had abducted me because he wanted me to find someone for him by venturing to the Veiled Between to ask the semelees, yet Jax hadn't known I couldn't do a calling for him because of my collar. Yet despite telling him that, he didn't believe this stopped his plan.

So now what? It was obvious Jax wasn't going to let me go today, so I could either be a pliant and willing captive, and trust him to release me in a few days' time when he finally accepted that I could never perform a calling for him with my collar in place. Or, I could take matters into my own hands and try to escape.

My brow furrowed, and I considered which was the smarter option based upon what I knew of the Dark Raider. What I *did* know was that the poor spoke of how the Dark Raider helped innocents and didn't hurt them.

But what I'd seen was entirely different.

Jax had murdered Mushil.

And Mushil had been an innocent.

Pain slashed through my heart when I recalled how quickly Mushil had been killed by that arrow. The old guard was dead because of the Dark Raider, even though Mushil had been one of the kindest fae I'd ever known and had been entirely innocent of any wrongdoings. All he'd been doing last night was guarding me. He hadn't deserved to die simply for doing his job, and who was to say my fate would be any different from poor Mushil's?

A sob threatened to rise in my chest as his death hit me anew, but I blinked rapidly and tried not to dwell on it. I needed my wits about me right now, but Mushil's murder solidified that I couldn't trust Jax to do the right thing.

Despite what the poor said of him, despite that Jax claimed he wouldn't hurt me . . . after thinking about it, from what *I'd* seen, I would be a fool to believe that Jax would ultimately release me. When he finally accepted that I could never do a calling for him, it was possible he would just kill me versus letting me go.

In other words, if I wanted to guarantee my survival, I would have to escape.

I eyed the Wood and contemplated how to do that impossible task.

Even though I'd always felt at home among the trees, having grown up in them, in my current state with an aching body, no food or water, and only a few rulibs in my gown's pocket, I was vulnerable. Not to mention my damned gown and protesting muscles made sneaking through the Wood difficult, and I didn't know any of the local wildlings here. We were too far from Emerson Estate to call upon any of my friends to aid me.

Escaping wouldn't be easy, but at least I had time on my

side, since Jax knew I couldn't perform another calling for a few days. That could work to my advantage.

I nibbled my lip more. I knew my guardian would eventually be in pursuit of me, likely with guards or the kingsfae at his side. And if he could find me . . .

My thoughts whirled as I began to form a plan. If Guardian Alleron had enough time, he could track me and catch up to me. Finding a way to help him rescue me was likely my best option, considering it would be difficult on my own in the Wood even if I could escape, which meant that I needed to help my guardian locate me.

But I had no idea where I was or how far I'd traveled, so I had no idea what distance I was up against. Sighing, I scrubbed my cheeks with both hands as the impossibility of everything nearly crushed my spirits.

A butterfly danced by on the wind. Its turquoise wings glistened with purple spots and blended into the bright foliage of the Wood's diverse plant life. And seeing that, along with the beauty of the Wood, helped to dispel some of the anxiety coursing through me.

I can do this. I'm not helpless. I'm in a bad situation, yes, but that doesn't mean there's nothing I can do about it. I will survive this.

"Use your wits, Elowen," I muttered to myself. "Find a way to stop them from taking you any farther."

"Elowen?" Jax bellowed.

I shot to standing, pain ricocheting through me, and

from the quietest rustle of leaves, I knew that Jax was nearly upon me, but by the Goddess, he was practically silent. If my senses weren't already on high alert and he wasn't almost on top of me, I never would have heard him coming.

Before I could round the tree, Jax was towering over me.

As before, all of him was covered, save for his eyes, but in the bright morning light, I was better able to see the planes and angles of his body. He was broad, built, and entirely . . . *male*. Rounded shoulders that reminded me of steel balls pressed against his shirt, and a defined chest that hinted at a male used to fighting made me remember how easily he'd murdered Mushil.

My heart hardened. Despite the poor's reverence for this male, I would *never* revere him again.

He arched a dark eyebrow. "Are you done? You've been gone awhile."

Nostrils flaring, I pressed my spine into the tree more. "Well, if I wasn't, this situation would be entirely more awkward."

A twitch came from beneath his mask. "You need to eat. There's bread and cheese by the tent. I'd advise you to eat now as we're leaving soon and won't be stopping often."

Somehow, I managed to keep my tone from being too sharp when I replied, "Yes, Guardian Jax."

His breath sucked in. "*Don't* call me that."

"Sorry . . . Dark Raider."

He huffed out a breath and then gestured toward camp. "After you."

I lifted my bulky skirt and slowly began to walk toward the camp.

The Wood quieted around us, as if the creatures eyeing us through the foliage were also mindful of the male in their vicinity. Despite most of the wildlings hiding, I still caught sight of a pair of thin yellow eyes, no more than a foot from the ground. The *beemi* was entirely hidden, and if I hadn't spent so much of my life in the Wood, I wouldn't have seen him.

But the moment I stepped toward him, pleading with my eyes for help, the wildling scurried silently away, not even disturbing the leaves hiding it.

Shoulders drooping, I gathered my skirts more and took my time stepping carefully over the foliage on my way back to camp.

I debated faking a fall to delay us, but since Jax walked so closely behind me, he'd likely catch me right away. Besides, a fall would only delay us by a few minutes.

I'd have to find another way.

Only minutes later, I was back to where I'd woken up with no solid plan in place, but as promised, near the disassembled tent I'd slept in, waited a plate with a wide slice of bread, a wedge of cheese, and a cup of water.

"Eat." Jax gestured to the food, then left to join Phillen and the other males.

Sighing, I did as he said, or tried to, but when I leaned

down to grab the plate, my gown's tight corset stopped me and pinched off my breath.

Grumbling, I straightened and rubbed my sore ribs.

"Excuse me?" I called to the six of them. "Do you by chance have a new gown for me? This one is quite heavy and cumbersome. Perhaps you have something less bulky that will make walking easier?"

One of the males, the one who had been farther back in the group initially, eyed me. Brown eyebrows and dark-brown skin were visible in the slit between his mask and scarf.

So there are two *brunettes in this group.* The male beside him remained quiet but had red eyebrows. *And a true redhead as well apparently.*

"We don't," Jax replied gruffly. "But don't worry, you won't have to walk."

"I won't?"

Jax shook his head. "No, you'll ride. I can get you a change of clothes after we're out of your kingdom. Two days at the most. You'll have to wear that gown until then."

I frowned. *We'll be out of Faewood Kingdom within two days? Goddess Above, how far have we gone?*

But then his words hit me. We were riding out of here, yet there were no *domals*, but if I remembered correctly, Jax had said the same thing when we'd been in the tent. And there'd been the sound of hoofbeats last night when they'd abducted me. But there weren't any domals anywhere.

I held my hands up in question. "What in the realm am I to ride?"

Jax hooked his thumb toward Phillen. "Him. He drew the short straw."

My lips parted, and annoyance flared through me. "You want me to ride your friend? Is that to be done in some kind of perverted stunt?"

A few of the males outright snorted, and I could have sworn a sly smile lifted Jax's lips from the way his eyes crinkled even more. "It's no joke, Little Lorafin. You'll ride him, but not in the way you're suggesting."

Before I could ask anything further, a flash of magic cut through the clearing, and Phillen's fae form disappeared.

The creature that stood before me made all hopes of delaying my captors' journey die a thousand times over. Now I knew what I was going to ride.

And there was no way Guardian Alleron would ever catch up to me.

CHAPTER 5

"You're *brommel stag* shifters?" My jaw dropped.

"What gave it away?" the lean, blond male replied dryly.

My mind raced. Animal shifters commonly hailed from Stonewild Kingdom, the kingdom north of us. That possibly meant Jax was from Stonewild. What the kingsfae would give to have that knowledge. As far as I knew, nobody knew what kingdom the Dark Raider came from, although I'd once heard that some thought he was from Mistvale. But that was likely a rumor.

The huge stag that stood before me—Phillen in his shifted form—snorted and pawed at the ground. He was *huge*. His shoulders easily reached five feet, and his large head rose a good three feet above that. And considering his chuffing noises, I would have bet that the brawny male was laughing at me.

As if to mock my surprise, magic flashed around the other

four males, and before I could blink, *five* brommel stags stood beside Jax.

They were all different colors. Two brown, one deep golden, one auburn, and the last a true red. Their colors obviously coincided with their natural fae hair shades. Each stood tall with broad chests that had thicker, denser, and darker colored hair compared to the rest of their bodies. Powerful haunches hinted at their superior running capabilities, and puffs of dense magic filled the air around them. Impressive antler racks stretched wide and high from each male's head. They were so big they nearly tangled in the vines that wove and dipped through the Wood's canopy.

Yet no remains of clothing fluttered to the forest floor. Their black disguises had disappeared entirely, making me think their shifter magic concealed it or perhaps stored their clothes somewhere I couldn't see.

Whatever the case, my shoulders fell. *Goddess, I shall never be rescued.*

Brommel stags were some of the fastest creatures in the realm. A naturally born brommel stag, a true animal and not a fae shifter, was known for its speed and ability to outrun any other animal. Most fae who tried to hunt them could never catch one. Not even the Nolus, Lochen, and Solis fae had developed a reliable way to ensnare brommel stags, and only those truly gifted with magic had ever been able to take one down.

Which meant I was entirely in over my head if I'd hoped to slow them.

"Are you a stag shifter too?" I asked Jax.

He made a noise, and I had a feeling he was smirking, but that damned mask covered his expression. "That would be telling."

Huffing, I aggressively snatched the plate from the ground and began to force the food into my mouth while I collected my thoughts. Since I was apparently going to ride Phillen, that meant I would have an even harder time impeding our journey.

As I finished the dry meal, Jax lifted pack after pack to his friends' backs until all of their supplies were secured. Long bows were also stored on each shifter, and numerous quivers of arrows were strapped to them. It seemed to be their preferred weapon of choice.

But even those huge bows didn't appear awkwardly packed on the stags. And none of the males so much as staggered under their supplies' weight.

Once everything was secure, only Phillen's back remained bare. With a sickening lurch of my stomach, I realized they truly intended for me to ride him.

Finally done eating, I drank the cup of water, then wiped my mouth.

"Ready?" Jax sauntered toward me.

"Wait." I held up my hands when he neared.

He paused, staying rooted to the spot several feet away. Once again, his gaze was unnervingly intent.

I chewed on my lower lip, and for the briefest moment, Jax's gaze dipped to watch the movement, but just as fast, he snapped his eyes up.

"I can't ride him. I don't know how to ride." I made a show of twisting my hands even though my claim wasn't entirely true. I was fairly versed in riding domals, but I wasn't practiced in riding any animal bareback.

"You're worried about falling?"

"Wouldn't you be?"

He prowled closer to me, and his eyes crinkled in the corners. "No need to be concerned. I won't let you fall."

My brows pinched together, and I cocked my head. "You won't let me—" My eyes flashed wide. "Wait, you're going to ride on Phillen's back *with* me?"

Phillen let out a loud snort, and I couldn't tell if he was enjoying my horror or if he was as offended as me.

One of Jax's dark eyebrows quirked up. "Of course, I'll ride with you. How else can we trust you to stay atop him and not tumble off?"

"Is that how you took me last night? You were riding Phillen?" I didn't remember many details about my abduction, but I distinctly remembered the feel of an arm sliding around my waist and the memorable sound of hoofbeats.

"Perhaps."

I ground my teeth together at another vague answer. "Perhaps?"

But instead of divulging anything further, the Dark Raider nodded toward Phillen. "Enough questions, Little Lorafin. We're leaving. *Now*."

EVEN THOUGH I'D been worried about falling off Phillen, it'd been for naught. Once I was on the stag, Jax straddled the natural groove of Phillen's back just behind me. My captor's solid chest and muscled thighs slid snugly against me. And to make matters worse, he also snaked an arm around my waist to hold me in a firm grip.

All breath left me. *Stars and galaxy.*

I felt every hard line of Jax, every divot, every pulse in his veins, every breath in his chest. All of him was molded to me like a form-fitting glove. Not one inch of my back remained untouched.

My heart throbbed in time with my aching limbs. Sitting like this made my abused muscles scream.

"Let's go!" Jax called.

I jolted when Phillen abruptly took off at a brisk trot, but Jax's grip only tightened.

"You can hold onto his mane if you want." He nodded toward the thicker hair around Phillen's neck. "Phil won't mind."

Phillen glanced over his shoulder and snorted as he and the other males fell into a single-file line, knees lifting high as they effortlessly pranced through the Wood.

The gait was bumpy and awkward, and each jar of Phillen's body felt like my arse was slamming into stone. At this rate, I would be black and blue by lunchtime. Not to mention, the pain from the callings roared back a thousandfold.

Phillen's pace increased, moving from a brisk trot to a slow canter as the stags cut through the thick Wood. A minute later, we reached a trail. A single strip of soil, trampled by so many creatures the footprints were hard to decipher, cut through the Wood.

Each stag stepped onto it and made a single line, nose to rear as they lined up, never once breaking stride.

"You travel on wildling trails?" I somehow managed.

Jax shrugged. "It's easiest. Keeps the path clear, and nothing tangles our antlers."

I stiffened. He'd said *our antlers*. I was guessing that meant he *was* a stag shifter too.

I opened my mouth to ask another question, but Phillen took off. I lurched backward, hitting Jax right in the chest, but since he was so damned tall, my slamming head missed his face entirely. Pity. I wouldn't have minded giving him a split lip for what he was putting me through.

The stag's speed increased, all five of them moving in perfect synchronicity. The realm rushed past me. We were moving even faster than an enchanted carpet, but then a rush of thick magic puffed from the brawny male, and then . . . we were flying. It was almost as if Phillen was no longer touching the soil, as though he glided along the air, kissing the forest floor in barely discernible flutters.

Phillen and the other shifters moved like the wind, and if not for Jax's solid form and unyielding arm locked around me, I would have indeed flown right off. But my captor's strong thighs seemed to cling effortlessly to his friend despite their impossible speed. Not once did his seat falter.

So this is why Jax insisted on being so close.

Wind whipped against my face, and I squinted my eyes against the wind that began to cut into me like needles. Eyes watering, I could barely breathe, the wind was so fierce.

"I can help with that."

Behind me, a puff of magic emitted from Jax, and the wind immediately stopped.

My hair, still braided thank the Goddess, no longer had wispy strands flowing around my face, and while Phillen continued to move in a blur, the air around me stilled even though the rocking motion of Phillen continued.

"What did you do?" I was too in awe of whatever magic he'd just woven not to ask.

"I created an air bubble around us to stop the wind."

"You created . . . Wait, do you have *elemental* magic?" Perhaps the Dark Raider wasn't from Stonewild after all. He'd never actually confirmed he was a brommel stag shifter despite saying *our antlers*, and if he had elemental air magic, then it was likely he was from Faewood—my kingdom.

"Perhaps."

I rolled my eyes at another vague answer. "So you're from Faewood?"

He shrugged.

At my throat, my collar rattled when my irritation spiked. I knew I needed to figure out a way to delay us, but Jax's clandestine responses were getting on my nerves, even if it was for the best that I didn't know much about him. Less reason to kill me and all if I couldn't find a way to escape.

Jax shifted behind me. "Why does it do that?"

"What?" I replied distractedly.

"Why does your collar vibrate by your skin?" With his free hand, he trailed a fingertip along the smooth metal.

I stiffened again. "It does that in warning."

"Warning of what?" His finger continued to trail along my collar, and if I didn't know better, I had a feeling he was assessing it more thoroughly.

"A warning to not use my magic."

His finger stopped. "You were just trying to use your magic?"

"No, but lorafin magic typically responds to emotions. I thought someone such as yourself would have known that since you sought me out?"

"I've heard that can happen, but I didn't know you'd just

had a strong emotion." He leaned closer, and his breath tickled my skin. "What was your emotion?"

Every fiber in my body locked up, and I tried to inch away from him, but his arm didn't budge. "Do you really need to ask? I've been kidnapped by the Dark Raider, and I'm currently atop a brommel stag shifter being transported to who knows where. Wouldn't that elicit a strong emotion in you?"

"You do make a fair point."

I huffed and tried to make sense of where we were, but the landscape was a blur. In a way, with Jax's elemental magic enacted, it was like being locked in a void—a rocking chair beneath me, a haze of color surrounding me, and a large male behind me.

It felt as if I'd been transported to an alternate reality, and somehow, I had to figure out a way to stop all of this.

"Where are we going?" I asked.

"You'll see."

"Is it truly so bad that you won't tell me?"

"No. I simply find it's best if captives know little about what's happening."

My insides chilled, and I was reminded that I'd likely end up like Mushil if I didn't find a way out of this. "I thought you weren't in a habit of abducting females?"

"I'm not."

"Yet the words you just uttered claimed otherwise."

"No, they didn't. How do you know I wasn't referring to male captives?"

"So you take male captives regularly but not females?"

"When I need to."

The chill in me morphed into annoyance again. "Do you always answer questions this vaguely?"

"Sometimes."

"What's everybody's names?" I asked, switching subjects since our destination was apparently guarded knowledge. "Or should I start calling the others Red, Blond, Brown One, and Brown Two? Oh, and of course there's Phillen." I figured there was no harm in learning their names. I doubted they were their real names anyway.

The stag in front of Phillen, Brown One I decided to call him, glanced for the briefest moment over his shoulder. I could have sworn he narrowed his eyes.

Jax pointed to him. "That's Lander, and the other brown-haired fairy, the one with the earring, is Bowan. The blond is Trivan, and the redhead is Lars."

"Lander, Bowan, Trivan, Lars, and Phillen." I didn't know if I would be able to keep them straight, but at least I had names for everyone.

Jax leaned closer, his thighs tightening around Phillen slightly. "So, tell me more about this collar."

Since I was currently at a loss for how to slow them down, I replied tartly, "What do you want to know about it? It's magical. It doesn't come off, and despite all of this effort you're going through, I'm entirely useless to you with it in place, so if you change your mind about my captivity, feel free to stop and leave me right here."

He touched my collar again, and when his fingertip grazed softly against my skin, a shiver fluttered down my neck. "And your guardian? What can you tell me about him?"

I stiffened. "Why do you want to know about him?"

"I'm just curious. He put this on you after all, didn't he?"

"So you're saying that you want *me* to talk while you refuse to?"

"I haven't refused to talk. Aren't we talking right now?"

"Right, but you get to ask questions, and I don't?"

"You seem to have been asking questions just fine."

"But you don't *answer* them, so they don't really count."

"I don't see how that's relevant."

A chuff came from the blond, who was named Trivan, if I remembered right. At least someone was enjoying my annoyance.

"Back to your guardian," Jax said, shifting behind me. "From what I learned, he's quite wealthy and only recently moved to that estate you were traveling to last night."

I started. "You researched Guardian Alleron?"

"I did."

"Yet you didn't know of my collar?"

A discontented sound came from him. "No, an embarrassing slight on my part, I'll admit, but what else can you tell me about him?"

My stomach began to churn. "Um . . . what do you already know of him?"

"That he's used you for full seasons to fill his pockets. He's now rich, conceited, arrogant, and smug since he's acquired so much. He's also a native to Faewood Kingdom and has finally secured the status he's relished since childhood—a name among the nobles with hopes of becoming a favorite of the king. All of this is to secure his ultimate goal, to become an appointed lordling who commands one of your kingdom's ten Houses, but without you at his side any longer, I don't see that goal being achieved."

Without you at his side . . . My pulse leaped. He'd just said *without you at his side.*

That had to mean that he *wasn't* going to let me go, because if he intended to ultimately release me after his calling, he *wouldn't* have said that.

Stars and galaxy.

A part of me wondered if he was even aware of his slip.

Not that it mattered.

Goddess, I must delay them. Now!

I cleared my throat, and my mind raced as I tried to figure out how. "It seems you've been watching him."

"Learning about him would be the more apt description."

"And all of this was so you could take me from him?"

"Yes."

My heart beat so painfully that I was certain he could hear

it. "And . . . how did you know that I'd be on that enchanted carpet last night at the time that I was?"

He leaned down to whisper in my ear, "Tongues have a habit of spilling secrets when the consequence of not doing so could result in that tongue being removed."

A trail of ice zinged through me all the way to my bones. The Dark Raider had just said that statement so casually, so matter of fact. As though cutting out tongues was no different from washing one's hands before a meal.

Or killing a kind guard who was only doing his job. My breath hitched. *Or disposing of a lorafin who couldn't access her magic.*

He's going to kill me. I'm sure of it. Nothing about this situation will end well for me.

And in that moment, an idea came to me at lightning speed.

I knew what I needed to do. It would be to my detriment, but it was the only thing I could think of that could ultimately lead to my escape.

CHAPTER 6

I curled my concentration inward, cringing at what was about to happen. The last time I'd done such a thing was when I was a teenager and had learned the hard way what would happen if I defied the collar, but at the moment, if I wanted to escape, I had no choice.

I squeezed my eyes closed and delved my focus down to my magic. Down to my bottomless depth of power.

Down.

Shadows unfurled within me, my lorafin essence cold and writhing. My magic swirled, growing more potent with every breath.

Rattling, my collar *zapped* against my skin, the sharp sting a clear warning of what would come if I continued.

"Elowen?" Jax said, confusion evident in his voice.

But I didn't stop. I didn't douse the power that was rising inside me. I called to it, crooned to it until it heeded my command.

Painful pulses of electricity emitted from the collar again, and again, and again. They grew sharper and more acute with each *zap* that was emitted.

I steeled myself for the inevitable punishment and demanded that my magic venture me to the Veiled Between.

My magic sang in response. Darkness. Power. Might.

I was the princess of shadows.

The walker between the veils.

The enchantress of the semelees.

I was a lorafin by birthright, and I would one day be the maker of my own destiny.

A shout came from behind me. A firm grip on my shoulder came next. Someone spun me from where I sat as more voices came, but I didn't stop, and I wouldn't.

My soul shot through the galaxy until the Veil appeared in the darkness, a wispy fog that called to me. *Come to me. Come to me, my creatures.* I was so close. I reached toward the Veil, and my fingertips parted the cool mist. The semelees on the other side stirred, sensing my presence.

I entered the Veiled Between, and a semelee swam toward me. *You've come, Daughter of Darkness. What do you seek?*

An electrifying *zap* skated along my limbs, nearly jolting me back.

For a moment, I hung suspended, pain ricocheting through me, but the second I regained control, I pushed myself farther through the Veil and clenched my teeth with each inch that I won. The semelee watched me, waiting for my command, but instead of demanding anything, I pushed farther, which triggered my collar even more.

Another paralyzing sting of magic slashed from my collar, so strong that for a brief moment, the Veil disappeared, and I saw stars.

Another bolt skittered along my nerves, setting me on fire. I screamed, and the collar unleashed a third explosive array of whips.

Its triggered magic zoomed through my system as the mist disappeared, and then I was falling. Falling once again into my body as the Veiled Between fell to the great beyond.

Burning sparks of lightning shot from the magical device and ignited my nerves. Scorched flesh encircled my throat. My body convulsed. My eyes rolled back in my head. The collar's dousing effects, on top of the pain I'd already been dealing with following the callings yesterday, made agony rip through me.

"Elowen!" Jax roared.

I seized in his arms, jerking so violently that I tipped to the side, but the collar didn't stop its punishment. It wouldn't. I'd gone too far.

Jax grabbed me, halting my spasms, but then I was on the ground, my limbs under the control of the collar. Legs and arms jerked out, contorting at impossible angles. Bones cracked. Flesh burned. A scream of pain escaped me as the collar punished me severely for using my lorafin powers without permission.

But it wasn't until terrified eyes stared down at me, pulling me into their impossible sapphire depths, that blessedly, the collar at last calmed.

I slumped to the side, my body broken and my mind bruised.

"Elowen!" Jax yelled again.

He held me in his arms, eyes wide with shock, as grass tickled my cheek.

Sheer agony sizzled through me. Everything burned and ached so potently I could barely breathe, but it didn't stop the small triumphant smile that parted my lips.

We'd stopped, and Jax and all of his friends had shifted back into their fae forms with looks of horror coating their faces.

It was the last thing I saw before everything went black.

I awoke to the sound of footsteps pacing by my ears. Someone was walking back and forth, back and forth. The scent of the Wood came next, that musky and damp fragrance that always reminded me of dewy mornings and curious wildlings scampering through the trees.

"What in all the realms happened, Jax?" a male asked.

Pain still barreled through me, but I forced my breathing to remain even, and my eyes closed.

"I don't know," the Dark Raider snarled. "She was just sitting with me, and then all of a sudden she began to tremble, her magic began to rise, and then out of nowhere she just"—his breath sucked in—"*broke*. I've never seen anything like that."

"Do you think she's sick?" Phillen asked, his deep voice easy to distinguish from the others.

"I thought lorafins didn't get sick," another of the males replied in a monotone voice. It was someone I hadn't heard before, so I had no idea who it was.

A snort. "Bollocks, Lander. Everybody gets sick at some point." That voice sounded like the blond—Trivan. "And now our time with her will be delayed even more. She can't perform a calling like *this*."

"But I thought lorafins were magically superior," Lander replied in the same monotone voice. "You know, how they have their own type of magic, which can also mend themselves, unlike most fae in the kingdoms?"

"They are incredibly powerful and can heal rapidly," Jax growled, "but I've never heard of them breaking like she just did."

"Do you still want to keep her?" Trivan asked. He sighed, the sound carrying a hint of annoyance. "Maybe it's not worth it. We could find another way without her because there's a reason lorafins are allowed to be slaves. If they're a danger to others, as she very well could be, then their guardians have to prove they can control them."

I bristled inwardly.

"Of course, we're keeping her," Jax snapped. "We still need her." More pacing came from above my head, and it hit me that it was Jax I was hearing walking frantically in the Wood.

A bird song trailed through the air, then the sound of more voices. Distant voices. Ones I'd never heard before. My ears pricked toward that sound. Fae were *talking*, not far from where we were. And they weren't my captors.

My eyes flew open.

The Wood still surrounded me, and all six males were covered once more in black clothing and masked faces. A faint green sky shone through the trees' canopy above.

Pain shot through me anew when I pushed to sitting.

"Whoa, she's awake." Phillen startled from where he sat.

Jax was immediately at my side, crouching down in the tall grass from where I lay at the base of a *babbo* tree. "Elowen?"

But I didn't pay him any attention. My gaze whipped about, even though a hiss parted my lips from that frantic movement. I searched for the sound of those distant voices. I needed to find them.

There.

Through the Wood, a group of fae were walking. Nothing impeded them. No vines, trees, or roots. They had to be

KRISTA STREET

walking on a road, a *road*, which meant that civilization wasn't far away.

I cried out, raising a desperate hand in their direction, but the second I uttered a sound, a heavy palm clamped over my face.

I screamed, or tried to, but Jax muffled the sound.

In a blurred move, he had me hauled against his chest and us hidden behind the massive babbo tree. His other arm wrapped around my waist, pinning me to him. "Stop. Stay quiet," he whispered into my ear.

For one crazy, asinine moment, I considered biting him as hard as I could and then screaming at the top of my lungs.

"Don't," he hissed. "Don't be foolish."

I breathed heavily through my nose. My chest heaved, and my heart was thundering. Vibrations began along my collar again.

Jax groaned. "Elowen," he said on a low whisper. "*Please.* I'm not going to hurt you."

Every fiber in my body ached and burned, but the damage that had been done to me by the collar—the broken bones, burned skin, and fizzled nerves—had mostly healed, but the effects lingered. Lander was right in one aspect. I rarely got sick, and most of my injuries healed quickly, but not the mental ones, and not the ones from a calling.

I attempted to thrash, but Jax tightened his grip, and I whimpered.

"Elowen, please, stop." His voice turned gruff. "I mean it. I don't want to hurt you, but I'll be left with no choice if you continue."

Realizing I wasn't going to win this, I slackened in his grip.

His arms loosened slightly. "Can I trust you not to scream?"

I knew that I could scream my head off once he removed his hand. But if I did that, the fae on the road would likely come to my aid, and then they'd happen upon the Dark Raider. While I knew that Jax's violent nature was reserved for the truly vile in our realm, I also knew that he didn't have any qualms with killing those to get what he wanted. He'd done nothing less to all four of Guardian Alleron's guards. So if I screamed for help now, and those fae came running, Jax would be forced to kill them to protect himself, and then they would all be dead, and their deaths would be on my conscience.

I shouldn't have called out to them in the first place. It was an impulsive thing to do.

Shoulders slumping, I accepted my defeat and nodded.

Jax slowly removed his hand while the other five formed a half circle around us. As before, I could barely discern any of their features since their disguises were in place, but Phillen hunkered down at my side.

The others were looking toward the group traveling on the road and were whispering to each other.

"Jax?" one of them called quietly. Lars signaled him over, then said something quietly in his ear.

Jax's attention whipped toward the travelers. Eyebrows

slanting together, I tried to see what all the fuss was about. Through the trees, a few features in the group became apparent. Snouts on two. Hooved hands on one. A long tail on another. Yet they all walked on two legs and had partially siltenite bodies.

Half-breeds.

Shock billowed through me. There were so many of them —fae of both wildling and siltenite descent. Usually, their kind remained hidden. They were scorned and looked down upon throughout the kingdoms, and most didn't often call attention to themselves. But the group traveling on the road was at least a dozen strong.

How odd.

"I'm glad you've decided not to do anything stupid."

Phillen's comment snapped my attention back to him. I arched an eyebrow as Jax continued whispering with the others.

Phillen scoffed lightly, and I guessed I'd communicated my silent, sardonic response quite effectively.

His brown eyes raked over my frame, but my limbs were already back to normal, the unnatural angles gone after the collar had broken my bones. The fact that I was already healed meant I'd been passed out for at least a few hours. *A few hours.* A sliver of triumph skated through me. I'd truly delayed them and was one minute closer to a potential rescue.

Eyes narrowing, Phillen asked, "What happened when you were riding me, Elowen? Are you sick?"

I contemplated my response. I didn't know if my plan would work. I had no idea if I'd just doomed myself to even more misery, but there was only one way to find out.

I gave a slight nod.

His eyebrows shot up. "You are?"

I kept my voice small when I replied, "It hurts."

"Jax?" Phillen called quietly. "She's still hurt."

In a heartbeat, Jax was at my side, his whisperings done. "Where?"

"Everywhere." My voice came out raspy and raw, and that wasn't even faked. The skin on my neck was still tender, and it smarted every time the collar rubbed on it. I knew if I looked in the mirror, a fresh burn mark would still be apparent, the skin red and angry. Burns could take hours to heal if they went truly deep.

The concern in Jax's eyes grew. "Can you move your limbs?"

I made a show of trying to but winced. Once again, I wasn't pretending. Fire raced up my veins from my still-frazzled nerves, and even though my bones were no longer broken, they *hurt*.

"Dammit," he muttered under his breath.

"So, she'll be in a bit of pain when we travel." Trivan shrugged. "Big deal."

But a growl from Jax had his nonchalance evaporating. "No, Triv . . . it *is* a big deal. She's of no use to me like this. This will prolong my calling even more, and she'll be even worse off when we get there if she doesn't heal completely. I doubt that intense travel will make her better. She needs to be fully healthy to venture to the Veiled Between for me. We can't keep going like this."

A flare of hope fired through me, and I said in a stuttering tone, "I just need some rest. Usually, when this happens, I . . ." I sniffed and took a shuddering breath. *Goddess*, the damsel-in-distress act was embarrassing, but if it worked, I'd do it to all three moons and back if needed. "I . . . I need a few days of sleep and recovery. That's all. Then I'll be able to ride again."

"*Days?*" Bowan—the male with light-brown skin, the earring, and a jovial-sounding voice—raised his eyebrows. "But we're supposed to be in—"

"I know." Jax cut him off. Pinching the bridge of his nose, the Dark Raider shot me an accusing glare. "How in the realm did this happen anyway?"

I shrugged. "I don't know. Sometimes, it just does."

But Jax didn't look away, and his eyes narrowed. For a brief moment, I thought he was going to call me on my bluff, but then he began pacing anew. "How far is Lemos?"

Lemos? I tried to keep my eyes from bugging out. If we were near Lemos, we were traveling much faster than I would have thought possible. And that also meant we were heading north, in the direction of Stonewild Kingdom.

Is that where he's taking me? I supposed it made sense if most of them were shifters.

"It's not far off." Lars nodded toward the road.

Trivan crossed his arms. "It's likely where that group was coming from. If we stick to the trail, we can probably be there within the hour."

"How are we gonna move her?" Bowan leaned against a tree, regarding me, and with a start, I realized he had green eyes, like me.

I twisted my hands in my lap. "My guardian usually uses an enchanted carpet."

Phillen snorted. "I'm afraid we don't have one of those, lovely."

"We can get one." Jax turned to the redhead. "Lars, shift and head to Lemos. Buy a carpet and bring it back."

Lars's eyebrows rose clear to his bandana.

"Go," Jax growled.

Another thrill ran through me. Venturing to Lemos to find an enchanted carpet would take at least an hour. Dealers of the magical forms of transportation could be hard to find.

I leaned my head against the tree, not even having to feign fatigue, but I made sure to wince again and act as though every breath pained me.

"What are we going to do in Lemos?" Trivan asked shrewdly. The lean blond cast me an annoyed glare.

Jax paced again in the grass. "I guess we'll find an inn, get a room, and let her rest for a day. But that's it. After that, we're getting out of Faewood."

CHAPTER 7

The fact that I'd managed to truly delay us caused me to feel wonderfully giddy. I'd actually beaten the Dark Raider at his own game, and that realization made a swell of triumph fill my soul. Suppressing that response, I forced my lips to stay pressed into a tight line as we glided on an enchanted carpet to Lemos.

Jax sat beside me, Phillen and Lander behind him. Bowan, Lars, and Trivan had all shifted back into stag form and pranced behind us. We were traveling much slower than we had while all of them had been running at full speed, and since Jax planned to let me rest for an entire night, with any luck, Guardian Alleron would now have a chance to reach me.

Wind flowed over my cheeks as I contemplated the night ahead. I knew that my situation was still precarious, and that at any moment, Jax could change his mind and insist that we move despite my state, but I didn't think he would.

If I wasn't such a rare creature, Jax probably would have carried on even if I'd been bleeding and all of my limbs had been broken. But the fact that he was changing his plans to ensure I returned to full health solidified how much he was counting on me to find whomever he was seeking. Even if I never could with my collar in place . . .

I peered up at Jax, curiosity filling me. He stood over me, staring ahead. His all-black attire hid his identity completely. From his actions, it was obvious he was desperate to find whomever he sought, so much so that he was going to great lengths to secure my power. And I couldn't help but wonder who it was. A lover perhaps. Or maybe it wasn't someone he cared for at all. Maybe vengeance was what drove him. Perhaps he was seeking a fairy who had wronged him, and the moment he found them, he would send them on a brutal journey to the afterlife, just as he'd done to poor Mushil, who'd never done anything untoward nor deserved that kind of punishment from anyone.

Closing my eyes, I glanced away. Wind blew over my cheeks, and fresh pain twisted my heart. The Dark Raider might care for whomever he desired to find, but he hadn't cared one bit for my dutiful guard.

Heart hardening, that reminder reaffirmed that escaping him was the smartest option. One way or another, I would find a way to free myself tonight. I wouldn't be another victim of the ruthless Dark Raider too.

Rooftops in Lemos soon appeared. They rose from the Wood, above the tree line, and hinted at a blend of stone, beamed siding, and slanted peaks. From what I could see, the small city was a bustling blend of the Wood, modern roads, and creative architecture. Gnarled branches wove through many of the homes and shops. Leaves sprouted from siding. Moss-covered bark climbed over roofs. The city's constructors had obviously welcomed the Wood versus deterring it when they'd built this town.

I'd heard of Lemos over the seasons. It was mostly known as a laboring city and produced some of our kingdom's finest wheat, but it wasn't until we crested a large hill that I finally saw the crops sprawling north of the city. Acres and acres of rolling hillside were covered in swaying stalks that shimmered in a rainbow of colors.

Yet those very fields were why I'd never visited this area before. The fae who lived here weren't lordlings, and they weren't wealthy, which meant they held no interest to Guardian Alleron since they couldn't afford his hefty fee even if they wanted to use his lorafin.

Jax muttered a command, and the enchanted carpet slowed as we began to descend the hill into Lemos. "Bowan, a glamour if you would."

I pushed up just in time to see the three following us in

their stag form shift back to fae and leap onto the carpet. In my next breath, a dose of magic altered all their appearances.

Their black disguises and ebony clothing morphed into one of normality. Before my eyes, the masks disappeared, the head scarves obliterated, and the dark clothing transformed. In a blink, all of them were fae wearing simple, laboring wear, and all of their faces morphed into fae males I'd never seen before.

And then my gown changed too. Even though I still felt my bulky skirt's numerous layers of tulle, my gown morphed into a simple home-spun dress. Nothing about it screamed for attention. It was a simple frock that any fairy could be wearing.

I seethed inwardly. Now, I wouldn't draw attention at all in Lemos.

Phillen laughed when his trousers turned baggy and worn. "My da used to wear pants like these."

Dammit. So Bowan is quite adept at glamours. Good to know.

Even though all fae could create glamours, some were more adept at it than others, and considering Jax had asked Bowan to do it, meant Bowan likely produced the strongest glamours in their group.

But I was under no illusion that what I was seeing was even remotely close to their true features. Despite their builds staying the same, all of their ears got sharper or longer. The noses that had pushed against their masks had either lengthened or shortened. Not even their hair remained true to their inherent coloring.

Jax's dark locks changed to a rusty brown. Phillen's turned as red as Lars's, yet the natural redhead shifted to being blonder than Trivan. Bowan and Lander remained brunettes, yet Lander's shoulder-length hair shortened, and Bowan's grew longer. And Trivan was behind them all, so I couldn't even see what he'd changed into.

It all happened so fast. As soon as their appearances finished morphing, I struggled to remember who'd turned into what.

I grumbled and lay back down. If I'd had any hope of understanding their identities before, I knew now I never would. Six strangers surrounded me.

"What's the matter, Little Lorafin?" Bowan asked in an amused tone. At least their voices hadn't changed, yet my grumble grew. "Don't like what you see?"

I peeled my eyes open to see him grinning down at me. His new face had a lovely smile, although the one I offered in return was anything but sweet. "Not at all. I was simply pondering why the feared Dark Raider would feel the need to hide." I slid my attention to Jax. At least I could identify *him* in the group. "Are you afraid of being arrested in Lemos, Guar . . . I mean, Jax?" I batted my eyelashes, my tone like honeyed syrup.

Jax shrugged, not rising to the bait of my intentional slip-up. "Not really."

"Then why the glamours?"

"As you pointed out, without them, our dark disguises are

rather noticeable, meaning we could be pursued by the kingsfae."

I pushed to sitting again, gasping when pain sliced through my stomach. In a heartbeat, Jax was beside me, propping me up.

He glowered. "You need to quit doing that."

"Quit doing what?"

"Hurting yourself."

"Ah, so you would like me to quit existing."

His forehead furrowed, or rather, the male identity that he'd taken on frowned. "Is it always this painful for you? Is every day like this?"

I lifted my shoulders. "Sometimes, yes. Other times, no." *And that's not even a lie.*

His gaze captured mine. The same cerulean eyes that I'd first seen upon waking this morning held firm. At least his eyes hadn't changed. "Does your magic hurt you intentionally?"

"No," I answered honestly, and truth be told, I wasn't sure why I hadn't thought of another lie to spill, anything to keep him thinking I was always this fragile. "It's the collar that does it."

"So, your guardian is the one responsible for the pain."

"How do you figure?"

"He created that collar, did he not? Therefore, he's to blame."

My heartbeat quickened when I thought of what I'd done

when I was only five. "Only because I'm a threat to everyone without it."

Air billowed against my cheeks as the breeze picked up, yet Jax didn't look away. "Is that what he told you? That without his control and collar, you'd be lost without him?"

My brows pinched together just as the carpet slowed when we entered the outskirts of the sprawling town. "How would you know? Are you saying I'm not?"

"If you've never been without it, not truly, how could you actually know if it's needed?"

I arched an eyebrow, but I had no intention of telling him what I'd done seasons ago. Instead, I said sarcastically, "And is that what your scholars told you? That lorafins don't need to be caged?"

But his voice remained calm when he replied, "They told me that only a lorafin can interact with the all-knowing semelees, and only a semelee can confirm if a missing fairy has entered the afterlife, and if they haven't, then only a semelee can reliably tell me where they are."

I had a feeling he was desperately hoping whomever he sought was still alive, but I still didn't know if it was love or vengeance that drove him. Regardless, that buzz of curiosity filled me again.

The carpet zoomed faster down a street and pulled my attention from Jax. We passed a few shops, but then the carpet flew behind them to a quieter lane.

We came to a stop at the back of a building. Before I could

say anything further, Jax hopped off the carpet and nodded briskly toward me. "Keep her here. I'll get rooms."

Phillen inched closer to me, and the remaining four fanned out. It wasn't lost on me that they had me surrounded. And since Jax had commanded the carpet to the narrow street behind the inn, there weren't any siltenites and wildlings around to see my arrival.

"What did he mean by that?" I asked Phillen despite knowing I should shove my curiosity to the far edges of the solar system. "What he said about wanting to know if someone's entered the afterlife? Is he worried whomever he's looking for has died?"

Phillen shrugged. "Suppose you'd have to ask him that."

My nostrils flared, but I figured it was probably for the best. The less I knew or cared about who Jax sought, the better.

The sound of fae walking not far away drifted toward us, even though I couldn't see them, and the five moved in even closer to me.

I snorted. "Afraid I'll run? Or cause a scene?"

One of the males grinned, and when he spoke, I knew from the teasing tone that it was Bowan, the male with brown hair and an earring. "Please do. Then I'll be tasked with catching you." He waggled his eyebrows. "I'll happily tackle you to the ground."

Huffing, I ignored him as I contemplated what to do next. I'd successfully delayed us from leaving Faewood Kingdom, and now, if only I could cause a big enough scene to bring attention to myself, perhaps someone would alert the kingsfae, and I would be able to escape in the commotion.

But before I was able to come up with a plan, Jax was back, and he was dangling three keys on his finger. "Two to a room, but one will have to have three."

"Let me guess, you'll be sharing with the lorafin." Bowan grinned.

Jax gave him a side-eye. "There's food and drink in the salopas below the rooms. It's mostly empty right now. We'll eat, then retreat to our chambers. It's bound to get busier once evening approaches."

"So you *are* afraid of being spotted," I taunted.

He arched an eyebrow at me, but instead of replying, he scooped me into his arms and hefted me off the carpet.

The abrupt feel of his arms enclosing me had my breath stopping. He carried me as though I weighed nothing, then kicked the door open to the inn and carried me across the threshold.

Lingering scents of smoke and fire from the night before permeated the air, and the low ceiling didn't allow much natural light in. The salopas was dimly lit with wood flooring and wood paneling on the walls.

As Jax had said, it was mostly empty. He proceeded down a short hall to the eating area. A lone employee stood behind the bar, and a young wildling female sat at a desk at the front door. Curved horns rose from her head. It was all I could see since her nose was buried in a book. She didn't even glance up when Jax carried me to a table in the corner.

The other five males were right behind us, and when they all crowded into the table, they cornered me—quite literally—and I knew they had no intentions of letting me out.

Jax signaled the bar employee over.

A large wildling male lumbered to our side, the floor vibrating with each step he took. He was a *fusterill,* a giant among the wildlings. His feet were so large that half of my leg could have fit in one of his shoes, and he had to stay stooped to keep from constantly hitting his head against the ceiling. *How uncomfortable to work in an accommodation like this.*

"Bit early for supper. What brings you lot in today?" he said by way of greeting.

"Just passing through," Jax answered easily.

"Actually, I—" As soon as the words left my mouth, a wash of magic shimmered over me, and my voice *disappeared.*

I gaped like a fish, sucking air in and blowing it out, but no matter what I did, I couldn't *speak.*

"Seven rounds of food, of whatever's easiest to make," Jax told the male without missing a beat.

I clawed at my throat, and my magic rattled inside me. Baffled disbelief barreled through me like a racing wildfire.

The fusterill eyed me, concern growing on his face, but Bowan made a comment about the upcoming Matches, drawing his attention away from me.

I tried to speak again. Nothing. I was mute. And then it hit me. *Sensory magic* . . . Jax was using *sensory* magic on me. Speech could also be manipulated by those who wielded sensory magic, although such an ability was uncommon due to the amount of magic it took. But that was a trait of *Ironcrest* fae, not Faewood or Stonewild. *Where in the realm is he from?*

The wildling employee glanced my way once more, frowning anew, but when none of the males showed any signs of concern, and I couldn't scream that I'd been abducted, he listened to the rest of Jax's order before turning and ambling back to the kitchen.

Panic began to cleave through me, and my collar was shaking so violently by the time the fusterill ambled away that my magic was on the brink of combusting.

Jax leaned closer to me, angling his body so I was blocked from view. "Your lost voice is temporary." He shifted closer, and his pine and spicy scent clouded the air around me.

And Goddess Above, he still smelled so *good*.

It made me hate him even more. I bared my teeth and despised myself for craving my captor's scent.

But even though my chest was rising swiftly, and I was glaring daggers at the Dark Raider, he didn't seem concerned. I was pretty sure if looks could kill, he would be dead.

He sighed and finally said, "I couldn't have you screaming that you'd been abducted now, could I?"

The strength of his magic caressed me in a warm cloud, and if I hadn't wanted to spit nails, I would have marveled at his ability.

Phillen leaned back on the bench, the seat groaning in protest. "Count yourself lucky, lovely. If Jax had wanted to, he could have taken your sight and sound too."

My eyes went wide, and I again tried to speak but couldn't. Jax controlled two senses *and* speech. Even for a powerful Ironcrest fairy, to command more than one or two senses was unusual.

Unease filled me again, making me want to retreat inward. I *needed* to get back to my guardian and away from the Dark Raider.

Glittering blue irises narrowed when my shoulders folded together. Jax inched back, putting several inches of space between us. "I'll remove my magic, but this is your only warning. If you cry out, cause a scene, or try to attract attention to us, I'll rob your voice again just as fast." His tone lowered. "Understood?"

I nodded, and even though I tried to stay strong, I began to tremble. Fear cascaded through me, and my magic tried to rise. Tried to come to my rescue. After all, I was a lorafin, a magically rare creature with the ability to venture to the Veiled Between. I wasn't caged by the magic of the four kingdoms, and I *wasn't* a pawn to be played with.

Yet, a pawn was all I'd ever been.

A violent rattle came from my collar, and a silent yelp left my lips.

Jax scowled at my collar. "Remember. Stay quiet."

Another wash of his magic caressed my skin, and when I opened my mouth a second time, a new lightness filled me.

My voice was back.

"You . . . have elemental power and can control multiple senses and speech? And you're likely a shifter too?" My mouth opened and closed, and I clasped my trembling hands. "What in the realm are you?"

Jax shrugged. "I'm a fairy just like you."

"No siltenite fairy that I've ever met has had that many abilities from that many kingdoms."

Trivan snickered and sprawled a leg out of the booth onto the floor. "You haven't even seen half of it, Lorafin."

Before I could ask more, an enchanted serving tray floated toward us. Magic held the tray aloft. Seven pints of beer and plates of steaming pasta with diced hen in a creamy sauce sat on the tray. When it reached us, the enchantment lifted everything and glided it to our place settings.

"What are you?" I hissed at Jax again, just as the steaming plates of pasta filled the air with its rich aroma.

"I told you, a *fairy*. I'm not a rare lorafin like you. I don't command otherrealm power. I simply was born with more magic than others."

For a moment, I couldn't reply. All of the males dug into the food and drink, but the reality of what he'd just revealed barreled through me. No wonder he was so feared among the kingdoms. With that kind of magic at his disposal, he could literally make a fairy completely defenseless.

That kind of power was godlike.

Bowan laughed. "I wish I could capture your face in a portrait right now." He laughed again before forking another bite of creamy pasta. "It never gets old when fae learn what he's capable of."

Lander nodded at Jax and said in his monotone voice, "Best to keep that in mind, Elowen, just in case you're thinking of trying to make a run for it."

Lars's gaze darted between all of us, but he remained silent.

I sagged on my seat, the food in front of me forgotten.

Jax continued eating, yet I knew in that defeated gesture, I'd just given myself away, basically telling all of them I'd been hoping to escape.

But can I? Despite delaying our journey, I was no closer to freedom, and if I couldn't call for help or cause a scene, then my chances at making a break for it were next to nothing.

In other words, I was entirely dependent on Guardian Alleron finding me and saving me.

CHAPTER 8

"Right. Off to our chambers then." Phillen stood from the table once everyone had finished eating and stretched his massive frame. The salopas ceiling nearly brushed the top of his head since their heights hadn't changed, despite their altered appearances.

"Elowen? After you." Jax gestured for me to slide out of the booth.

"Such manners for a male who spends his time kidnapping females," I replied dryly.

His lips lifted in a sly smile. "What can I say? My mother raised me right."

I gave him a side-eye, not liking that on some level I believed him. He was the savior of the poor, after all. I couldn't help but have a modicum of respect for him because of that, but he'd still taken me against my will and was holding me hostage for purely selfish motives. *And* he'd murdered Mushil.

That murder was entirely evil—Mushil had done nothing to deserve that. So even if Jax helped the poor, killing innocent fae like that, I couldn't forgive.

The smooth wooden bench slid against my rump as I sidled to the edge. Once all of us were up, Jax nodded toward the stairs. "Let's get her out of here."

My lips pressed into a tight line. I was so tired of being referred to as if I wasn't even there. My entire life I'd been treated like that.

But I could understand Jax's haste. More fae had entered the salopas, not all travelers either. Local fae were ambling in through the front door, calling out greetings to the wildling and siltenite staff. Yet none of them gave us a second glance, probably because Jax and his friends all acted so at ease, and we appeared like simple laboring fae.

Trivan led the way out of the salopas, a swagger in his step. He even bowed when a pretty siltenite female passed him, and got a slug to his shoulder from Phillen.

The female giggled, flashing Trivan a smile, and I wanted to scream at her to run the other way and not be fooled by their antics.

When we passed the wildling staff member at the front door, she glanced up from her book. Trivan gave her a flirtatious grin too, at which her horns turned pink, but she quickly stuck her nose back in the pages and hunched over her novel.

I chewed on my lip, wondering how I could signal to her that I was in distress. But considering she seemed more interested in reading than working, I doubted I would be able to grab her attention.

Still, I could try, and if I was subtle, maybe Jax wouldn't notice.

I drifted closer to her table, my fingers reaching out, but as soon as I'd moved two feet from the others, a hand pressed to my back. The warmth of it, along with the intoxicating pine and spicy fragrance that accompanied it, told me immediately who the hand belonged to.

"Don't."

Jax's single warning was all I got before his magic appeared again. It clouded around me, not stealing my voice, but I knew if I so much as uttered a peep, he would render me mute again.

Glaring at him, I abandoned my attempt to engage the wildling but still jerked away from him before following his friends up the stairs.

Music began in the salopas, drifting to us, and more voices carried to me as we climbed the stairs. Creaky steps groaned beneath our feet as we trudged to the second floor.

"We'll stay here." Jax stopped at the first door in the hallway, then threw the remaining keys to his friends. The Dark Raider unlocked the door, pressed his hand to my lower back *again*, and then ushered me inside before I could so much as ask why I had to share a room with him.

The lone sleeping chamber I stepped into contained a narrow bed, barely big enough for two fae, a chest of drawers, a cold fireplace, a wash basin in case a fairy preferred traditional cleansing, and a lavatory.

That was it.

Blue paint covered the walls, similar in shade to my wrinkled gown, and the window overlooked the main street below, a street much larger than the narrow back alley we'd arrived by.

It was still early, the sun hadn't set yet, but Jax waved toward the bed. "Rest. We won't be staying more than one night. Bowan?"

His friend stepped forward, and a rush of Bowan's magic cascaded around me. My glamour disappeared, my gown appearing once more.

I swung toward them, a million questions on my lips, but Bowan and Jax were already in the hall, and Jax was closing the door behind them.

"Wait!"

The sound of the bolt sliding into place followed.

I rushed to the door and immediately tried to disengage the lock, but a pulse of magic flowed over my hand, and the lock *froze*. He'd used a spell to solidify it.

"Bastard!" I pounded on the door. "Let me out of here!"

"My name's Jax, not Bastard. Now, rest. I mean it." Jax's command penetrated the door, but his voice was muffled. "This is your one and only opportunity, Elowen. Don't make me regret this. We won't be stopping again."

Faint footsteps reached my ears from the other side. I pounded on the door again. "Jax! Let me out!"

But if he heard me, he didn't care.

Seething, I swung back around and glowered at my newest cage.

Music thumped from below, along with rowdy singing and laughing. Jax and his friends hadn't returned, which meant they were either standing silently in the hall, were in one of their rooms, or perhaps were even back downstairs in the salopas enjoying a few more pints with the locals and other fae staying at this inn. The Goddess only knew.

Wherever they went, they weren't here, and since it'd been *hours* since Jax had locked me in this chamber, I had no idea when he would be returning.

And, as I'd come to learn, the Dark Raider had not only spelled the door, but he'd also spelled the windows. He must have done that when he first retrieved the keys, and the rest of us had been waiting in the back alley. Or maybe his magic was so powerful that it flowed throughout the room on his way out, sealing every entry and exit point within this chamber. Whatever the case, he'd caged me completely.

Yet he didn't know I knew several counterspells for such an event.

Or, that I'd been waiting for the right time to use them . . .

Joke's on you, Dark Raider.

I waited until the sun set, just so it wouldn't be entirely visible what I was doing, and I didn't put my efforts into the door. That would be the most obvious path of escape, and I worried Jax or his friends would see me in the hall.

Instead, once the sun cast only a dim glow through the streets, I concentrated on the window.

I whispered the most universal spell my tutors had taught me as a child for such an event, and no sooner had the unlocking spell left my lips—my magic rising just enough to wield it—a shimmer appeared around the window's seal.

Jax's sealing spell evaporated.

"Not so powerful now, are you?" I whispered, gloating inwardly that it'd been so easy.

I couldn't take all the credit, though. Guardian Alleron had hired multiple tutors when I'd been young, not scrimping on my education since he sought to impress the wealthy in the realm, who were always supremely educated.

I'd been taught well as a child, and since Guardian Alleron was always on the lookout for someone trying to steal his things, I'd also been instructed from a young age on how to wield the intricate spells to disarm locking mechanisms. And now, that training had come in handy.

I grinned, then grabbed the fireplace poker and wedged it under the window, cracking the paint in the process. I didn't stop, not even when the old wooden frame creaked in protest at being breached. Paint flecked off its rim, but after putting more of my weight into it, the pane squeaked up half an arm's length.

I swallowed my squeal of glee. "Thank you, tutors."

Fresh air swirled around me, and another hoot of laughter came from the salopas below. On the street outside, several fae ambled into the inn's salopas or wandered by on an evening stroll.

I carefully laid the poker on the floor, then focused my attention on the shop across the lane.

By some miracle or gift from the stars and galaxy, the shop across the street was exactly what I needed.

I peered behind me again, but the door remained closed. Even so, I knew if Jax had any inkling what I was attempting, he would return and use his horrid Ironcrest magic on me once more, robbing me of speech entirely and probably for the full night.

A tremor ran through me. To not have the ability to speak had been terrifying. I usually never felt that kind of vulnerability, even when my guardian was selling me off to the highest bidder.

"Bastard. I hope he rots in the underworld." I seethed quietly under my breath, then pulled my gown down my chest more, so all one could see was bare skin, before squeezing my upper body through the window. It was narrow enough that it was a tight fit, but I managed to get one bare arm out, which was all I needed.

"Pardon!" I called quietly and waved in a friendly manner to a passing wildling.

He glanced upward, his beady eyes narrowing when he saw me. "Armarus Above, what are you doing? And undressed nonetheless," he added with a sneer.

I forced a sheepish grin. "Sorry, sir, but could I trouble you to fetch me a *dillemsill*?" I nodded toward the shop across the street.

He frowned, his whiskers twitching and shimmering in the moonlight. "Why don't you get it yourself?"

I brought a hand to my mouth, feigning embarrassment. "I haven't got any clothes on at the moment. I gave them to the inn staff to launder, and well . . ." I shrugged sheepishly.

The wildling rolled his eyes. "Dillemsills aren't free, you know."

"Oh, I know! I have a half rulib to pay for it." Before he could protest, I dropped it to the ground, thankful that I always kept a few coins in my gown's inner pocket. "That should cover it."

He snatched it off the ground, muttering that he didn't have time for this, then stalked to the shop across the lane that had a bright blue sign in its window advertising dillemsills.

I glanced nervously over my shoulder again, certain that at any moment, Jax would burst through the door.

But the door stayed closed, and the music below remained as rowdy as ever.

The wildling returned a few minutes later, carrying the small bird in his cupped hands. He whispered into its ear, then released it.

The small creature, covered in purple feathers with a long yellow furry tail that trailed along the ground when it walked, flew up to me, then hopped onto the sill beside me.

"Thank you!" I called to the wildling.

But he was already halfway down the street and didn't bother replying.

Several other wildlings and siltenites walking by glanced up at me curiously, but nobody interfered or paid me much attention.

I took a deep breath, working to calm my breathing as I carefully held out my palm for the dillemsill to hop onto.

It came readily, then cocked its head, its sharp and intelligent eyes regarding me impatiently. "What's your message?" it asked in a shrill voice.

I brought it closer to my lips and whispered, "I need you to venture to Emerson Estate near the palace, ask for Guardian Alleron, then tell him that the Dark Raider has taken his lorafin, and I'm currently being held captive on the second floor of the Lemosilly Inn in Lemos. And if he's already left Emerson Estate, then you need to find him on the road and warn him. Tell him to bring all of his guards or the kingsfae. He'll need them."

The dillemsill's eyes grew rounder with every word I spoke. "The Dark Raider?" it finally said with a squeak.

"You've been commissioned and accepted my fee," I reminded it sternly. I knew it also understood why I wasn't asking it to go to the local kingsfae. In all likelihood, there was only one or two kingsfae patrolling this small town. And given Jax's strength, dozens would be needed to take him down.

But Guardian Alleron had many trained guards at his disposal, and he could bring more if needed. They would be able to save me if they were prepared for what waited. Sheer numbers alone would do it. My brow furrowed, but I reassured myself that they *wouldn't* end up like Mushil if they arrived on high alert.

The bird's small eyes narrowed, and it ruffled its feathers. Finally, it nodded. "Very well, my lady."

I sagged in relief against the window as the dillemsill began to spin. Its wings flapped. With every movement of its feathers and twirl of its body, the small creature's magic grew. The bird whirled and spun, moving like a mini tornado, and then . . . it disappeared in a wink of magic.

The second it was gone, a small smile formed on my lips. It would take only minutes for the little bird to arrive back at my guardian's estate, and if Guardian Alleron wasn't there, a servant would tell the bird where to venture next.

With any luck, I'd bought enough time for my guardian and his hired hands to get here by tomorrow, and if they traveled through the night, they would make it.

Smiling, I closed the window, made sure I put everything back to where it'd initially been, and then re-engaged the locking spell.

Once certain there were no signs of anything being amiss, I sat down on the bed and waited.

CHAPTER 9

By the time the three moons were high in the sky, the galaxy was alight in a myriad of colors, and the hooting and hollering were so loud from below that I wondered how anyone managed to sleep at this inn, Jax still wasn't back.

I crept to the door, pressing my ear to it to listen.

Nothing.

Nobody stirred outside the room. The only sounds were the loud yells that crept up the stairs from drunk fae below.

I paced back to the bed and lay down. Or rather, I tried to lie down. My large gown made that difficult, but I did my best to heave the opulent skirt out around me, which made the mattress squeak and bounce a few times since it was such a fuss. I loosened a few of the stays too but had to bend and twist to do so. Not for the first time, I cursed the tight corset and bulky design.

Finally settling back, I did my best to relax, but my collar wouldn't stop vibrating, and the mattress kept squeaking. It didn't take much imagination to figure out *why* the bed was so loud. Even though I'd never been privy to such bedchamber activities, it didn't mean I was entirely naïve of them.

Grumbling anew, I eyed the door again, and my collar emitted a small *zap*. "Stars!"

I took several deep breaths, and finally, my collar calmed. Fingers tapping on my thighs, I contemplated what to do. Since Jax still wasn't back, and he thought he'd sealed the windows and door, it was possible he had no intention of returning tonight. Perhaps he figured I was his secured prisoner who he'd fetch in the morning. Given the late hour, that seemed the most likely option, which meant I would probably be alone in this chamber all night until Guardian Alleron arrived. *If* he arrived . . .

Whatever the case, I had a feeling I would be alone for the foreseeable future. Decision made, I heaved out of the bed and thoroughly set to work on my gown. Several minutes and many curses later, I finally had the horrid contraption off me.

I sighed in bliss when the heavy clothing dropped to the floor. *Galaxy above, that feels amazing.* Dressed in nothing but my underthings and a thin shift, I pulled back the covers and fell between the sheets.

Despite the squeaks, the bed was soft and better than the Wood's hard ground. And considering so much had happened in the past two days, it wasn't long before my eyes closed, and exhaustion overtook me.

A HAND CLAMPED over my mouth. "Elowen?" a low voice hissed.

My eyes flew open, a scream lodged in my throat, but when familiar eyes and the scent of smoky leather clouded around me, my panic eased. *He made it!*

The inn's chamber was dark, although traces of gray light streaked through the window, hinting that dawn was coming.

"Do you understand that it's me?" my guardian asked.

I nodded behind his palm.

Guardian Alleron removed his hand, and I had the urge to throw my arms around his neck, but his savage and terrifying smile of victory stopped me. He looked positively . . . sinister.

"You're not hurt?"

"No, Guardian. Are you?" I eyed his shoulder. A thick bandage was apparent beneath his jacket where Jax's arrow had penetrated him.

He scowled. "It's a deep flesh wound, but I'll live."

Relief barreled through me, and I threw the covers off me. At the same time, I slid my hand across the bed to the other side.

Smooth covers greeted me. Jax had never returned, just as I suspected he wouldn't.

That realization hit me at the same time I took in my guardian's appearance. Guardian Alleron's face was covered in unshaved stubble, his usual clean-cut appearance gone. He was also dressed all in black, perhaps in mockery of the Dark Raider or simply as a way to hide in the night, but from the looks of the rising dawn sun, that clothing wouldn't hide him for long.

My guardian crouched at my bedside and hurriedly retrieved my gown. "Get up. We need to get out of here."

I grabbed the large dress and peered around. "Have you seen him?" I pulled on the silky material with hurried movements and cursed when the voluminous skirt caught on my heel.

"No, but you're certain it was the Dark Raider who attacked us in the Wood?"

"Yes."

I finally got the gown on and smoothed it down. My guardian signaled for me to turn around. His movements were rough and jerky as he tightened the stays and did quick work of securing the gown at my back. "You're sure?"

"I mean," I said over my shoulder. "I'm fairly certain it was him. He claimed to be the Dark Raider, and he looked like he was. Not to mention he'd been seen in our kingdom the day prior, but I guess"—I nibbled my lip—"I guess I don't know for certain he's who he claimed to be."

Guardian Alleron scoffed. "I highly doubt it was him. The Dark Raider would never be this easy to trick, and I'm starting to wonder if the three-dozen hired hands I brought along were even necessary. I turned back to retrieve them after that dillemsill found me, but now I'm thinking that was also unnecessary and only delayed me further. Not to mention, the cost of so many is extraordinary."

I bit my lip harder as he finished securing the last ribbon. "I'm sorry. He said he was the Dark Raider, so I thought it best to—"

"It's fine. You can do a few extra callings this month to recoup the cost. Now, get moving. We're going home."

More callings? Fatigue hit me at just the thought, but then I recalled what else he promised. *Home.* We were going back to Emerson Estate. I finally had a home, and all of the fantastical stories I'd read as a child had instilled the belief in me that home meant safety.

Soon, I would be back in my bedroom chambers, enjoying my large soft bed, and I would finally be able to relax and soak in my new huge tub. The wardrobe would be filled with silky gowns and endless tulle—even if I hated those types of dresses —but Lillivel would fuss over me the second I arrived, which made up for the clothing I was expected to wear.

For the first time in two days, anxiety didn't coil my stomach, even if the thought of doing extra callings to fund my rescue made me want to weep. But at least now, I wouldn't have to fear death.

I was going *home.*

I followed Guardian Alleron to the door, but when he

reached for the door handle, he hissed, and his hand shot to his upper arm.

I laid my palm gently on his forearm, but he jerked back so quickly that my hands fluttered awkwardly before I forced them back to my sides. "I'm sorry. I was just concerned. How's your shoulder?"

His nostrils flared. "It's healing. Slowly."

I made a noncommittal noise just as Guardian Alleron swung the door open and ushered me out. He'd obviously already dismantled Jax's locking spell from how easily it opened.

I was about to follow him, but I stopped short.

Down the hall, four guards stood in the dark, like malevolent sentries in their black attire. All were large and heavily armed. I didn't recognize any of them, but they weren't kingsfae. None of them wore the king's seal on their arm or had uniforms of brown, turquoise, and white.

Guardian Alleron huffed. "They're mine. Don't be concerned. *Move*, Elowen."

Hired hands then.

The four males all peered down at me. One of them took in my haphazardly dressed form and gave me a sultry smile.

I quickly hurried past them to follow my guardian, and all of them stalked behind us, their armor clanking softly.

Nobody was in the salopas when we drifted through it downstairs. Neither was anyone at the front door's desk. The female who'd been reading the book and occasionally checking in guests was long gone. It seemed everyone had retired for the night.

Within minutes, we were outside on the quiet street. Fresh air filled the breeze, and the scent of juniper blossoms carried on the wind. If I inhaled long enough, the sweet smell of wheat also permeated my senses.

Only a few wildlings and one siltenite were walking by on the sleepy lane, yet the second they caught sight of us, they scurried the other way or dipped into alleyways between buildings.

I had a feeling that six enchanted carpets and over thirty armed males outside of the Lemosilly Inn had something to do with that.

"On the carpet, Elowen, the one in the middle," Guardian Alleron barked.

I hurriedly did as he demanded but couldn't help but peer around. Confusion filled me when, once again, I didn't spot Jax or his friends anywhere.

Galaxy and Stars, they left me.

That realization struck me so suddenly that I paused mid-step. Whoever Jax was, he'd probably decided that I wasn't worth the trouble after all. Perhaps he accepted that since he couldn't remove my collar, I truly was of no use to him, so he abandoned me in the inn's chamber and fled.

A wash of hurt filled me, which was ridiculous, but anytime anyone left me, it ripped open the old scar of what my mother had done. Once again, I'd been discarded without a second thought.

Irritation filled me that I was allowing such a male to affect me. *He abducted you, murdering innocents in the process, and then left you. Why are you upset by that? Leaving you is a good thing.*

Simmering at my stupid reaction, I settled myself onto the center carpet, dismissing the rumbling of my empty stomach while I prepared myself for the long, full-day journey back to Emerson Estate.

Guardian Alleron hopped onto the carpet I rode and nodded toward a male I'd never seen before, then snapped his fingers. "I need a ward. Now."

The male stood and began to weave his hands through the air while mumbling beneath his breath. A hazy dome appeared around us, visible for only a second before it disappeared.

My eyes widened at the precaution. Guardian Alleron had wards around his estate, but he'd never commissioned one before when traveling.

When the spellcaster finished, my guardian inclined his head. "Let's go."

All of the guards positioned themselves on the carpets around us, weapons raised, postures ready.

The carpets, hovering an arm's length above the sleepy street, lurched forward and then picked up speed.

Wind blew across my cheeks. In the east, the horizon began to glow as the sun crested it. With every second that passed, the eastern sky lit up more, carrying with it a pulse of magic that bathed our realm in the rich essence of a new day.

Normally, I loved sunrises. I loved the feel of our realm billowing around me as the galaxy blessed us with a sprinkling of her magic. The feel of it called to my lorafin abilities, igniting that spark of power within me each day.

But today, all of my concentration lay on the disappearing buildings flying past us.

Within seconds, we careened out of the town and left the swaying wheat fields behind us as we flew up the hill and back into the Wood.

The carpets quickly set on a glided path, hovering above the road and heading south. We were safely on our way back to familiar territory, and we would soon be far away from Jax and his band of raiders.

"Make yourself comfortable. It'll be a long day." Guardian Alleron sat beside me, his injured arm cradled in his lap.

The strongly flowing breeze continued to brush against my cheeks, and the scent of the Wood filled my senses. We traveled swiftly, but the carpet abruptly banked left to avoid a group of fae also heading south.

I pushed the stray strands of hair from my eyes as I peered behind us. "Are those . . ."

"Half-breeds?" Guardian Alleron arched a perfectly plucked eyebrow. "They are. The Centennial Matches are allowing their kind to compete this time around." He made a disgusted noise under his breath. "Those competitors are likely on their way to the capital now in hopes of passing the preliminary tests to compete. I've seen more half-breeds this week than I care to share."

Another group of half-breeds. Just like yesterday. I snuck a second glance over my shoulder at the quickly disappearing group. Several of them sported tails, hooves, and other animalistic features, but they also had the builds of siltenites, pointed ears, and features that were distinctly high fae.

Turning back around, I settled into a seated position once more. "I think it's a positive change that they're being accepted and welcomed into the Matches, don't you think? Some have magic like siltenites, and just because they're part wildling doesn't mean they're any less intelligent. What's the harm in letting them join?"

"You know how quickly they can breed. Any acceptance is repugnant."

"I know they breed faster than us, but is that truly something to fear?"

My guardian eyed me coolly. "The fact that you think they should be accepted tells me you're both ignorant and uneducated. Really, Elowen . . . that's quite disappointing."

A rush of shame crept up my neck, and I ducked my head, not commenting on it further.

We careened around another corner, and the Wood grew denser. The trees' canopy spread over us, blocking out the early morning sun as the dawn's spread of magic slowly receded.

I cleared my throat. "How's Lillivel?"

"Anxious to see you. She's been worried."

"And—" I swallowed, my throat bobbing. "Mushil, Zale, and the other two guards who died, are their families—"

"The guards didn't die."

I blinked, then blinked again. "*What?*" Surely, I'd misheard him. I *saw* them die.

"They still live."

"But they . . . I mean, I saw them . . . *How* are they still alive?" I sputtered.

"I'm unsure, but all four of them showed up at Emerson Estate right before I left. Each complained of a fierce headache and a bruised chest, but they were all alive."

It felt as though the wind got knocked from me. Slumping back, I tried to understand how that was possible. "Mushil's fine?"

"Yes, your favorite guard still breathes." He sneered. "Although, I've since fired him, so you shan't be seeing him again." He scoffed. "And now, after rescuing you so easily, I'm certain it wasn't the Dark Raider who took you. Everyone knows the Dark Raider ruthlessly kills, so the fact that the guards were spared is proof it wasn't him. And considering how easy you were to rescue, just further proves how wrong you were. They fooled you, Elowen. Most likely, it was a group of cowardly thieves who the kingsfae will execute as soon as they find them." He gazed down his sharp nose at me. "I thought I taught you better than that? How did you let them fool you so easily?"

I dipped my head. "I'm sorry. He said he was the Dark Raider, and his powerful magic was so . . ." I sighed, and a huge rush of relief pummeled me that Mushil hadn't been murdered after all. *But how did it appear that he had?* Shaking my head, I added, "It doesn't matter. It's done and over now."

Guardian Alleron clicked his tongue, then gazed ahead, but his cold disappointment clouded around me like a cool mist.

Shoulders slumping, my heart suddenly felt heavy. Sighing, I settled back, closed my eyes, and tried to dispel how foolish I felt. Guardian Alleron was right. Jax wasn't the Dark Raider, and I'd been an idiot to believe my captor.

Another sigh lifted my shoulders, and I tried to get comfortable. It would indeed be a long day. *Best to make the most of it.*

But just as my mind began to drift to the promise of sleep, I stilled.

Nothing was around us.

No sound.

No movement.

The Wood had entirely *stopped*.

I bolted upright, my eyes flying open. Trees flew past us, and all of the guards still had their weapons raised. None of them appeared worried, and all seemed normal, yet . . .

The silence persisted.

I whipped around to face my guardian. "Guardian Alleron! I think—"

Dozens of arrows abruptly whizzed through the air, their tips glowing with a magical essence. All of them hit the dome encasing us simultaneously.

Explosive magic pummeled the ward. It shattered into millions of glittering green sparks that cascaded all around us, falling in tiny glass shards to the road before disappearing.

I screamed just as the guards roared to one another and began to fire.

A dozen more arrows abruptly rained down on us, coming from everywhere.

Fifteen guards fell at once, tumbling off the carpets just as Guardian Alleron shouted, "The ward! A stronger one, *now*!"

The spellcaster clambered to his feet, his hands shaking and his face pale. Whispered words tumbled from his lips, but before he could repair the damage that had ripped through his ward, another arrow whizzed through the air and sliced clear through the spellcaster's throat, like a hot knife cutting through butter.

My stomach lurched when the spellcaster tipped off the carpet. Blood smeared along the carpet's edges, soaking into the fibers. Behind us, dead bodies lay in a pile, but the enchanted carpet didn't slow. If anything, it picked up speed.

Tremors shook my entire body, and my magic sang inside me. The collar zapped and shocked me, wrestling my powers into submission, but my darkness tried to rise up anyway, clouding me protectively until the collar electrified me entirely.

Screaming, I fell back when a fresh burn scorched my neck, but the dousing worked. My magic settled back inside me just as the remaining guards jumped from the outer carpets to the inner one that Guardian Alleron and I rode on.

All of the hired guards continued firing even though neither Jax nor his friends were visible. The guards were firing blind, but Jax's arrows continued to sail through the trees as though a phantom had shot them. And each arrow hit its mark.

Just like the first time. As before, everyone he hit died.

Or did they?

"Where is he?" Guardian Alleron seethed.

Faint hoofbeats abruptly reached my ears, the steady pattering of them growing louder and louder. In a burst of awareness, I understood how their attacks were always unseen.

One of them was using Mistvale magic to hide their appearance until the last moment. An *illusion* was covering them. *Yes!* Everything clicked into place. The guards hadn't died. Whatever coated Jax's arrows didn't impale them but instead penetrated them with a potion that likely knocked them unconscious, yet his *illusion* made it appear that they died. The only arrow that had actually caused harm in the Dark Raider's attacks had been when he'd shot at my guardian, probably doing so to fool my guardian into believing the others had actually perished.

Stars Above, only a fairy capable of wielding immensely

powerful Mistvale magic would be capable of that, which meant—

"Get down!" I screamed.

But the guards didn't heed my warning. They continued standing, still firing, completely oblivious to the fact that they were about to be knocked from the carpet.

A burst of movement *exploded* from the Wood.

Jax, Trivan, and Bowan appeared out of thin air atop three brommel stags. Whatever illusion had been covering them dispelled.

All of them wore black. Their masks and scarves were firmly in place, leaving only their eyes visible, and the glee shining from Jax's gaze had my stomach tumbling.

Before I could utter another scream, each of them shot three arrows at once from their long bows.

And each arrow struck true.

Nine more guards tumbled off the carpet, but before the remaining guards could fire back, Jax and his friends moved in blurred speed and sliced through them.

Every. Last. One of them.

Their bodies hit the ground with a sickening thump. Limbs splayed out at unmoving, unnatural angles.

"Oh Goddess." Horror rose in me, making bile rise in my throat. Utter carnage was left in our wake, and my magic again swelled inside me, threatening to rise above my collar's dousing even though I kept telling myself it wasn't real. But by the gods and goddesses, it *looked* real.

Either oblivious to how vulnerable we were or so arrogant he didn't think they would dare fell him, Guardian Alleron shot to standing and roared, "You can't have her!"

Posture defiant, the wind whipped around my guardian as he stared down the Dark Raider. Lips thinning, fire elemental magic flew from my guardian's hands, flames erupting from his palms.

But the second that fire reached Jax, it fizzled out of existence. My guardian sputtered and tried again, but the same thing happened. His magic was no match for the Dark Raider's elemental power.

My chest heaved. Jax was more magical than any fairy I'd ever encountered, and I knew in that moment, I'd been right. Jax *was* the Dark Raider—the most feared male in the kingdoms, and more powerful than my guardian would ever be.

Jax wielded his stag to the front of our carpet, and Trivan and Bowan closed in on our sides. The enchanted carpet had no choice but to stop since its magic didn't allow collisions.

The wind abruptly died, and the Wood went eerily still. Only my ragged breathing filled the quiet.

Heart threatening to jump up my throat, I sucked in breath after breath as I tried to stop my magic from rattling inside me. I clutched my chest while gaping at the three males surrounding us. *Stars Above, I need to calm down.* I was damned near hyperventilating, and my collar was about to blast me to oblivion if I didn't regain control.

Guardian Alleron hissed and bared his teeth. "You're not taking her!"

A sound came from Jax that sounded suspiciously like a scoff. "It's not just *her* I'm after." He slipped off Phillen, his booted feet landing on the road so quietly, it was a faint whisper.

I lurched back on the carpet, yet the Dark Raider's attention stayed fixated on my guardian. Magic clouded around Jax, then it speared right for Guardian Alleron.

My guardian's mouth opened, then closed, but no sound came.

Oh, Goddess!

My guardian's hand flew to his throat. He clawed at his neck, and his eyes grew so round all of the white was visible.

"No! Don't hurt him," I cried, and I couldn't help my whimper when I pleaded, "Please, *please* just leave us be."

But Jax's focus remained on Guardian Alleron. The Dark Raider's eyes narrowed to slits, and power stirred around him.

In a move too fast for me to fully see, he had Guardian Alleron's face to the carpet and both of his hands behind his back. Guardian Alleron silently kicked and screamed, but it did no good. In my next blink, my guardian's hands were bound in a rope of stinging magic. Jax had him entirely restrained, and his Ironcrest magic had robbed my guardian of his voice.

Nobody in the surrounding Wood would have heard a thing.

My heart leaped into my throat. Even though I suspected that Jax didn't kill as freely as I'd initially assumed, that didn't mean he wasn't dangerous. I contemplated running. Contemplated jumping off the carpet and fleeing through the Wood. But from the crazed look in Trivan's gaze as he watched me, followed by Bowan's crinkling eyes as he no doubt grinned, I knew they would all relish hunting me down.

"Why can't you just leave us alone?" I yelled.

Jax's nostrils flared. "Because I need you, Elowen. I thought I made that clear."

Rage fired through me. Even if all of the guards who had appeared to fall still lived, it didn't make abducting *me* any better.

"You're a monster," I hissed at Jax.

His attention snapped to me. "No, Little Lorafin. The true monster here, is *him*." He shoved his knee into my guardian's back before hauling him upright.

Twisted pain seared across Guardian Alleron's features at the rough treatment of his injured shoulder, but Jax didn't seem to care. He maneuvered Guardian Alleron as though he relished his pain.

Before I could protest or utter a sound of disagreement, Bowan sidled to my side. "Enjoy your night alone, Lorafin?" he asked in a teasing tone.

My head whipped from him, to Jax, and then to Trivan. All three stags also chuffed. "You . . . you planned this?"

Bowan dipped his head, his earring twinkling in the

morning sunlight. He swung his leg over the red stag—Lars obviously—and dropped to the ground. "And it worked out exactly as we hoped."

Jax grabbed Guardian Alleron and threw him onto Lars's back. He did it so easily, as though picking up my guardian's two-hundred-pound weight was nothing.

Only shifter magic gave fae that much strength.

So Jax truly is a shifter too? If that's the case, that means he wields magic from Stonewild, Faewood, and Ironcrest kingdoms. It seemed too impossible to believe.

My stunned surprise grew as the implications of what Jax being a shifter meant. The male harbored magic from *three* kingdoms. Three. *Stars and galaxy.*

But what about the Mistvale magic? Does he wield that too, or does another in his group?

Bowan jumped back onto Lars, landing just behind my guardian. Roughly, he pushed Guardian Alleron forward and tied him to the stag's neck.

A silent cry of pain opened my guardian's mouth wide, but none of the males seemed to care.

Once secured, Bowan jumped off of his friend again, leaving Guardian Alleron alone and restrained on the stag's back.

Both Trivan and Bowan shifted into their stag forms in my next blink, and then the Dark Raider approached me, his aura vicious, his intent obvious.

Even though I knew my attempted rescue had failed, I still

kicked out when he neared, almost connecting with his thigh before he dodged.

He *tsked*, and the magic inside me threatened to rise anew. The collar hummed at my throat, its warning vibrating along my limbs.

Jax eyed the collar, his magic smoldering in his irises. "We ride first, since we need to reach Stonewild, but once we do"—his gaze locked onto my throat—"then I'm dealing with *that*."

CHAPTER 10

We flew through the Wood, moving as fast as the wind. Phillen rocked beneath me. Jax sat behind me. They acted as though all was normal, as if everything that had just occurred was all part of an average day's work, yet I still couldn't move.

Couldn't think.

Could barely breathe.

Shock wrapped around me like a suffocating noose. Because one thing had become apparent. Jax had *wanted* to capture my guardian, which meant the Dark Raider had foreseen my attempted escape. He'd anticipated me calling for help. He'd known I was going to do everything in my power to get away from him.

And he'd been one step ahead of me the entire way.

In front of us, atop Lars, my guardian sat hunched forward, still tied to the stag. Worst of all, I couldn't tell if he was conscious or not.

Guilt speared me that I'd dragged Guardian Alleron into this. If only I'd been smarter, thought of a better plan, or anticipated the level of cunning Jax was capable of . . . none of this would have occurred, and I would have actually gained my freedom from the Dark Raider.

But I hadn't. I'd failed—failed *miserably*.

"How?" I finally whispered. "*How* did you do it?"

Jax shifted behind me, his muscled form hard and unyielding. The solidness of his chest reminded me of carved stone, and given his immense magic and ability to plot things in such a calculating manner, trying to defeat him seemed as impossible as scaling a treacherous mountain.

He shrugged. "Simple. I saw enough of your personality yesterday to know that you wouldn't give up easily, so I offered you a way to seek your guardian out, and you took the bait, exactly as I hoped you would."

My brows drew sharply together. "What do you mean?"

"There's a reason I picked an inn across the street from a shop that sells dillemsills."

I nearly choked. Coughing, I bit out, "You chose that inn for that lone reason? You *knew* I would find a way to acquire one and call for Guardian Alleron's rescue?"

"I didn't know for certain that you'd be capable of it, but I hoped for it. When I sealed the room with a locking spell, I chose one that could be broken out of."

"In other words, you wanted Guardian Alleron to come for me."

"Yes. When I took you, I didn't know about your collar. I saw that you wore it, but I thought it was a piece of jewelry, not a magical device, and when its complexity became apparent, and you confirmed that the only fairy capable of removing it was your guardian, I knew I needed to capture him too. Yet returning to Leafton wasn't an option. I needed him to come to me."

I stilled, freezing so completely that I was like a wall of ice on the Solis continent's Cliffs of Sarum.

When my mind began turning again, I rasped, "So *everything* was set up? All of it? Taking me to the inn, choosing an inn across from that shop, leaving me alone to meddle?"

"Yes."

My cheeks burned. And I thought I'd been so clever, fooling all of them and feeling so superior behind their backs. *So foolish, Elowen . . . You're an absolute imbecile.*

Shame fired through me. "You must have had a good laugh at my expense."

"No, actually, we didn't. Truth be told, we were all quite impressed when you broke through my sealing spell so quickly."

"It was an easy spell," I mumbled, but then my head snapped back. "Wait . . . you were *watching me*?"

"The entire time."

I gritted my teeth. "From where?"

"Across the lane. We were on one of the shop's rooftops, hidden under an illusion."

An illusion. I'd been right. One of them did harbor magic from Mistvale.

But any sense of smugness I felt that I hadn't been wrong about everything dimmed when the depths of his plan took root. He'd played me like a fiddle.

"Stars and galaxy," I whispered.

No wonder he'd never returned during the night. If my cheeks had been pink prior, that was nothing compared to the flaming scarlet they felt like right now.

Jax nudged me. "Don't be embarrassed. You truly surprised me. I thought it would take you half the night to find a way to open the door or window, but you did it much faster than I would have thought possible."

I snorted. "Right. Now, you're truly making a mockery of me."

"I'm not, actually." His voice turned softer, more sincere. "Most females would have lain on the bed crying or screaming for help, but not you. You took matters into your own hands and found a way out."

Some of the heat in my cheeks abated, even though I told myself I was stupid to believe anything he said, but he seemed . . . genuine, which I wasn't sure how to interpret.

I entwined my fingers through Phillen's mane. "And the thirty guards who my guardian brought with him? Did you truly kill all of them as it appeared?"

He was quiet for a moment. "What do you think?"

My chest rose with a deep breath. "I think they all still live.

I think your arrows were dipped in a powerful potion that rendered them unconscious. And I think someone in your group wields Mistvale illusion magic, making it all appear that they'd died when, in reality, they haven't." I paused. "Am I right?"

He chuffed. "Stars."

When he didn't say more, I frowned. "Well, am I?"

"You are." He laughed, a hint of surprise weaving into that sound. "I can't believe how quickly you put that together. Most have no idea that we don't kill those caught in the crossfire. You're quite intelligent, Elowen."

I brushed off his flattery, since I was more interested in getting to the bottom of it all. "So it's true? You pretend to kill, but you don't always?"

He released a breath, then made a sound low in his throat. "I will say this . . . I don't kill innocents, Elowen, and I never will. Those who fall at my hand deserve nothing less for what they've done, but as for others . . . no."

Hearing that made my stiff shoulders soften, and it felt as though the fist that had been squeezing my lungs—constricting each breath since my abduction had occurred—loosened. For the first time since he'd taken me, it felt like I could breathe because Jax might be the Dark Raider, but he *wasn't* as brutal as the kingdoms claimed him to be. He'd simply allowed his reputation to become the monstrous tale that it was, even if the truth remained hidden.

And the reality of that revelation meant he *wasn't* going to kill me.

"Thank you," I finally said. "For not killing Mushil. I thought you had."

He grunted. "I'm assuming that Mushil is one of your personal guards?"

"He is, or rather, *was*. I guess he's been fired." I threaded my fingers more through Phillen's mane, the course hair grounding me as a rush of sadness coasted through me. In all likelihood, I would never see the older guard again.

Jax shifted behind me, his chest brushing my back. "You sound . . . upset by that."

I lifted my shoulders. "Mushil was always kind to me. He was the only personal guard I ever had who was nothing but good to me. When I thought you'd killed him—" I swallowed the thickness in my throat. "Well, he certainly didn't deserve death, so I'm glad you didn't murder him. But I will miss him. I didn't even get to say goodbye."

Jax's chin bobbed against my head, as though he was nodding. "I'm sorry you've lost him, but you're right, I wouldn't have killed him. He was simply doing his job by trying to protect you. I cannot willingly kill a male for doing his work. If I did, then what the kingdoms believe of me would be entirely warranted, so at least now you can rest easy knowing that the guard you cared for still lives."

I sat for a moment in silence, processing exactly what this

new revelation meant. The reality was that Jax might be the Dark Raider, but unlike what I'd thought of him—what everyone thought of him—he wasn't actually evil. He just allowed his reputation to precede him.

I shifted again, my thoughts turning as more questions came to me. "How long were you watching me for, before you took me?"

"About a month."

"And you knew I was a lorafin who catered to the wealthy and had a guardian who kept me under lock and key, so an abduction at night in the Wood was the only way?"

"Yes."

"And you knew I would have the education and training to know a counterspell to break through the locking spell you wielded in Lemos?"

"Also yes."

"What else do you know about me?"

"I know that you're twenty-eight summers old. You've lived a vagabond lifestyle in three of the kingdoms and have only settled in Faewood within the past full season. I know that you don't have any siltenite friends, only wildlings, because your guardian forbade you from forming close friendships with others. And I'm guessing he doesn't know of the wildlings you've befriended, because if he did, he would likely put a stop to it. I know that the king favors you and is likely going out of his mind at this very moment now that I took you and he can't use you for callings, and I know that you treat others with kindness and respect. I saw that very early on while I was watching you. It didn't matter if they were nobles or servants, you were polite to everyone."

I scoffed lightly and for a moment couldn't respond. Finally, I said in a wry tone, "Is there anything you don't know about me?"

"I don't know who your blood family is."

It felt as though he'd punched me in the gut. Gasping, I couldn't speak, but then I managed to rasp, "But you know that my mother left me in the Wood to die?"

A heartbeat of silence passed before Jax replied quietly, "I know that your guardian claims that she left you."

A whirring sound began in my ears, like a high-pitched scream. The realm spun around me, and I leaned forward, trying to dispel the dizziness.

"Elowen?"

I inhaled sharply through my nose as darkness cascaded through me. *Why? Why do I still have such a visceral response whenever anyone mentions my family?*

"Elowen?" Jax ran a hand up my back, softly, lightly, as though afraid the collar would once again break me if he moved too fast.

I slowly straightened, and his hand fell away. But his concern did little to lift my spirits. I couldn't stop thinking about what he was accusing Guardian Alleron of.

No.

The little voice inside my head, the voice that had also whispered things to me throughout the seasons, making me question if everything my guardian told me was a lie, threatened to rise.

No!

I squeezed my eyes tightly shut and dropped my chin. My guardian loved me. I knew he did. He wouldn't have lied to me about my mother, yet once again I was questioning if there was more to it than he claimed.

But until I reached thirty, I would never know.

Defeat swam through me. It was so potent that for a moment, I couldn't breathe.

"Elowen?" Jax said softly again. "I'm sorry if I've upset you."

I took a deep breath and forced myself to calm. When I was certain that my tone wouldn't waver, I replied, "It's fine. It's nothing I haven't considered before." I took another deep breath and exhaled. "But you're wrong. My guardian loves me. If he said my mother abandoned me, then she did."

Jax fell silent, but eventually, I felt him nod.

"So now what?" I asked. "You have both me and Guardian Alleron, which means my guardian can wield the adaptor so I'm able to perform a calling for you. So what's your plan? Do we stop soon so I'm able to find whom you seek?"

"Eventually, yes, but I also know it's too soon for you to perform a calling, especially after the stunt you pulled when your magic broke you. That had to have taken a toll on you."

My cheeks warmed again. Jax knew that the injuries I'd suffered from hadn't been an accident and weren't something my magic occasionally did to me involuntarily. I cleared my throat and hoped he didn't sense my returning embarrassment. "And after I perform your calling, then what?"

"Then I'll let you go."

"You will?"

"Yes. I told you. I'm not a slave guardian. I have no interest or intention of owning you, Elowen."

My breath sucked in, and my heart beat so wildly it felt like a trapped bird in my chest. Before, I wouldn't have believed him. I would have felt it was another pretty lie to manipulate me to do his bidding, but after knowing he hadn't killed Mushil . . .

"Do you mean that? Truly?"

"I do," he replied gruffly. "After you do as I ask, I'll set you free."

Hope surged in me. If he let me go, then my life could return to normal. Guardian Alleron and I could return to Emerson Estate. I could continue counting the days on my calendar until my thirtieth birthday arrived, and then my guardian would permanently remove the collar, and everything I'd been working for could still come true.

I just needed to do Jax's calling, and everything would be set right.

I sat straighter, and a new sense of determination slid

through me. "All right, Jax. You have a deal. Once I'm able to do a calling for you, I will, and then you'll let me go."

A smile filled his words when he replied. "We indeed have a deal, Little Lorafin. Now, no more self-harm on your part and no more stunts to escape. In two days' time, you'll venture to the Veiled Between for me, and then, I'll release you."

CHAPTER 11

By the time we stopped for the night, we'd reached the mountain range that separated Faewood Kingdom from Stonewild Kingdom. A pulse of magic washed over my skin when we crossed the barrier into the new territory. Heady power filled the invisible border. Land that had once bred elemental power now birthed shifters.

I'd never been to this kingdom before. As the most reclusive kingdom on our continent, Stonewild wasn't generally welcoming to outsiders, and since Guardian Alleron had found such success peddling his lorafin in the other kingdoms, he'd never felt the need to venture this far north. So I took it all in, soaking up each new sight and sound as though it were a new day.

Here, if I were to give birth to a siltenite—not a lorafin like myself, a rare anomaly that nobody could explain—the magic in the soil would infuse the infant with shifter magic, igniting each bairn with the ability to turn into a cawing bird or fluffy wolf or prowling cat or some other creature that roamed the Wood.

One never knew which animal the land would choose, but an animal it would be. Or, if the child was blessed, they would develop abilities from more than one kingdom, able to wield not only shifter magic from Stonewild, but psychic magic from Mistvale, or elemental power from Faewood, or sensory magic from Ironcrest. It was uncommon to have magic from more than one kingdom, rarer still to have magic from three, such as the Dark Raider at my back. And I'd never heard of any fairy having magic from all four.

Nostrils flaring, I breathed in the new scents that came with the new kingdom. Dry, dusty air floated around us that carried hints of herbs, magic, and rocky minerals. It was boggling to realize we'd traveled over a thousand miles since leaving Leafton. The stags had moved impossibly fast. In two short days, we'd managed to traverse more land than most fae did in a week of travel.

The sun was falling behind the jagged Ustilly Mountains, like a blazing orb of angry red light, when the stags cantered down the mountain into the new kingdom. Pines covered in sapphire needles rose like spindly cones. Rock littered with sandy soil and course vegetation brushed against the stags' hooves. Above, the three moons began to glow as the stars winked. And with each breath that passed, the colors of the galaxy came more alive.

Around us, the thick Wood filled the sloping mountainside. Cool air swirled, the breeze dancing around us. It lifted my hair and made the loose strands—that had finally escaped Lillivel's intricate braids—flutter in front of my face.

Halfway down the mountain, the stags finally slowed to a walk. The slower movement had my muscles protesting. We'd been traveling all day, and despite Phillen's gait being even and comfortable, his back was hard, my arse was sore, and my thighs felt like mush.

"We'll camp here for the night," Jax said quietly into my ear, then signaled for his friends to stop.

I gave a small nod, not replying. Jax and I had barely spoken since we'd reached our tentative truce hours earlier, as though each of us was afraid to break whatever fragile bond had been born between us.

My captor jumped off his friend, his movements practiced, but I sat on Phillen a moment longer. I couldn't help the sliver of awe that coursed through me when I looked down at Stonewild Kingdom. The kingdom north of mine cascaded down the mountain's slope to spread out before me like a vast blanket.

A sandy valley waited at the bottom of the mountain. The desert seemed endless, sprawling as far as I could see.

Far in the distance, though, twinkling lights waited. I had no idea what city it was, but I knew it wasn't Jaggedston, Stonewild's capital. Jaggedston lay much farther north, near the coast, and its palace was whispered to be constructed of black rock and sheets of onyx stone, so different from the palace in Faewood.

Finally, I slid my leg over Phillen and fell lightly to the ground. Stiff muscles greeted me when I landed, but I forced myself to walk and shake it off.

Magic billowed around the stags, and they shifted one after another. In a blink, all of them were disguised fae dressed in black attire. Masks covered their faces, and bandanas covered their heads. Once more, six male siltenites and my guardian surrounded me.

I arched an eyebrow. "How convenient that you don't all end up naked when you shift back to fae."

Bowan's eyes crinkled, and his earring flashed in the growing moonlight. "Oh, you'd like that, would you, Lorafin?"

"Hardly." I gave him my back and strode to an area in the forest that had a large break in the trees. The view opened, allowing me a perfect spot to see the last remnants of the sunset.

A huff came from behind me, and with a start, I realized Guardian Alleron was watching me. His hands were still bound, his mouth an angry slash of a line, and his eyes . . . They were staring daggers at me.

Guilt hit me when I realized that even though I'd made temporary peace with my captor, my guardian certainly hadn't. He'd been bound and robbed of his voice all day.

I hurried toward him to offer what help I could, but before

I reached him, Jax pointed to a tree and addressed his friends. "Tie him up over there."

The Dark Raider cast a glance my way, that intent look in his eyes again, but then he strode out of the clearing and disappeared into the Wood.

I scowled after him. "Is that truly necessary? I thought we had a deal."

But if Jax heard me, he didn't respond.

"Come on, Slave Guardian." Bowan made a move toward him.

Guardian Alleron stumbled back, and Lander *tsked*.

I rounded on both of them. "Please, don't hurt him. He's done nothing wrong."

But my begging didn't alleviate their rough handling. They had my guardian pinned between them two steps later, and even though my guardian kicked and seethed, they dodged his blows effortlessly, and then hauled him toward a pine and slammed him to the tree.

A squeak of rage emitted from me, but even that didn't deter them. Within seconds, Guardian Alleron was entirely bound with lashing strands of the same ropelike magic Jax had used to hold him in place. The glowing strands had grown from Bowan's hands this time, as though they were a part of him, and I couldn't help but wonder what spell was used for that, or if *he* was the one who harbored Mistvale magic.

After Bowan's magic tethered my guardian to the tree, the

magical rope shone like stars around him, and every time my guardian moved, the bindings hissed and sizzled.

Despite their humming warning, Guardian Alleron fought against the restraints.

Bowan chuckled. "I'd advise against that."

Ignoring him, my guardian wrestled more, but when the magic dug deeper into his skin, cutting into him like barbed knives every time he twisted or kicked, he finally stopped.

Blood trickled from small cuts under the magic, and my guardian grew completely still. I had a feeling if he hadn't, Bowan's magic would have cut right through him.

Bowan winked. "Tried to warn you."

He and Lander ambled away, and my guardian's nostrils flared as he shot me another look. The accusations wordlessly flying from him had me instinctively going to help him again. I wasn't sure what I could do, but perhaps I could put a pillow beneath his legs or behind his back. Something to make him more comfortable.

"This will all be over soon," I whispered as I fussed at his side, but Guardian Alleron only seethed more and glared at me, and it struck me that with his voice still gone, he couldn't say what he was thinking.

And perhaps that was for the best. Given the rage strumming from him, I had a feeling I would be getting a tongue-lashing if he could.

I fussed more, trying to please him and do whatever I

could to help him, but it seemed no matter what I did, he only grew more irritated.

"Don't worry about him, lovely," Phillen called from where he was erecting his tent. "He'll live."

I swung around to face him. "You're really just going to leave him tied up like this? That's cruel."

Bowan laughed, the sound unnervingly joyful. "We sure are, Little Lorafin, and cruel or not, it's what he deserves."

"Says who?" Huffing, I bent down to help my guardian again, but Trivan was suddenly there, forcing me upright.

The blond shook his head at me as he pulled me away from the tree. "You're not to help him, Elowen. Jax's orders."

Jaw dropping, I glowered at him, and the truce Jax and I agreed on threatened to fizzle away. "And what about me? Am I to be bound and gagged too at the Dark Raider's *orders?*"

"Do you want to be?" Jax's question had my spine snapping to attention. The Dark Raider entered the clearing, carrying an armload of dried wood he'd collected from the forest floor. "But to answer your question, no, you won't be bound. You've done nothing wrong. Not like your guardian. Have a seat." He nodded toward the makeshift firepit that Lars had constructed, then tossed the firewood to the redhead.

Eyeing Jax, I tapped my fingers on my hips. Collar vibrating, I fought to calm my rising tide of anger, but I was done with following his commands. I wasn't going to sit, and if he was hurting my guardian and refused to hurt me since he needed me, then I wasn't going to stay quiet.

"How does my guardian deserve this?" I demanded.

Jax's eyebrows rose. "Do I really need to explain? He's a *slave* guardian. And you're his slave."

My breath sucked in. "Just because I'm his lorafin slave doesn't mean that's all I am. He's also my *father*."

Jax's irises turned into deadly chips of ice. "If you say so."

My jaw dropped, and it felt as though he'd punched the wind from me.

"Please," Jax added in a softer tone. "Have a seat. I don't wish to fight with you."

I crossed my arms. "I'd rather not sit."

He sighed. "All right. In that case, don't sit. Stand or walk in circles or do whatever else your heart desires."

My hand flew out and slapped him across the face. "*That's* what my heart desires."

Jax's head whipped to the side, and he brought a palm to his cheek.

I gasped, and my hand flew to my mouth. *Goddess Above, I'm losing it.*

For a moment, stunned silence descended on the camp, but then Phillen let out a bark of laughter, and Bowan and Trivan howled. Lander snickered, and I could have sworn that beneath his mask, even Lars was fighting a smile.

Trivan slapped his knee, still laughing. "She has a point. You did tell her to do whatever her heart desires. You kind of asked for that."

Phillen guffawed. "The lorafin's got a temper. I knew I liked her."

"Goddess, help me," the Dark Raider muttered under his breath. Jax lifted his mask just enough to wipe a trace of blood from his mouth. In that brief moment, I caught a glimpse of his lips. Full yet firm. But in a blink, that telling detail was hidden.

Jax wiped his hand on his pants, the smear of blood visible despite their dark color.

I staggered back. "I'm . . . I'm sorry. I was angry at how you're treating my guardian. I didn't mean to do that."

Tensing, I waited for him to strike me back or shove me to the ground or do *something* in retaliation.

It wouldn't be the first time I'd been hit. Guardian Alleron typically avoided physical punishment, but sometimes, when my temper got the best of me—as it just had with Jax—and I refused to do a calling, he would hit me. Whenever that happened, his blows had been hard enough to make me see stars. But it was usually only one punch or a back-handed slap. Never more, and afterward, he profusely apologized and begged me to listen to him so he wouldn't have to hit me.

So, I waited. Waited for Jax to strike me in return.

But the blow never came.

Jax straightened and put his hands on his hips, regarding me coolly.

My self-loathing grew when I saw the trail of crimson glistening again on his pants. *Stars and galaxy, I did that to him.*

It didn't help that he didn't say another word, just kept

assessing me. And to make matters even worse, he still didn't lash out. He just looked at me, as though asking, *Are you done?*

Cheeks heating, I waved toward the valley and ignored the guilt that spiraled through me. "Is that a desert down there?"

"It is." He nodded down the mountain's slope, not even a trace of anger evident in his words. "That's the Shadow Valley. Magnificent, isn't it?"

"Um . . . yes." I frowned. I hadn't intended to have a random conversation about the scenery, especially after abusing him nonetheless. If anything, his calm reaction to my fierce one was making me feel like the biggest pile of domal dung that had ever existed. With flustered movements, I waved at the northern horizon. "Where are we ultimately—"

"Hungry?" Bowan called before I could finish my question. The brunette threw me a piece of dried meat, and I caught it automatically.

Beside him, Lars was quietly cooking food over the fire. Flames now roared in the pit. Crackling and snapping sounds rose as well.

The redhead was placing thick buns on a metal grate and holding it over the heat. Next to that, a hearty stew was simmering, coming from one of their containers.

My shame grew even more as I watched the males work. They'd continued readying the camp and cooking supper, carrying on despite my theatrics. And other than wiping the blood away that I'd drawn, Jax hadn't shown any reaction to my momentary display of rage either.

The feeling of being a *huge* pile of domal dung grew exponentially.

Absentmindedly, I chewed on the piece of dried meat as Lars dished heaping ladles of stew into large bowls.

"Supper's ready," Lars called.

"Elowen?" Jax indicated for me to go first. He gave me a bowl filled with fragrant soup, then grabbed one for himself, the others doing the same.

Feeling even more foolish, I sat on the ground by the fire and picked up a spoon. Delicious aromas of tender meat, thick gravy, and root vegetables rose from the bowl. My stomach howled in anticipation.

"Try one of these." Bowan winked, his earring flashing in the firelight. "Best honeybuns in all the kingdoms." He pushed a plate with two doughy buns toward me. Rich butter was melted all over them.

Stomach rumbling in appreciation, I picked up the plate but was too hungry to bother watching what everyone else was doing. I dug into the stew, closing my eyes in rapture when the first taste hit my tongue. The thick, soft buns complemented it perfectly, and I wolfed all of it down.

"Galaxy, that's good," I whispered more to myself than anyone.

A chuckle came from beside me. "A female who likes to eat *and* isn't afraid to fight." Phillen sat on the ground next to me, his thick thighs straining against his pants in his crossed-legged position. "My wife would like you."

Wife? I eyed him curiously as he tucked into his food. He ate with as much gusto as I did despite his mask staying in place.

I set my empty bowl aside and wiped my lips, then cleansed my buttery fingers with my magic. Around me, all of the males were still eating.

Jax sat directly across the fire from me. His eyes never left me despite eating quickly and efficiently. It amazed me that he could bring his spoon under his mask so easily, the fabric not slowing him even slightly.

Still reeling that I'd hit him, I hastily looked away.

Sounds of spoons scraping on bowls and the crackling fire filled the space. I waited for one of them to order something of me now that everyone was settled. My entire life, orders had come regularly.

Sit straighter, Elowen.

Wear that gown, Elowen, not this one.

Wake at sunrise, Elowen. We have a calling just past seven.

You're to entertain this lordling, Elowen. He wants more than just a calling, so flirt with him, make him feel special.

For full seasons, my life had been a string of demands and expected responses. I'd learned to be dutiful and appeasing, and after hitting Jax, a part of me was hoping he would ask something of me. Demand it. Orders were familiar. Orders I could handle.

But this companionable silence, after I'd abused him so egregiously, made me want to jump out of my skin.

I eyed my guardian again. He was still tied to the tree. No food had been offered to him, and he was staring at me as though all of this was my fault, which it was.

My stomach sank, and as the minutes ticked by, I grew tenser and tenser, yet the easy quiet continued. Everyone finished their meals, and other than Jax silently watching me, nobody seemed to even care that I was there.

The only thing that seemed out of place was that nobody fed Guardian Alleron.

"What about him?" I finally asked when my guardian's angry gaze practically burned a hole into my back. I knew he had to be as ravenous as I'd been.

"You want me to nourish your slave guardian?" Jax cocked an eyebrow.

"I'm sure he's hungry. He hasn't eaten all day."

Jax set his bowl to the side. "No, Elowen. He won't be eating."

Before I could ask anything further, Jax rolled to his feet and prowled toward Guardian Alleron. I tensed and shot to standing, but Jax only crouched at his side.

The Dark Raider whispered something, and a cloud of magic lifted from my guardian.

The second it did, Guardian Alleron sucked in a breath and spat, "You're a cunt of a male!"

It took me a second to register that Jax had just removed his Ironcrest magic from my guardian, and my guardian's first words to him had been an angry curse.

The Dark Raider glanced nonplussed over his shoulder as everyone else began to clean up. "Did you hear that? I'm a cunt of a male."

The others all laughed or chuckled, and a moment of unease stole through me.

A spark of energy simmered around the Dark Raider. His aura felt like a storm that had begun churning over the sea, the waves beginning to rise as the clouds rolled.

Jax exhaled, his posture calm and non-threatening, but in my next blink, he had his hand locked around Guardian Alleron's throat.

I shrieked, but Jax ignored me and said in a low, lethal tone, "I hear there's a device you use to control her. Where is it?"

Guardian Alleron kicked, but the stinging magic tightened around him. "I don't have it."

"That's a lie. She said you always carry it."

My guardian shot me a glare, his eyes narrowing to slits. Ice sped through my veins. I knew that look. Punishment was coming, usually in the form of a full dousing from the collar when he looked at me like that.

I'm sorry, I mouthed.

Jax growled and jerked my guardian's chin back in his direction. "You don't look at her. You look at *me*."

Guardian Alleron spat right in Jax's face. Unfortunately for my guardian, it landed on Jax's mask and not his skin, and in a whisper of Jax's magic, the spittle fizzled and then was gone.

"Bowan?" Jax said calmly.

A rush of magic clouded the air, and the bands encircling Guardian Alleron disappeared.

But before my guardian could begin swinging, Jax hefted him up and slammed him to the tree, dangling him a foot above the Wood's floor.

Everything happened so fast it was as if it happened simultaneously.

Jax's hand tightened more around my guardian's throat as he held Guardian Alleron aloft, and my guardian clawed at him but to no avail.

"I'm not asking again," Jax said in a deadly calm voice. "Where is the device?"

Feeling entirely helpless, I twisted my hands. "Please stop! Please don't hurt him, Jax."

But the Dark Raider ignored me.

My guardian kicked, his hands continually trying to claw Jax off his throat, but Jax's grip only tightened.

"*Where?*" A pulse of magic shot into Jax's word, and the urge to please Jax and do whatever he requested fired through me.

"It's in his pocket!" I called just as my guardian shouted, "In my pocket."

My heart thundered, and my jaw dropped. *What in the realm was that?*

But whatever magic Jax had just used in that command disappeared on the wind. He loosened his hold on my guardian, and Guardian Alleron sank to his feet. The Dark Raider kept his grip on Guardian Alleron's throat, however, and used his free hand to fish the device from my guardian's pocket.

A flare of triumph surrounded Jax when he pulled the adaptor free. The device was a slim wand constructed of smooth metal. At its center, a purple gem glittered—a stone identical to the one in my collar.

"How does this work?"

Guardian Alleron's nostrils flared so dramatically that his skin looked sharp enough to cut glass.

"*How does this work?*" That same strange magic channeled into Jax's words again, but this time it was more streamed, directed entirely at my guardian, so I didn't feel the overwhelming urge to respond.

Goosebumps rose along my arms despite that, and I shot a wild look at the other five males. Strange sorcery seemed to be at work here, but all of them continued cleaning up the remains of supper and unpacking sleeping rolls from their sacks, as though completely unimpressed at what Jax was doing.

Breaths coming faster, my eyes bulged when Guardian Alleron replied through gritted teeth, "The stone on the adaptor connects with the stone in her collar. It responds to my fingerprint only"—he gritted his teeth more, as though fighting whatever magic had gripped him, but then his mouth opened again, and more words poured out even though rage twisted his features—"so when I activate it, the power containing her lessens, and she's able to call upon her lorafin magic and wield it. If I don't minimize the collar's power, her lorafin magic stays suppressed, and if she tries to use her magic without permission from me, the collar punishes her."

I'd heard this explanation so many times I'd lost count. Every lordling who desired my services had been curious how Guardian Alleron's device controlled me. My guardian had always been more than happy to boast of its superior magical ability, touting that it was a one-of-a-kind creation and not to be found anywhere else in the realm.

Jax cocked his head. *"How do I remove her collar?"*

Veins strained in Guardian Alleron's neck, and his entire face turned red. His jaw worked, and his hands fisted, but that strange magic clouded around him even more. Teeth clenching, almost as if the words were physically pulled from him, he growled, "You . . . can't." His teeth gritted more, but it was no use. The words still came. "It can . . . never be removed."

My head snapped back. *It can never be removed? What?* No. Surely, I'd misheard him . . . Or he'd misspoken. Guardian Alleron had probably meant it could never be removed unless he commanded it, which he'd never done before.

Jax glanced my way, his jaw working beneath his mask, before he addressed my guardian again. *"Can her collar be removed if you remove it?"*

Guardian Alleron side-eyed me. His jaw pumped, his teeth grinding, but then his mouth opened, as though physically forced by a phantom. Hissing, he said, "No, it can never be removed. Not even I can remove it."

I stumbled back. "You're lying. He's lying!" I proclaimed to Jax. "He's going to remove my collar when I turn thirty. That was always our plan."

Jax glanced at me again, concern evident in his gaze.

"Don't move." The Dark Raider released my guardian and took a step back, then he began to prowl back and forth. It reminded me of the pacing he'd done when I'd been unconscious, following the collar's full dousing effects in my kingdom's Wood.

But that thought flitted through my head like a shooting star, there and then gone. I was still reeling at what my guardian had claimed. Surely, he was lying. Somehow, he'd *lied* despite whatever truth magic Jax was using on him.

Gasps soon emitted from Alleron's mouth, and Jax said dismissively, *"You may breathe."*

A suck of air lifted Guardian Alleron's chest, and his lips, which had started turning blue, bloomed with color.

The complexities of Jax's magic hit me like a clap of thunder. With stunning clarity, I realized who in the group commanded Mistvale magic. "You can not only wield the elements, control one's senses, shift into an animal, but also command one psychically too?" I whispered more to myself than anyone in particular.

"He sure can, lovely," Phillen said from behind me. He stood near his tent, arms folded over his massive chest. But his brow was furrowed, and it struck me that he'd also been watching me as I denied what my guardian was claiming.

Blood thundered through my ears. To command one psychically, that was Mistvale magic. Goddess. *Jax* was the one who commanded magic from that kingdom, which meant he had magic from all *four* kingdoms.

But nobody had that kind of power.

I swallowed the thickness in my throat, not wanting to believe what was staring at me right in the face.

It was as though someone else was speaking when I said, "So what Guardian Alleron just said . . . It's true? Jax's magic is like a truth serum? It forces responses from fae, which means there's no way my guardian can be lying?"

Phillen's eyes dimmed. "Correct, Elowen. Nobody can lie when Jax commands them like that."

My breaths came faster, my chest heaving. "That means my collar can't be removed, and I'll never be free of it."

Phillen's eyes dimmed even more.

My throat grew so thick I could barely speak. I blinked my eyes rapidly as quickened breaths lifted my chest. I shook my head, not wanting to accept the truth.

It will never come off.

It will never come off.

It will never come off.

Yet my guardian had promised to one day set me free.

He'd promised to remove my collar.

My entire life he'd told me that all I had to do was be a good, dutiful lorafin, and once I reached my thirtieth birthday, that pliant behavior would be rewarded. He would remove his device, I would go to the supernatural courts, I would be awarded my freedom, and then he and I would be father and daughter only. No more callings. No more ownership. No more demands. We would be a true family in every sense of the word.

But if what he'd just told Jax was true . . .

The full blow of Guardian Alleron's confession hit me like a million strikes of lightning.

I jolted in place, my entire body going rigid. Because if my collar could never be removed, then my guardian had never planned to release me.

My entire life he'd been lying to me.

He'd never planned to let me go.

Which meant he intended for me to always be his slave, and I was never to be his true daughter.

CHAPTER 12

I stood frozen in place, my heart like carved ice. Zings from my collar skittered along my nerves, flashes of pain following. But I didn't move. I stood rigidly. Listening. Processing.

Jax continued his questions, and I digested every damning answer and soul-slicing comment that emitted from my guardian's traitorous mouth.

My guardian was forced to verbalize honest answers under Jax's Mistvale magic. But with each answer Guardian Alleron gave, my heart withered more and more until it felt like a dried husk.

Most of my guardian's responses were entirely new information to me. Such as, not only could my collar never come off, but it was also only Guardian Alleron's fingerprint that could ever wield the adaptor. Jax would never be able to wield it, not even if he took it.

And, the crystals within the adaptor and my collar came from a land far away, so far that it would require crossing the Adriastic Sea to reach it. And since my guardian had never traveled there, but had merely hired someone to retrieve my collar and his adaptor, he wasn't even sure of their exact origins.

There was also nothing Guardian Alleron could do to alter any of my collar's strength. It'd been set long ago when the collar had been initially forged.

In other words, I would always be caged.

Hearing that confirmed a deep-down fear that I'd been carrying in my cracking heart for full seasons—that my freedom and hope for a real family were merely a dream. And now, since I knew the collar would *never* come off, I would always be contained, even if I proved I was no longer a danger to others. The harsh reality was that everything that'd been whispered in my ear since I was a child . . . It'd all been false.

Jax had been right.

Guardian Alleron had never intended to release me from slavery.

Because the most damning information he confessed to was that he'd specifically requested the forger to make my collar irremovable, which meant that all of the seasons my guardian had promised it would one day come off had all been a deception—a way to make me pliant and eager to do his bidding. He'd never intended to remove it.

And now, I saw my mistake. My guardian and I had never made a fairy bargain. We'd never been bound by the gods and goddesses to ensure his word was true, because I'd been stupid and naïve and believed that he loved me. Because I'd *trusted* him, the male who'd been the only father I'd ever known, to keep his word.

I stood in the clearing, entirely numb, as Jax continued asking question upon question. He kept looking for some way around all of the restrictions Guardian Alleron had crafted for my collar.

But there wasn't a way out of this, and several absolute truths slowly began to sink in.

Guardian Alleron had only sought to use me.

I was a permanent slave.

I would never be free.

And that meant I would never know what had become of my blood family.

Devastation hit me so suddenly, and my knees threatened to give out. If the collar never came off, then I would never be able to fully access my magic, which meant that I could never ask the semelees for my own calling.

No, don't think about that. Don't feel that. Feel anything but that.

I piled on layer after layer of denial to that soul-lashing pain. I wouldn't feel this. *Couldn't* feel it. Slowly, a thick wall of stone erected itself around my withered heart.

Questions finished, Jax finally released Guardian Alleron

from his commanding voice, and my guardian fell to the ground.

My captor stood over him, chest heaving. Jax placed his hands on his hips, his fingers tapping, and a look of absolute disgust yanked his eyebrows together.

None of the other males gave Guardian Alleron so much as a pitying glance when he rubbed his throat. Instead, Bowan immediately called forth his binding magic and tethered Alleron to the tree again, his magic unyielding even when my guardian hissed in pain.

"May I please have some water?" Guardian Alleron croaked once completely bound.

Everyone ignored that request. Including me.

"Or food, or perhaps—" He hissed again when the ropelike magic cut into him anew. "Perhaps slightly less tight restraints?"

Bowan grunted but did nothing to change his magic.

I still didn't move. Didn't respond. I couldn't *think*. Fog grew in my mind, and only one thought penetrated it.

I'll never be free.

Jax inhaled sharply, then took a tentative step my way. "Elowen? Are you all right?"

But I barely heard him. Twilight lit the sky in a dusky glow, and I gazed upward at the shining moons.

Trembles began to rack my body. I thought of my calendar. Thought of how I crossed off one day each morning. For *full seasons* I'd been counting the days until my freedom was won and my life truly began.

But it'd all been a lie, a cruel, vicious joke that my guardian had played. He'd probably been laughing at me all along, smirking over the eager lorafin child who had gazed up at him with adoration and every intention of pleasing him. All so that one day, the collar would be removed, she could be a daughter and daughter only, and she could finally ask the semelees what became of her mother so that mystery could be laid to rest.

Now, I'll never know.

And that was all because Guardian Alleron had chosen to make my collar irremovable. He'd always held the lock to my freedom, but he'd willingly thrown the key away the moment he commanded the collar's forger to make my collar permanent.

Now, I would never be able to perform a calling for myself. I would never be able to ask the semelees what happened to my family. I couldn't when the collar suppressed my magic so much. For a lorafin to request a calling of her own, she had to be able to command the semelees fully similar to what was needed to twist fate, and because of the restrictive collar, I'd never been able to.

Wind blew over my cheeks, feathering across my stinging eyes.

Only feet away, Jax continued to watch me. He stared at me with the intensity of a blazing sun, his attention firmly fixated on my face as his pulsing aura flowed out of him.

Cursing, Jax shot daggers at my guardian, then waved toward a tent and said gruffly, "Elowen, you're sleeping in here. Come. You should rest."

Numbness continued to seep through me, but I automatically stumbled forward on stiff limbs.

"Elowen!" Guardian Alleron called hoarsely.

My entire body froze mid-step, but before I could respond, Jax snarled and rounded on him. *"You don't speak to her. You never speak to her again unless I command it."*

The power in those enraged words cascaded through the air.

Guardian Alleron's lips clamped close, his eyes bulging when Jax's commanding Mistvale magic speared him.

I watched his struggle, and it felt as though I observed him from a great distance even though he was only a body length away. He stared at me, mouth opening and closing, but robbed of voice when trying to speak to me, he banged his head against the tree, then bared his teeth at Jax.

But I didn't feel pity for him. I would have earlier, but now . . .

Now, I felt nothing.

The numbness spread, moving like an icy river through my chest, along my limbs, down to my toes, and burrowing deep into my bones.

Guardian Alleron lied to me. Lied through his teeth to me since I was a child.

Stiffly, I walked past him.

His eyes stayed on me, stayed pleading, but I refused to acknowledge him.

Nothing. I felt nothing, because I was nothing, and I had no one.

I was entirely alone now.

Vibrations strummed along my collar—the collar I would never be rid of. Somehow, I managed to cross the distance to the tent even though it felt as if I was floating.

Jax's brow furrowed, and I could have sworn that beneath his mask, his jaw was working. Hand gently encircling my forearm, Jax's warm fingers met my cool skin, yet I barely felt it.

"Elowen?" An ache filled that one word. "Would you like to see him suffer for what he's done to you?"

I looked at him blankly.

"Elowen?" he said hoarsely.

"Do whatever you deem fit."

Jax gave a curt nod, and magic speared from him to cloud around Guardian Alleron. I could *feel* the Dark Raider's vengeance. It coated the air, snaking around my guardian like vicious, deadly serpents.

A look of sheer panic coated my guardian's face. His head whipped around, more silent screams coming from him. For a brief second, he thrashed against his restraints but then stopped when Bowan's magic cut into him, and fresh blood rose.

"What did you do?" I asked, not even sure if I cared.

"I took his sight and ability to hear in addition to his voice. He currently has no senses other than taste and smell, but I could take those too. And now—"

Guardian Alleron abruptly twitched and thrashed, sheer terror and agony twisting his features.

"And now, I'm causing him pain. He currently feels like he's being burned and stabbed."

"At the same time?"

"Yes."

Shrugging, I moved automatically into the tent.

Inside, a soft mat had been placed on the floor. Bundles of furs and blankets lay on top of it. There weren't two distinguished sleeping areas. It was all one large pile, but considering all that had happened, it was the least of my concerns.

I would now eat, sleep, travel, and exist wherever Jax told me to. He now controlled me and my guardian fully, even if he'd never wanted to.

I fell to my knees amidst the thick, soft furs. Shivers ran through me. A part of me knew I was cold, but . . . I didn't care.

I listened to Guardian Alleron's thrashing limbs that beat and thumped against the ground just outside of the tent. It was the only sound of his torture.

And I thought of how that male had molded me into the female I was today.

A dutiful lorafin—his prized trinket.

It was all I would ever be.

I lay down and stared up at the tent's ceiling. Soon the

pounding thumps of my guardian's agony drifted away on the wind. I no longer heard them as the numbness spread.

Shivers continued hitting me intermittently as I stared at the billowing canvas above. Outside, darkness grew as twilight bled into night, and I thought of what else Jax had said today.

"I know that your guardian claims that she left you."

A thought suddenly struck me, and I bolted upright, the first rush of warmth cascading through my limbs that I'd felt since Jax's questioning had begun.

"Jax?" I called.

In a blink, he was there, at the tent's opening. "Yes?"

"Can you ask him what he knows about my mother?"

He gave a curt nod, and I lay back down, biting my lip as the feel of Jax's magic again speared the air. *"What do you know of Elowen's birth mother? You may speak only to answer my questions."*

I waited on bated breath, and a surge of hope began to rise up in me. Maybe he knew who she was. Maybe he knew where I could find her. Maybe he'd known all along and had been lying about that too, and there was still hope that I would one day locate her.

A hiss came, then my guardian said slowly, as though the words were pried from his lips. "She's . . . dead."

A clash of pain exploded inside my chest. *She's dead.* Vicious vibrations zapped along my throat, coiling all the way around my heart. *My mother's dead.*

"How did she die?" Jax asked in a deadly tone.

"I killed her."

My heart stopped.

It just . . . stopped.

"How did you kill her?"

"I saw her bathing in a stream in the Wood with Elowen lying on a blanket near the stream's edge. I saw Elowen's shadow mark and realized what she was, so I drowned her mother and then took Elowen."

I squeezed my eyes shut, not wanting to hear more. I couldn't. Pain barreled through me. Intense, vicious, all-consuming pain.

I couldn't bear it. I fell back on the furs, my heart reeling.

A disgusted sound came from Jax. "I knew it. You're the worst kind of fucking scum that walks in this realm."

Rustling sounds came from the other males. They spoke quietly, their voices blending together in concealed rough whispers. I didn't try to discern any of it.

Because my heart was ripping in two. I was being killed from the inside out.

Not only had my guardian made me a permanent slave, but he'd murdered my mother and then claimed my entire life that she abandoned me.

I knew I could ask Jax to reveal the details. He could force my guardian to tell me all of the gruesome facts of what had transpired the day my guardian had taken me. The day he murdered my mother.

But I didn't want to know. Because the thought of hearing anything further about her last moments of life . . .

I squeezed my eyes shut even tighter.

The tent's flap lifted a moment later, and I opened my eyes in time to see Jax hesitantly step inside.

His mask still covered him, his bandana was still in place, yet the raw emotion pounding in his aura was anything but hidden.

"Elowen . . . are you okay?" Jax's deep tone cut through the quiet. He stood there, waiting for me to reply, but I remained silent. Harshly, he ran a hand over his bandana before saying gruffly, "No, of course you're not okay. What a stupid question."

He toed closer to me, as though afraid he would spook me if he got too close. Sapphire eyes glittered in the firelight as he watched me. "I'm sorry," he finally said, and strangely, he seemed to mean that.

For the briefest moment, my attention drifted to the Dark Raider. He stood hunched over, since the tent was too low for his full height. Inching away from the middle, I gave him room and then turned on my side and stared at the tent's wall.

The tent's canvas billowed in front of me, the material flapping lightly in the wind. Sounds from the other tents drifted to my ears. Quiet conversations. A few grunts as the other males settled onto their sleeping furs. But then all fell silent. I didn't even hear Guardian Alleron. I'd tuned him out completely.

Jax finally settled behind me, his large body making the

furs and blankets dip in his direction. "Stars, Elowen, I'm so sorry. Truly, I am. I know your entire realm was just shattered."

I swallowed the lump in my throat. "It's okay. That's not your fault. I stupidly believed—" I shook my head.

The rustle of shifting furs came again, and then Jax's energy pushed more into my back. He leaned over me, and a cloud of his fragrance enveloped me—spice and pine. "You believed what?"

I closed my eyes. "Nothing. It doesn't matter anymore."

Silence followed, but Jax's energy strumming into my back kicked up a notch. "What if it matters to me?"

Matters to him?

Those three tiny words stirred something inside me, worming through my broken heart until I turned to face him, slightly surprised to find him so close.

He still wore his black clothes, mask, and bandana. All of him was concealed from me. All except for his eyes. Dazzling cerulean irises gazed at me in the dying firelight. He had beautiful eyes, a myriad of varying blue shades.

I swallowed the lump in my throat. "Even if it did matter to you, Jax, nothing changes."

Energy pulsed from him. His hand lifted, and he trailed a finger along my collar.

The intimate gesture stole my breath.

"I know there's nothing I can do to bring back your mother, and I know you think you'll never be rid of this." His words turned rough. Sharp. Magic pulsed from his hands, even stronger than before, and a part of me wondered if he'd tempered his power when we first met, as if he'd deliberately kept himself at bay so as not to frighten me when I'd awoken in his tent yesterday morning. "And perhaps that's true, but that doesn't mean you can never be free of *him*." He growled the last word, and the pulsing energy from him kicked up even more.

Jax pulled the adaptor from his pocket and ran his finger along the purple gem. He had long fingers, strong hands, yet he held the adaptor gently. But unlike when Guardian Alleron touched it, the purple stone in its center didn't begin to glow. "Without your guardian's fingerprint, this doesn't control you anymore."

"It still contains me."

"True, it does."

"I tried to tell you that, and that without my guardian wielding it, I'm of no use to you, but you didn't listen."

"You're right. I didn't." He shook his head and sighed roughly. "I hate to ask you this, Elowen, especially after what you learned tonight, but will you still help me? Will you still travel to the Veiled Between if I ask you to, even learning what you did tonight? Your guardian will have to wield this for me, but I can assure you he'll never hurt you again."

An ache shook his voice, and I wondered who he wanted to find so fiercely that his goal had never wavered. No matter all that had happened in the past two days, Jax's sole purpose for taking me was still his guiding light.

"You could just command it of me, Jax. Your Mistvale magic would ensure I stay obedient." It would be so easy for this male to control me. He could make me his puppet, his forever dutiful servant.

Yet even that thought didn't instill any emotion in me. Not even a flicker of terror. It was as though nothing mattered anymore.

"I don't want to do that," he said gruffly. "Not just do I not want to, but I *won't* do that to you. My psychic magic is . . . evil. Only those who are just as vile will ever feel its wrath. And you, you're an innocent in all of this, Elowen. You don't deserve that."

"Even though I struck you?"

He chuffed softly. "I deserved that for all I've done to you."

A flicker of relief coursed through me, just the barest glimmer since the numbness had spread.

Jax's brow furrowed, and his voice dipped. "I've been telling you all along, Elowen. I'm not going to hurt you."

My gaze shot to his. Startling blue eyes met mine, and for the first time since he'd taken me . . . I believed him, truly *believed* him.

Something inside me shifted. Softened. Maybe I was crazy, desperate even to make some kind of sense amidst all this chaos. And perhaps I was just making another stupid, naïve decision, but I looked at him in a different light.

"Who do you want me to find, Jax?" I whispered.

His eyes dimmed. "Somebody very important to me."

"But . . . *who*?"

A single breath heaved his chest. "I can't tell you. I'm sorry, but nobody can know who they are. Not even you."

My brow furrowed, and a moment of silence passed between us, but the forlorn energy surrounding the Dark Raider couldn't be faked. It was too raw. Too visceral.

And maybe it was feeling that aching emotion he had for another—love, no doubt. Because what else but love could form a response like that . . . Vengeance certainly couldn't. No, it had to be love. Somebody he loved had gone missing. And it was a love powerful enough that he'd ventured to my kingdom, stalked me for weeks, and then had taken me when the opportunity presented itself. Even though I'd been King Paevin's favorite pet, Jax had still risked it.

He'd done all of that for love.

And maybe it was knowing love like that existed, even if it was something nobody would ever feel for me, that had me nodding my head.

"Yes, I'll still help you, Jax."

"You will?" he replied gruffly, hope evident in those two words.

"Yes, I will."

A breath escaped him, a huge sigh of relief. "Thank you, Elowen."

"Don't thank me yet. I haven't found anyone."

"But you said you will."

"When I can."

"How much longer will you need to recover from the last callings before performing another?"

A heartbeat of silence passed between us. I knew I could lie. I could prolong it, tell him that it would be weeks until I could, but . . . I didn't want to lie. For the first time, I felt that I was being given a choice about my callings. As though that fragile truce that had been born between us was growing stronger, more resilient, and I didn't want to shatter whatever understanding was being formed between us.

"Honestly, I probably could do one the day after tomorrow."

Eyes glittering, his aura rose sharply. Jax lifted the adaptor. "Your guardian will need to wield this to make that happen, but once he finishes, I can command him never to use it again without your permission. That is the gift I can give you for helping me in addition to letting you go."

I managed a small smile, even though inside it still felt like I was breaking. It was the best he could offer, and he and I both knew it.

"All right, our deal is settled."

Jax nodded and finally lowered himself to the furs until he was lying beside me. I shifted to face him, then placed both hands beneath my cheek. He studied the adaptor, holding it up in the dying light, so I studied his profile.

He lay on his back, and the outline of his face was more

discernible beneath his mask in his current position, and I wondered if he was even aware of that. He had a straight nose, not long but not short either. A strong nose, one might say, and his jaw appeared defined with how the cloth draped over it.

"How often does he use this on you?" he asked quietly.

I shrugged. "Whenever he wants me to do a calling. Or, when he wants to severely punish me. The adaptor can also hurt me, like what happened yesterday to me in the Wood."

His gaze whipped to mine. "He *punishes* you with this?" he all but snarled.

I took an unsteady breath. Rage pounded from Jax, filling the tent. "Not often, but he has."

He took a deep breath, then lay back but his chest still lifted too quickly, and it felt as though he was struggling to control himself. "And how often does he demand callings?"

"Twice a week at most. That's the maximum my magic allows, but usually only a couple of times per month."

He took another deep breath, his eyes narrowing, and a puff of magic emitted from him. Outside, Guardian Alleron's thrashes increased.

Another moment passed, and Jax finally broke the quiet once again. "And each time he uses this, you venture to the Veiled Between?"

"Yes."

"And how long have you been doing this for him?"

"Since I was a child."

His head snapped in my direction once more, the adaptor falling to his side. "Since you were a *child*?"

I nodded, and the magic inside me warmed, reacting to the stirring energy swarming around Jax. A slight vibration hummed along my neck, and Jax took a deep breath and relaxed his shoulders, but his voice was still gruff when he said, "I've been told that when lorafins travel to the Veiled Between, it can be dangerous, that some become lost."

"That's true."

"And that if one becomes lost in the Veiled Between, her soul is forever linked to the semelees."

My breaths sped up. "That's also what they say."

"And has that ever been the case with you? Have you ever come close to becoming lost?"

I closed my eyes and fought off the horrific images that came. All the times that my guardian had pushed me reared in my memories. He'd forced me to learn my magic and wield it when I was so young and still didn't fully understand it myself. Just the other day, when I'd done three callings for the king, I feared that I would become lost.

But I hadn't been. The collar's horrific shocks had pulled me back.

I licked my lips, and Jax followed the movement, his eyes dipping to watch my tongue dart out. "There've been many times."

He grew still, so still I wondered if he was breathing. "Many times?" he repeated.

I nodded. "This is what saved me from becoming fully detached." I rubbed along the collar again. "I suppose in a way, it's both a blessing and a curse. The collar keeps me grounded. It's forced my soul back into my body so many times I've lost count." I didn't tell him that the collar was also responsible for the unbearable side effects that plagued me every time I did a calling. Part of what kept me grounded was the collar connecting me to the fairy who was demanding the calling, and that connection meant I suffered from the fairy's magic.

Jax inhaled a long, deep breath.

I pulled my bottom lip into my mouth to nibble on, and again, his eyes tracked the movement. "Do you know I'd planned to remove myself from our culture once I was free of it? I was going to live in the Wood, free and alone without my collar, until I knew for certain that I wouldn't hurt anyone, then I thought I'd return to my guardian. I thought I'd truly be the daughter he never had." My breath caught.

Jax's gaze became so intent that for a moment, I couldn't speak. I shook my head. "I guess that won't happen anymore."

"Why do you think you need to isolate yourself without that collar?"

My memories turned to what I'd done as a child, to that horrific moment that had defined me and allowed the supernatural courts to make me Guardian Alleron's indefinite property until he or I proved I was safe to be free otherwise. "Because of my magic. Even as a child, I couldn't be trusted."

"Is that what he told you?" Jax growled.

"No. It's what *I* did as a child that proved that. It had nothing to do with Guardian Alleron." A flush worked up my cheeks. "But I was a fool to believe I would ever be given a chance to prove that I was no longer a danger to others. I was a fool to believe I would ever be free."

"No, you're not a fool. Whatever happened, you were just a child."

"No lorafin is ever truly a child," I whispered.

"And whatever happened, did your guardian try to help you?"

I ran a finger along my collar. "He put this on."

Jax's eyes hardened. "So he enslaved you to him with that collar, and you trusted him because he was the only thing you ever knew." His voice softened. "He took advantage of your innocence, Elowen. That doesn't make you a fool. That makes him a—" He took a deep breath, and swirling magic stirred around him anew.

I closed my eyes again, not wanting to hear it. Because while a part of me felt incredibly betrayed by Guardian Alleron, I also felt other things for him. I couldn't help that. He'd been like a father to me, even if our relationship could be tumultuous at times. He'd cared for me, nourished me, and provided me with clothes and a home when I had no one. He truly was my father, even though we shared no blood, and a part of me still clung to him because of that, wanting to believe that some part of him did love me, even if he'd hurt me and murdered my mother.

I brought a hand to my forehead and scrubbed my eyes. My feelings for Guardian Alleron had always been twisted and complicated, but the truth was, he was the only family I'd ever had. But the irony of that wasn't lost on me. He was my only family because he murdered my mother.

Jax's voice fell to a whisper. "He's used you for your entire life, Elowen. Filled your head with lies, seduced you with his sweet words, but he's nothing but an evil snake."

My brow furrowed, and one thought and one thought only penetrated my mind.

He's right.

Silence again reigned in our tent as soft snores from the one next to us filled my ears, yet despite being tired, despite pain still running through me, I couldn't relax.

It seemed Jax couldn't either. He lay still, his breathing deep and even. Yet despite our silence, he continued watching me. Watched me so closely that once again, it felt as though he saw into me.

Sitting up, I finally undid the braids that I'd been wearing for the past two days. Jax watched that too, his intent gaze upon each of my fingers threading through my hair until my long chestnut strands tumbled down my back.

His throat bobbed in a swallow, his mask not hiding that. "You're absolutely beautiful, Elowen," he said so softly that I almost didn't hear him. "And I can see that you're not just beautiful on the outside but on the inside too. Despite everything he's done to you, your heart is still good."

Jax closed his eyes before I could fully process his tender words, and once I did, my heart pounded, my breaths turning shallow.

Sinking back onto the furs, I closed my eyes and let Jax's heat warm my side. And when I finally drifted off to sleep, it was only to dream of masked fae, a yearning for a family I would never have, and inevitably being lost in the Veiled Between.

CHAPTER 13

Footsteps padded by my ears. Soft steps like ghostly whispers. They disturbed the Wood's soil littered with fragrant pine needles, each step inadvertently creating puffs of aroma that tickled my senses and roused me from sleep.

I opened my eyes groggily. Darkness greeted me. Beside me, a male slept. Soft, even breathing reached my ears, and a warm, hard body was turned on his side. His chest was pressed flush against my back, and his arm rested around my waist, as though completely unaware of the casually intimate way he held me.

Jax. Every inch of him was heated, as impenetrable as stone, and strangely, being held by him felt nothing but safe.

I roused more. I'd never been held by a male before. Not ever. Guardian Alleron had never permitted it since he wouldn't allow me relationships. He'd only ever granted males the right to touch me during callings, and that was under his ever-watchful eye, except for the time he'd left the room and Lordling Neeble had . . .

I shoved that thought away and settled back more.

Jax's arm tightened around me, as though sensing my fear. And even though he still slept, he dragged me closer to him, even if the movement was slight.

My cheeks pinked. His heat wrapped around me, keeping me warm in the chilled air. I closed my eyes again and was about to settle back to sleep, but then abruptly started. *Wait, if Jax is still sleeping beside me, then who's outside the tent?*

A faint whisper on the breeze reached my ears, but it was so quiet I couldn't decipher it. I scrubbed more sleep from my eyes, and my heart began to pound.

Somebody was outside our tent.

I was certain of that.

My collar vibrated along my throat, and my breathing sped up with every passing second. It was possible I was hearing the other males. Perhaps Phillen or Lander had gotten up to relieve themselves. But if that was the case, they wouldn't be trying so hard to conceal their movements.

I turned over to jostle Jax awake, but before I could, the tent's canvas door flew open, and a large siltenite fairy dove inside.

Gasping, I lunged out of the way.

But he wasn't going for me.

The glint of metal in the moons' dim light caught my eye. The blade streaked upward, its intent clear.

"Jax!"

But my warning came too late.

The dagger fell and impaled the Dark Raider.

I shrieked and flew back. A groan came from Jax, his hand going to his upper stomach, right by his heart. The blade had sunk all the way to the hilt, and an eruption of blood gushed from the wound.

My heart felt as though it'd stopped.

"Jax!" I screamed again.

Rough hands grabbed me and yanked me from the tent. Before I could scream again, I was outside, and the cold night air whipped my hair in front of my eyes. My collar vibrated so strongly that painful jolts traveled down my arms. Thrashing, I tried to pull free from whomever held me, but his grip tightened.

"Let me go, you—"

A large hand clamped over my mouth, the male's skin rough and damp with sweat.

"Is that her?" another male hissed.

More canvas flapped on the tents, and with a start, I realized the clearing was crawling with male siltenites. Ten, no fifteen . . . no, *twenty*. My eyes bulged. So many.

Hair tangled in front of my eyes. Another breeze blew through the clearing, shifting my hair from my face and allowing me to see. My entire body quivered when none of Jax's friends emerged from their tents, and considering that several of the unknown males did, I could only guess that what had been done to Jax had also been done to his friends. They were likely all dead.

Oh Goddess.

Groans came from each tent, and my fear halted. Not dead, but obviously wounded. But from the placement of the dagger in Jax's stomach . . . If it hadn't gotten his heart, it'd been damn close. He would likely be dead from bleeding out within the hour, his friends probably in a similar state even if they currently lived.

A twist of regret cleaved my heart. Those males had taken me from my guardian and shown me the truth of him. And now, they were all as good as gone.

"Bring her here." A rough voice reached my ears, and I stiffened. I recognized that voice.

No, it can't be. I'm dreaming. This has to be a dream.

But the male I was presented to was indeed Lordling Neeble. Faewood Kingdom colors adorned him. All the males accompanying him wore similar garb. My gaze sharpened in the moonlight, and a few more familiar faces appeared, then more.

Every part of me locked up. These siltenites were Neeble's fae, the notoriously brutal guards who he'd hand-selected to guard his properties. Most had come from prison, after spending full seasons behind rock walls for their atrocious crimes that usually involved violence against females. They were known for their vicious and abusive behavior. Nobody dared enter Lordling Neeble's grounds due to what these males were rumored to do to fae.

"Is this her?" the male holding me asked.

Lordling Neeble grabbed my chin and angled my face in the moonlight. A cruel smile curved his lips.

Bile rose in my throat. My skin crawled, remembering the last time he touched me.

I tried to pull away, tried to inch back, but his fingers tightened their hold.

"That's her. She's mine now." He cast a vindictive look over his shoulder to where Guardian Alleron was still bound and deprived of his senses. My former guardian sat entirely still. Jax must have released him from his pain-inducing psychic magic. It was possible Guardian Alleron was sleeping. With only his taste and smell senses activated, he probably had no idea that Jax's camp had just been overrun, and the Dark Raider and his friends were close to entering the afterlife.

That knife-like feeling again cleaved my heart.

"Stupid fool," Lordling Neeble said under his breath, then spat on the ground toward my guardian. "He got himself caught."

"What are you doing here?" I muffled behind the male's palm, my voice trembling.

Lordling Neeble smiled, a terrifying twist of his lips that had my insides churning. "Before he left for Lemos, Guardian Alleron told the king of your abduction. Naturally, the king wasn't happy to hear that his favorite lorafin had been whisked from his capital, so he ordered your guardian to send regular updates via dillemsills, and when word arrived that you'd been found in Lemos and your guardian had you, the king sent several teams out to patrol the borders, just in case your rescue failed. Lucky for me, I had just arrived in the north via a ship, so the king asked me to remain on standby, and when Alleron failed to send word back to the king at the appointed time, the king sent me and all teams out looking for you. Hundreds of fae are scouring the borders for you, Elowen, and it's a good thing our king is so diligent or you never would have been found." He cast another disdainful glance at Guardian Alleron. "Really, such a disgrace. Even with three dozen guards, he couldn't bring you back." He scoffed. "Your former guardian has proven he's no longer capable of keeping you. He's obviously lost his edge, so I shall now take on that task." He smiled, then licked his lips and eyed me hungrily.

Vomit threatened to rise in my throat, and I shrank back more, but the male behind me stopped my retreat.

"Where to now, Lordling Neeble?" the one holding me asked.

"Get her on the domal. If we move fast, we'll get her to port by sunrise."

I thrashed again, but the guard's grip dug into my bare skin, and the stupid gown I wore offered little protection.

Another groan came from the tents, and with a sickening realization, I knew those were the last sounds Phillen, Lars, Bowan, Lander, and Trivan would make. They were all dying.

Even worse, the tent that I'd come from was completely silent. Jax was likely already dead.

A horrible aching regret filled me. And even though a part of me knew my reaction was ridiculous since Jax and I had only just met, it'd truly felt like something had shifted between us last night. On top of that, Jax had never abused me. Despite me physically hitting him, he still never roughly handled me or struck me.

Unlike the male standing before me—a despicable Faewood lordling, who was apparently here to abduct me as well. My *third* abduction. A laugh of hysteria threatened to rise inside me. The absurdity of the situation nearly made me cackle.

The guard holding me shook me. "Quiet."

But his rough treatment did little to stop my hysterics, and an unhinged laugh escaped me.

Lordling Neeble seethed. "Shut her up, and get her on the domal."

The guard holding me spun me around and slapped me across the face. He did it *so* fast.

The sting it left on my cheek was sharp and smarted enough that my laughter stopped. Searing pain coasted over my features, and I winced.

The males moved swiftly, throwing me on top of a domal as though I was a sack of flour before righting me, and then tied my legs with leather straps to the four-legged animal. My hands were still free, but I wasn't given any reins, and my collar began to sing in warning as fear cascaded through me.

This is really happening.

The male who'd thrown me on the animal snickered. "I'd advise you to hold on."

The domal's eyes gleamed in the moonlight as it danced on its hooves, but domals were intelligent animals. This one was no exception, given its concerned looks my way and angry snorts at the males.

"We move. Now!" Lordling Neeble growled.

My domal took off, falling in line with the males who were already mounted, just as Lordling Neeble swung onto his steed.

Within seconds, we were flying through the Wood, galloping back up the Ustilly Mountains, moving south once more.

I struggled to stay upright but somehow managed to twist my fingers through the domal's mane and hang on even though *zaps* emitted continually from my collar.

I jostled and groaned with every patter of the domal's hooves. My newest captor hadn't cared about my comfort. I was tied so tightly to the saddle that my legs burned from the stinging ropes.

A whip cracked on my animal's backside. Whinnying, the domal leaped forward, moving even faster.

Wind flew through my hair, and I yelped when the domal careened around a sharp rock on the steep mountain slope.

The sound of rocks scattering along the ground and tumbling off the mountainside had my stomach lurching.

With every step that we climbed, the Wood disappeared behind us until only towering rock and jagged peaks surrounded us. Moonlight lit the way. My eyes flashed wide. I hadn't been able to see any of this when I'd traveled on Phillen's back. It'd all been a blur, but on the slower-moving domal, terror engulfed me. The domals hooves weren't equipped for the steep rock slopes, and all of the animals slid and whinnied in fear as the males pushed them to move faster.

I lurched forward when my steed tried to leap over a rock and instead swung precariously to the side before it landed, then skidded sideways.

Pain from the stinging ropes cut into my legs even more. My collar activated anew, sending a smattering of shocking bolts through my limbs, making my nerves burn and my mind go blank.

"Keep moving!" Lordling Neeble yelled.

The domals finally reached the peak of the mountain range and began to descend on the other side, but the downward descent was even more treacherous. Several times, the animals nearly plunged off the steep ravine, and Lordling Neeble was forced to slow us. The entire time, I clung to the domal's mane, my fingers entwined so tightly around it's dark-purple strands that its course hair cut into my skin.

"We're almost to the Wood," Lordling Neeble called.

"Once we're there, head back to the wildling trail and head east. There's a ship—"

An enraged howl echoed across the valley from behind us, like a snarling beast emerging from its cave.

I swung my head around, wildly searching for the source of that sound. I was convinced I would find a treefang or wildesnare, or another mythical creature that was said to inhabit the mountainous Wood. But . . . nothing.

A whistling sound abruptly cut through the wind, and a blade impaled one of the males in front of me. I screamed.

Blood glistened in the moonlight when the tip appeared on the front of his chest, piercing right through his heart. The male tumbled off his domal.

Heart thundering, I leaned back on my domal, trying to get it to slow, but the animal must have sensed the death and blood in the air. Its head reared back, another terrified whinny emitting from it.

"Get her to the Wood!" Lordling Neeble shouted.

More blades and arrows suddenly zinged through the air, coming from behind us, and then I heard it.

Hoofbeats.

A swell of disbelief and joy tumbled through me simultaneously. Out of the darkness, cascading down the mountaintop like Lucifer himself, the Dark Raider, Phillen, and Trivan appeared atop their friends, having come into view only when they reached the lordling's group and slowed enough to no longer be a blur.

They tore through the group of Faewood males as though demons possessed their souls, turning into a tornado of death and destruction.

The lordling's males fought back, using their swords and daggers to counter the blows, but the stag shifters moved like the wind, dodging and swiping their weapons in moves so fast they were impossible to see.

I'd never seen any males move that fast. Ever.

A rough hand abruptly yanked the domal I rode, then I was careening down the mountain once more, the animal screaming in fear as Lordling Neeble brutally forced it into the Wood.

We galloped into the trees at full speed. Leaves and branches cut into my skin.

"Elowen!" Jax's bellow came from behind me, but the noble didn't slow.

Magic speared the air, filling the space around me, and then Lordling Neeble gasped.

"My eyes!" he screamed.

He let go of my domal, clawing at his face while Jax's sense-stealing magic clouded around him.

The sound of more galloping hooves came from behind me, and then Jax was there, and his huge stag slammed into Lordling Neeble's mount.

The noble fell off his steed, landing with a crash in a patch of barnbrambles. The lordling cried out when the sharp thorns mercilessly impaled his flesh and tore his skin.

"Elowen!" Jax grabbed my domal, slowing the frightened beast until he danced around where Lordling Neeble lay.

Jax's sapphire eyes practically glowed in the moonlight. He jumped off the stag, and a flash of magic flared in the night, and then Bowan stood before me too, dressed in black with a weapon raised.

"Go," Jax snarled.

Bowan disappeared in a blur back the way he'd come.

The domal I rode whinnied again and pranced, but Jax kept hold of its halter, stopping the poor animal's terrified movements. Leaning closer, Jax whispered something, and some of its frantic movements slowed, but its eyes still rolled white.

I sucked in a breath, alternating between trying to breathe and attempting to stifle my heightened emotions so my collar would stop punishing me. It didn't help that my legs ached from the vise-like ropes or that cuts lined my palms from the domal's course hair, but none of that compared to the absolute fury emanating from Jax.

Jax quickly tied my domal to a tree, then rounded on Lordling Neeble.

The male was still stuck in the barnbrambles, trying to untangle himself from the wooded stalks as he thrashed in his blinded state.

Jax shoved his hands into the bush and seized the male's shirt before hauling him out.

Lordling Neeble bared his teeth and punched for Jax's

mouth, but Jax easily dodged it, then slammed his forehead right into the lordling's nose.

Bone cracked, and blood gushed from his nostrils. Lordling Neeble howled, but he continued trying to fight.

In the distance, sounds of hacking flesh and pitiful moans carried on the wind. Farther up the mountain, the fighting still waged, but given that the sounds grew less and less, I had a feeling I knew who the victors were, and from the sounds of it, Jax's friends were ruthlessly killing every single male who had accompanied Lordling Neeble. This time there would be no survivors.

"How?" I managed in a strained whisper as Lordling Neeble continued to blindly swing. "He stabbed you. Right in the heart. You were dead. I saw it."

"He missed my heart."

It was the only explanation I got before Jax hauled Lordling Neeble clear of the thorny bush, staggering slightly under the lordling's weight.

My eyes widened. "Jax, you're hurt!"

He groaned under his breath and slammed Lordling Neeble to a tree, but he sagged and took several deep breaths. Moonlight shone off his complexion, highlighting the pale skin around his eyes.

The domal danced more beneath me as my worry grew. "Jax . . . you're *injured*."

"Still healing," he rasped, then turned his attention back to the noble. "Who are you?" he demanded on a low growl.

But Lordling Neeble just kicked and thrashed, and my worry tripled even though Jax continued to dodge his blows.

"He's Lordling Neeble from Faewood Kingdom. He rules one of the ten Houses," I said in a rush. "The king sent him to retrieve me when Guardian Alleron failed to make contact."

Jax's eyebrows drew together. "You know him?"

I gave a swift nod, and a sharp swell of nausea roiled my stomach as the memories of how I knew him hit me anew. "He's . . . used my services before."

Jax inhaled sharply, his eyes narrowing in my direction.

The domal pranced more, and I rubbed my hand along the animal, trying to soothe it since I was still tied to the poor thing.

"Elowen?" Jax growled. "Did he do more than use your lorafin powers?"

My brow furrowed. *How can he know that?*

Somehow, I managed a nod. "When I woke from his calling, he was . . . touching me. Guardian Alleron wasn't in the room. I was alone with him."

The air around Jax completely stilled, and the Wood grew entirely silent.

Magic suddenly pulsed from the Dark Raider, growing stronger and more potent with every breath he took. The male felt like a storm brewing and writhing, growing and swirling as the power within him threatened to unleash.

Leaves rustled from the north, and then Phillen, Trivan, Bowan, Lander, and Lars appeared. All were coated in blood and smelled of death. Yet even though every single one of them had been stabbed, they were all still breathing.

"Did you take care of all of them?" Jax growled in a beastly tone.

"The bastards are all dead, on their way to Lucifer's kingdom as we speak," Trivan said, a smirk in his voice even though he slumped against a tree and breathed heavily.

"Untie Elowen," Jax replied. He released Lordling Neeble, and in another cloud of magic, the noble gasped.

Lordling Neeble blinked rapidly and gazed around. "I can see again!" he whispered more to himself than anyone here.

Jax clutched his stomach and staggered back before righting himself. I had the most ridiculous urge to go to him, even though I couldn't since I was still tied to the terrified domal.

Forcing himself to stand tall, the Dark Raider prowled toward the House noble. "Yes, you can see, Lordling Neeble, and I intend to have you keep *all* of your senses. Because I plan to ensure you experience every bit of torture I'm about to inflict on you."

HOURS LATER, the sun was rising steadily over the Ustilly Mountains. We were back at camp, and Jax and all of his friends had eaten a mountain of food, probably diminishing their supplies completely. But the food seemed to assist whatever magic healed them. None of them appeared tired or weakened anymore.

I sat before a fire that Lars had silently lit. Lander had given me a jar of cream, telling me it would help with the quickly healing welts on my legs. Bruises had formed on my upper arms from the guard who'd roughly handled me, and I'd had a swollen lip from the vicious slap across my face, but those were already gone. My magic had taken care of that.

Around me, the tents were still standing, but everything else was a mess. Lordling Neeble's raiding party had trampled over all of the supplies, leaving dirty footprints in their wake.

Across the fire, Jax watched me, and I could have sworn that his eyes glowed as he meticulously sharpened a blade against a rock. He observed every dip of my hands into the salve, every spread of the blessed cream over my wounds. His expression, what I could see of it, was entirely indecipherable, but his motions with the blade increased as I tended to each cut.

Strangely, though, I didn't feel fear when I gazed across the fire at my captor. Despite the dark energy strumming around him, it wasn't directed at me, but rather at the male who'd been stripped bare and was currently dangling from a tree branch by a rope that cut into his wrists.

Lordling Neeble's body swung slowly in circles. With his arms overhead, bound at the wrists, and the long rope holding him aloft so his feet couldn't touch the ground, he was entirely vulnerable.

The other five stag shifters all prowled around the camp. They'd washed the blood away from their clothes and hands and now waited for whatever was to come.

"Tell me what he did to you," Jax said in a low tone, breaking the quiet. His knife continued to move languidly across the stone, the scraping motion the only sound apart from the quietly snapping fire.

My hand stopped mid-movement from dipping into the cream again. I set it aside, trembling. To hide the movement, I wrapped my arms around myself. Before I even knew what I was doing, I was rocking silently. Memories I didn't care to ever relive threatened to rise.

Biting my lip, I shook my head. "I can't."

Jax watched me, his eyes glowing slightly. His aura swelled, pulsing throughout the camp. He glanced down at his knife. "But he touched you?" he finally asked, his voice gruff. "In places he shouldn't have?"

"He did."

Jax rose in a blur. "Hold him still," he barked at Phillen. "Lars, take Elowen away from here. She doesn't need to see this."

"What are you going to do?" I pushed to a stand as the magic inside me stirred.

"What he deserves. It's best if you're not here to see it."

Lars approached me, his demeanor nonthreatening, but I sidestepped the redhead. "What if I want to stay?"

Jax inhaled, then said in a dark tone, "I don't intend to be gentle. Do you remember when I said I reserved my brutal side for the truly vile in our realm? Fae like *this* are who I was referring to." He pointed his knife at the noble.

But I still refused to move. "Tell me what you're going to do."

I could have sworn Jax's jaw worked beneath his mask. "I'm going to carve into his flesh and make him bleed. Slowly at first, because he attacked my camp. He tried to kill me and my friends. For that, he will pay. But what he did to you tonight, and at that calling . . ." Energy slammed into the trees around us. "For *that*, I'm going to fillet the skin from his bones, strip by strip. I'm going to do it slowly, agonizingly so, and at the very end I'm going to cut that dangling tiny cock off." His eyebrows rose as the dawn sun lit his face in a myriad of colors. He still wore his mask. All I could see were those startling blue irises. But despite the malicious gleam in his gaze, his words gentled, and his tone softened when he added, "Are you sure you can handle watching that?"

I wrapped my arms around myself, trembling more. I didn't relish hurting others. Violence was never something I'd cared for, but after being abused by this male in the worst way I'd ever been hurt, I wanted to see Lordling Neeble in pain.

With a swift nod, I relaxed my arms and stood straighter. "I can handle it."

CHAPTER 14

Guardian Alleron had wet himself. The stink of urine filled the air as the midday sun beat down on us. That stench, along with the smear of blood that trailed from the rocks into the Wood, made this clearing hardly desirable for another night of sleep.

Jax wiped the remains of blood from his knife and slipped it back into its sheath. A dark gleam filled his eyes, practically glowing in intensity, and all of the whisperings I'd heard throughout the seasons about his brutality, his thirst for blood, his willingness to carve into fae's flesh . . . Now I knew. It was all true.

I should have been frightened by that, perhaps even disgusted, but neither filled me. I believed Jax when he said he only did this to those deserving it. That this kind of horrific punishment was only dealt to the fae who'd used their powerful statuses to intentionally and maliciously hurt others.

It wasn't unheard of for nobles to slip through the judgment of the supernatural courts, but when that occurred, the Dark Raider came in. He was the judge and jury for the vile fae who'd never been held accountable for their crimes.

And I had a feeling he would continue to be as long as he was never caught.

Even though a few specks of Lordling Neeble's blood had splattered on my blue gown, which was now entirely tattered and sullied from his attempted abduction during the night, it wasn't terror I felt as I watched Jax cleanse the blood from his clothes and then mine. No, it was *power*. Vindication. Nobody had ever sought vengeance on my behalf before. Nobody had ever cared enough to do that.

But Jax had.

"I'm glad you did that to him," I said quietly. The fire lay in smoky ash at our feet as Jax's five friends packed their dwindling supplies into sacks.

Jax finished cleaning my gown, his gaze unrelenting. "You are?" His irises bore into me. I was coming to realize it was something he did often—study me—as though I was some kind of creature he was either trying to assess or was entirely transfixed by. "I didn't know if you'd have the stomach for it."

I shrugged. "I didn't either."

He stared at me for another moment, and I could have sworn that the energy around him rose when he asked, "Did Alleron know what Neeble did to you?"

For the first time, hearing the lordling's name didn't cause a shiver to run through my soul. The male was dead, butchered beyond recognition. He would never hurt me again.

"Initially, no. When it started, my guardian wasn't in the room, but when he came back, he saw Lordling Neeble holding me down. His fingers were—" I wrapped my arms around myself.

A swell of energy rose from Jax. "And did he stop him?"

I closed my eyes, tears threatening to rise. "No. He said if the lordling wanted to touch me in that way, then he would have to pay more."

Jax stilled. "He *allowed* it?"

"Only that one time." A shiver wracked my entire body. "He apologized afterward, saying he was caught unaware and didn't know how to respond. I forgave him because I believed him, but now . . ." I cast a look toward my guardian, who was still tied to a tree. "Now that I know he murdered my mother and took me only to fill his pockets—" I couldn't continue. Betrayal still lashed through me so sharply when I thought of the male I'd considered my father.

Jax inhaled sharply, and he rhythmically tapped his fingers against his thigh. "Since that pile of dung obviously didn't help you, did anyone else? Did you ever report to the kingsfae what Lordling Neeble had done?"

I shook my head. "No. I never told anyone."

Jax took a step closer to me. I dipped my chin as something stirred inside me, something I couldn't name or identify as Jax's potent aura and alluring scent clouded around me.

With a gentle clasp of my chin, he tilted my head up, forcing me to meet his gaze. "Why did you never tell?"

Tears threatened to fill my eyes again, but I blinked them back. A grinding noise came from beneath his mask, and I could have sworn his jaw locked. "Because of *this*." I ran my finger along my collar. "I have no rights as a caged lorafin, Jax. Not really. And it never happened again. At least my guardian kept his word in that aspect."

Jax's breath hitched, and a tidal wave of power rose around him. Stepping even closer, he lowered his head, then whispered in my ear, "If any male ever does that to you again, I want to know. Do you hear me? *I* want to know."

When he pulled back, I was trembling but not from fear. Instead, disbelief at the quiet rage that strummed from him coiled around something inside me. He'd meant every word that he just uttered. I would have bet my life on it. And even more startling, I had a feeling if any male did hurt me again as Lordling Neeble had, Jax would dish out punishment that was just as cruel and savage as what he'd done to the dead noble today.

"Understood?" He let go of my chin, and for the merest moment, his finger trailed along my jaw. A slight glow filled his eyes again, but it was gone so quickly, I wondered if I'd imagined it.

A shiver pulsed through me all the way to my toes. "Yes, I understand."

"Good." He looked me over, his brow furrowing. His gaze

lingered when it reached my dress's ragged hem and torn sides. "We'll be in Fosterton by the end of the day. I'll find new clothes for you then. Do you think you can ride?"

My arse ached, and the welts on my legs still throbbed even though my lorafin magic had healed most of them, but I nodded. "I'll be fine."

By the time the sun began setting in the vast Shadow Valley, lights from Fosterton blurred the sky ahead like pearls of sparkling sand. Jax had created another bubble around us, allowing us to travel in relative comfort. We'd ridden most of the day, moving in blurred speed as Phillen rocked beneath us and Jax sat right behind me.

Due to the heat and dry terrain, we'd had to stop more often for water, but other than that, it'd been a day similar to the previous. The Dark Raider had held me close the entire time, his arm locked around my waist and his chest moving in rhythmic, deep breaths against my back.

He hadn't asked or spoken of the calling I was to perform for him tomorrow, and given the crazy events of the night, I was no longer certain I could. I hadn't slept more than a few hours due to the lordling's attack, and consequently, I still felt aches and pains from the callings I'd done for the king.

But I'd promised Jax I would, so I slept for most of the ride, trying to help my magic fully recharge. But it was hard to rest when sitting up, and each time I jostled awake, it was to Jax's strong hold and warm breath on my neck.

At first, knowing that Jax held me so intimately had caused a moment of embarrassment to hit me, but when I realized he didn't seem to mind me sleeping in his arms, I'd eventually fallen back into a light slumber, letting the soft lulling motion of Phillen's gallop soothe me to rest.

It also helped that every time I grew conscious once more, I became aware of the fact that Jax's hand had never strayed from its position on my hip. No matter what state I was in, Jax's touches had always been respectful.

I was slowly coming to realize that the Dark Raider might be many things, and the brutal reputation he'd earned throughout the kingdoms was definitely warranted, but the one thing Jax *wasn't* was an abuser of females or innocents who didn't deserve his wrath. Somehow, I knew that to the depths of my soul.

"Where are we?" I finally asked when I roused completely. The remains of sleep still filled my eyes, but in a small burst of magic, I cleansed my breath, teeth, and body, but my stomach let out a loud rumble, letting me know that another long day of riding had left me famished. Yawning, I arched against Jax. "Are we almost there?"

He sucked in a breath so quietly I almost didn't hear it. My eyes flew open when I realized I'd just pushed my backside right into his groin. He shifted slightly, just enough that our contact broke.

Cheeks blazing, I worked to subtly put another inch of distance between us.

Jax waved ahead with his free hand. "We're . . . uh, still in the Shadow Valley. We'll stop for the night in Fosterton." He rubbed his cheek, then added in a gruff voice, "Should be there within ten minutes or so, but we'll stop at a shop first, to get you new clothes, before we find an inn and supper."

Ahead of us, Guardian Alleron was atop Trivan since the blond had drawn the short straw today. As before, my former guardian was strapped to the stag, and given his hunched-over position, he probably slept too.

Jax had released his sensory magic on my former guardian before we'd left and had allowed Guardian Alleron some water and a small amount of food. My former guardian could once again hear, speak, and see, but the time without his senses and the tortuous pain that'd been inflicted upon him seemed to have left a lasting impression. Not once had Guardian Alleron talked back to Jax since being released. Instead, fear now filled his eyes every time he beheld the Dark Raider.

"How are your legs?" Jax asked quietly.

"They're okay," I replied automatically.

"Are they?"

I nodded. "They are. The sleep helped. My magic still isn't charged enough for a calling, but I'm fully healed physically. Although, I don't heal as fast as you." I frowned, thinking again of the wound Jax had suffered from. I'd never asked him about it.

"I'm glad to hear it. In that case, we won't also stop at the healer in Fosterton."

I angled my head slightly to see him better, but I was met with the underside of his jaw and black mask. "What about you? Do you need a healer?"

I could have sworn that he smirked beneath his mask. "No, Little Lorafin, I do not."

"But . . . *how* is that possible? How did you recover from a stab wound to your abdomen? I saw the blow. The blade sank into your body to the hilt, right by your heart." I shuddered, remembering the blood and what had come next. If Jax hadn't recovered, I would now belong to Lordling Neeble, at his mercy—forever.

"It's because I'm a stag shifter."

I bumped him mischievously with my elbow. "Now you admit it."

Chuckling, he caught my arm before I could bump him again, and wrapped my forearm around my middle, holding it with his. I was entirely held within his embrace, and . . . *Goddess*, my heart began to pound.

I was barely able to breathe through the sensations spiraling through me, and my head spun when he whispered in my ear, "Yes, I'm a shifter, and brommel stag shifters in particular have extraordinary healing abilities. It's part of our magic. We can move like the wind, heal almost any ailment, and . . ."

"And what?"

He cleared his throat. "Nothing. I think I've revealed enough. We don't usually talk about our kind."

"Then why tell me at all?"

His gaze shifted. "I suppose because you asked."

Phillen abruptly slowed beneath us, and the blurry realm came into focus.

My attention drifted away from my captor to the small town waiting down the sandy road. The quaint village was the only city for miles, and I had a feeling it wasn't the brightly lit one I'd seen last night. We likely already passed that one, given how far we'd traveled.

Dry, sandy soil still stretched for miles around us, though, and I wondered how big the Shadow Valley was, especially considering the Ustilly Mountains were now tiny peaks so far away I could barely see them.

"Is most of Stonewild a desert?" I asked just as Jax swung off Phillen.

His booted feet hit the ground. "No, this is the only desert in our kingdom, but it's a big one."

Our kingdom. He just said *our* kingdom, confirming he was from Stonewild. I wondered if he was even aware of his slip or if he no longer felt concerned that I knew details of his life.

My stomach fluttered at that thought, so I quickly shifted my attention to the desert that I could at last see clearly. Flat ground stretched forever. The Wood was long gone, but desert plants bloomed and grew throughout the barren land.

Dry air filled my lungs, and a pleasant scent carried on the breeze.

"What's that smell? It almost smells like an herb."

Jax cocked his head, then hunched down. He snapped off a small branch from a low-lying shrub. Prickly leaves coated it, but they didn't seem to bite his skin. "Is this what you're smelling?"

I took the outstretched plant and brought it to my nose. The tiny spikes on the plant's leaves were more fuzzy than sharp, and when its rich aroma filled my senses, I inhaled deeply.

Grinning, I nodded. "What is it? I've never smelled it before."

"*Saggerwire.* It's a common shrub throughout the drier areas of Stonewild. Many animals eat it. At the leaf's center is thick water that can sustain one for days." He snapped off another branch from the ground and cracked a leaf. Blue drops formed on its broken surface, and he brought it to his lips before sucking it out. "Try it."

I did as he said, and when I snapped my leaf, even more of that herby scent rose in the air. Tentatively, I brought the leaf to my mouth, and the second a drop of the blue moisture hit my tongue, my entire mouth flooded with water. Startled, I nearly dropped it, but I recovered and swallowed the mouthful of cool liquid in one gulp. "How?"

His eyes crinkled. "Magic. This shrub is particularly magical."

"It must be to survive out here." I waved to the area beyond the town. So many miles of empty land surrounded us that I wondered how anyone could walk them, but then I remembered that I was in the land of shifters. Who knew what kind of animals or creatures fae here could turn into. It was possible fae could fly that distance or easily run it as Jax and his friends had.

But the distance to the north did promise more mountains, another range appearing on the horizon. To the west, though, there were only distant hills. Pale green with a smattering of pink and blue wispy clouds spanned the entire domed sky above us.

"It's so dry here," I added.

"The sea's that way." Jax jerked his chin to the east.

I cocked my head since he was sharing information so freely. "And what about Fosterton?" I nodded toward the small town ahead. "Is this our final destination? Will I be performing your calling here?"

"No, you won't, and it isn't." I waited for him to continue, but he didn't.

"Why stop here if it's not where you want to go?"

"You need clothes, and we need to rest. Besides, Fosterton is one of the smallest and poorest villages of Stonewild. I usually check in with the fae here. And I also have this to give to them." He pulled several heavy bags from the sacks draped over Phillen.

"What are in those?"

"Rulibs. Courtesy of Lordling Neeble." His eyes crinkled in the corners, and I had a feeling he was grinning.

I huffed a soft laugh, and he held his hands up to help me down. I took them without a moment's hesitation, and when his strong fingers and large palms closed around me, my attention fixated on the roughness of his callouses and the strength of his grip.

A flush worked up my neck, and my magic spiked inside me. Collar vibrating, I took a few deep breaths and swung my leg over Phillen.

Jax held onto me until I regained my footing, then he went to my guardian and hauled him off Trivan.

Guardian Alleron grunted when he landed on the sandy soil. He was still bound at his wrists, and his knees buckled slightly, but with stiff movements he straightened, his pride no doubt ensuring that. He had to be sore from the long day's ride, but I knew he would never admit it.

Magic stirred in the air around the stags, heating and pulsing. In a swell of power, the remaining five shifters all transformed back to their fae forms. As before, the five of them stood clad in black attire and concealing masks. Packs were slung over their shoulders that had been draped over their haunches.

"Finally, we're here." Trivan huffed. The blond wiped at his shoulders, as though dispelling whatever feeling remained from hauling my guardian around all day.

"Go okay?" Phillen clapped him on the shoulder. "You didn't buck him off. I'm surprised."

"I thought about it." Grumbling, Trivan shoved Phillen's hand off. "I'd rather carry the two of them than that arsehole again." He sneered at Guardian Alleron, but my guardian's gaze only found mine.

He cast me a veiled look, as though he was trying to communicate something with his eyes, but a simmer of betrayal bubbled up inside me, and I quickly looked away.

"This way." Jax indicated for me to walk at his side, so I joined him.

At my back, Guardian Alleron followed. With every step he took, I felt his silent demands digging into me. Pleading with me to address him.

I stiffened and kept my attention forward. If my guardian thought I was in a position to assist him or that I *would* help him escape, he was sorely wrong. I was still so angry at him for his total and complete betrayal. *He* was the reason I never knew my mother, and it wasn't like I could help him escape even if I wanted to. Bowan's magical bands still bound him.

Bustle from the small village carried to us on the wind. Fae milled about, walking along the dusty streets, standing in small yards, or selling goods from their canopied shops. Poverty was evident in the simple, tattered clothing most wore, but they weren't entirely without.

The sounds of children laughing rang through the streets, and fragrant scents from eating establishments wafted through the air, making my stomach growl again. With every step that took me closer to the tiny city, my stomach howled louder.

Jax chuckled. "We'll get food soon. I promise."

I slapped a hand to my stomach, casting him a sheepish smile, but soon the wonders of the foreign city overtook me.

"The south side is where the markets are." Jax gestured for me to follow him into a labyrinth of twisting streets and narrow alleys filled with canvas tents and wobbly tables. Every which way I looked were ramshackle shops, simple eating establishments, and small entertainment venues.

Jax handed the sacks of rulibs to his friends, and they all doled out coins to every fairy who approached. Murmurs of thanks and blessings from the stars poured out of everyone's mouths, and for the first time, I was seeing the *good* deeds that Jax did for the fae of our kingdom.

"Care for a flower, my lady?" A male stepped into my path and held up a blood-red rose. Thorns poked up from its stem, but the bud was large and velvet soft. A part of me wondered how in the realm he grew that here.

"I don't have any rulibs," I replied with a regretful shrug. "But it's a beautiful rose."

"Nonsense." He placed the rose carefully in my hand. "Any friend of the Dark Raider is a friend of mine." He bowed and stepped back as he cast Jax and his friends reverent looks and whispers of thanks.

Other fae stepped forward as we wove deeper into the market, holding out their hands eagerly as Jax and his band of friends filled them with coins. They kept it up until all the rulibs were gone, and it wasn't lost on me that they didn't keep any for themselves.

In return, every fairy we encountered offered their goods and wares at no charge even though it was obvious these fae didn't have much. Deferent glances at Jax and the other five all filled their expressions, but Jax and his friends declined their offers.

Puzzled, I frowned. "I don't understand. I mean, I know that you provide for them, but why don't they fear you? I thought everyone was afraid of you to some extent."

Jax shrugged. "Not here. Stonewild Kingdom is our home, and these are fae who we strive to protect. They know we would never hurt them."

"Is that why none of you are wearing glamours?"

He nodded. "They know us. They would never turn us into the kingsfae. Here, we don't need to hide."

I nibbled on my lip and thought back to all of the tales I'd heard of the Dark Raider. Stories stretched throughout the kingdoms, speaking of his violence, malicious attacks, and unforgiving nature, but those acts had all been done against nobles or rich fae who wielded their wealth and status like a weapon. But he never hurt the poor, and he provided for the less fortunate in all four kingdoms.

"A silk shawl for your beautiful mistress?" A middle-aged fae female held out an array of colorful scarves and bits of silk when we passed her shop. She bowed low to Jax, her expression similar to what one would see when a fairy worshiped the gods.

A blush heated my cheeks that she thought I was his mistress, but Jax fingered the material and nodded. "Better yet, do you have any clothing that would suit her? We still have another day of travel ahead."

Only another day? That implied we were almost to our final destination. My throat worked when the female bobbed her head and gestured to the inside of her shop. "You know I do, Dark Raider. This way, if you would. I have several gowns and dresses that would suit her perfectly."

THE NEXT HOUR passed in a blur of trying on dress after dress. Each one was bolder, more extravagant, and more constricting than the one before. I couldn't help but wonder where the shop owner had obtained her supplies or who she sold them to. Nobody I'd seen here wore anything this grand, yet after sneaking peeks at the other racks and shelves in her humble shop, I saw that the majority of her clothing was simple. Cottonum pants, long-sleeved tops, home-spun dresses.

But that wasn't what she chose for me.

I was reminded of my many seasons under Guardian Alleron's care. Once again, I became a doll to dress up and admire versus a female fairy with a beating heart and a mind of her own.

Dutifully, I fell into the role I'd been conditioned to play since I was a child. Turning. Holding my arms out. Stepping into gown after gown when asked.

The entire time, the shopkeeper clucked and fussed, having me turn every which way so she could smooth the skirt, fluff the tulle, or clasp bobbles to my throat and ears.

And with each dress I wore, I stepped out of the fitting room to parade before Jax as the shopkeeper gushed and gazed at him with adoring eyes while asking if he liked it.

By the time an hour had gone by, my smiles had turned wooden, and my gaze fixated on nothing in particular.

"Well, Dark Raider, what do you think of this beautiful material?" The shopkeeper beamed at him as I gave a slow twirl. "It's made of silk from the Nolus continent, over ten thousand stitches that are so fine you can barely see them, and the jewels at the neckline were mined in Ironcrest. It's a true work of art."

Jax leaned back on the sofa and cocked his head. "Is this dress from my raid the other month?"

She bobbed her head. "It is, Dark Raider."

I perked up for the first time in the past hour, understanding hitting me that *Jax* was the reason the shopkeeper had such grand goods.

And she indeed had many fine items. The dark-green gown I currently wore clung to my curves, hugged my breasts, and draped down my body like liquid silk.

"I agree that it's beautiful." Jax nodded.

I wouldn't have been surprised if a sun lived within the shopkeeper since she glowed so much from his praise.

Jax cocked his head at me. "Elowen? Do you agree?"

"Yes, Dark Raider," I replied automatically.

Jax's brow tightened, pinching together as the shopkeeper continued to gush about the gown's pattern and cut. Her hands fluttered around me, picking up and smoothing the dress until it lay at just the right angle. "I have several more similar to this if it suits you. You can have whatever you like, obviously at no cost—"

"Can you give us a minute?" Jax interrupted her.

The shopkeeper immediately bowed. "Yes, of course." She stepped away, heading outside to the lane to join Jax's friends and Guardian Alleron, who stood watch at the front door, leaving me alone with the Dark Raider.

Jax rose to his feet, his head nearly brushing the top of the shop's low stall. I stayed rooted to the spot, even though my collar hummed.

The energy strumming from Jax turned visceral, pulsing through the room in soft waves. He prowled toward me and only stopped when he towered above me, his chest less than a foot away. Clearly defined pecs were visible through his black shirt, and I wondered if they were as hard as they looked.

"What's wrong?" he asked quietly.

I quickly averted my gaze. "Nothing's wrong. Everything's fine."

"That's a lie." He growled low in his throat. "You've

become more silent and despondent with every dress you've tried on." He reached for my hip, as though he was going to touch me, but he stopped himself at the last moment and shoved his arm behind his back. "I thought you wanted new clothes?"

"I do." I licked my lips. "I'm sorry. I don't mean to seem ungrateful. I honestly would like something else to wear besides that blue gown."

"Then what's the problem? Why aren't you happy?"

"I'm happy." I gave him a dazzling smile, one so rehearsed that I could have done it in my sleep.

He took another step closer until his chest was only inches from mine. "Elowen," he said gruffly. "The truth, please."

My gaze flew to his, and I was once again awarded a clear view of his piercing blue eyes. They stared at me so intently that it was hard to look away, and once again, I had the feeling that he was studying me, trying to see into me.

"It's nothing." I ran a flustered hand over my chestnut-colored hair, but when another low growl came from him, I blurted out, "It's just that, my entire life I've been dressed up. Asked to perform. Expected to play the part of the dutiful lorafin. I've been on so many shopping trips like this it's hard not to fall back into the role I've always played."

"And what role is that?"

"A lorafin slave who does her guardian's bidding."

Jax stilled. "Is that what it feels like I'm doing? Dressing you up so you can prance around before me while I admire you?"

"I don't understand." I twisted my hands, for the first time not knowing how I was supposed to react or what was expected of me. "I've been putting on each dress, turning every time I've been asked to, yet you're angry."

"Goddess." He raked a hand over his scarfed head. "Take it off."

My stomach sank. "Oh . . . okay." My hands automatically went to the dress's clasp at my neck, and the gown began to slide down my body, the swell of my breasts appearing as the dress slid lower.

Jax's breath sucked in, and his hands shot up to catch the dress before more of me was exposed. "Fuck, Elowen. Not here," he said in a low, rough voice. "In the privacy of your dressing room."

"Oh . . . *Oh* . . . I'm sorry. I misunderstood." Flustered, I stopped the gown from falling lower. "But I thought you said to—"

"I didn't mean that you had to undress for me." Energy soared around him, washing over me in hot waves. He quickly clasped the gown together at the back of my neck, his fingers brushing against my skin.

Feeling like the biggest fool, I hurried to change, and once I was fully covered again, I joined Jax, only to find him pacing and agitated.

"Is that what *he* would make you do?" Jax nodded to the

outside, toward the front of the shop where his five friends and Guardian Alleron were waiting, before prowling to the other side of the shop and back.

"No." I quickly shook my head. "Guardian Alleron never touched me or watched me undress, but some males asked to see more of me when I'd perform callings, and sometimes, he'd allow that."

Jax froze, not one muscle moving. I could have sworn the air chilled around him too. "He did?"

I shrugged, and my stomach churned. "Not often, and he always gave me extra rulibs in my allowance when I wore more revealing dresses or bared parts of my flesh that I normally wouldn't. If I agreed to it, it would always require a higher fee at the calling, but he never allowed me to be naked. Only small parts of me were exposed at a time. It was just to tease the nobles. *That* he would accommodate, depending upon the price, but he didn't let them touch me. Lordling Neeble was the only one who did that." I bit my lip, and those conflicting feelings rose within me again for Guardian Alleron. He'd protected me in many ways, but in some ways . . . he'd exploited my vulnerability. I'd always known that on some level. Yet, other than Lordling Neeble, he'd never allowed anyone to touch me. It was looking only.

I shook my head. Anger for him again simmered within me, and the sense of betrayal was sharp and stabbing. But that sense of love and devotion I'd always felt for him was still present too. I couldn't deny that. He was still my father, the only parent I'd ever had. And hope still lived within me that maybe in his own messed up way, he loved me too, because Guardian Alleron was, and had been, the one and only constant in my life. Despite everything he'd done.

Jax's chest rose faster with each breath that he took. "So he treated you like a whore."

My head snapped back. "No, he never asked that I bed a male."

"But he had no problems with them looking." His jaw locked again, that telltale sound of his snapping teeth drifting through the mask.

I gave a quick nod.

"Elowen, may I ask you something?"

"What?"

"Do you favor these types of gowns?" He waved toward the fluffy lavender one I'd changed into.

I glanced down at it, again not wanting to appear ungrateful. "I mean, it's beautiful. I would never offend the shopkeeper by saying it wasn't."

"That doesn't answer my question."

My heart hammered when I glanced up to find him watching me again in that intense, all-seeing way of his.

"I asked if you preferred these types of dresses."

With a start, I realized nobody had ever asked me that before. Not a shopkeeper, not Lillivel, and certainly not Guardian Alleron. I pulled my lower lip into my mouth again, nibbling on it slightly before shaking my head.

"No." I shook my head more forcefully. "No, I don't think I do. These kinds of gowns are constricting and always draw attention to me. Sometimes when I wear them, I feel like I'm suffocating."

"And the blue gown you were wearing when we took you, did you choose that one?"

My lip curled. "No, I hate that gown."

His voice dropped so low it was nearly a whisper. "Have you ever had any choice in what you wear, Elowen? Ever?"

Out of nowhere, tears threatened to fill my eyes. It was entirely preposterous. We were talking about *clothing*, nothing more, yet the way Jax was looking at me and the questions he was asking . . . We both knew this had nothing to do with gowns. "Never."

He gestured to the dressing room. "Take that off in there."

Before I could utter another word, he disappeared out of the front door.

I didn't waste any time heeding his command, but my hands shook, and I felt entirely flustered when the shopkeeper's voice abruptly trilled through the room, "My lady! I have a few more selections for you!"

Cringing, I peeked out from behind the curtain, but Jax was gone, and it was only the female shopkeeper. Her smile was wide and bright, yet her expression was strained. "I do apologize if the dresses weren't to your liking. I've brought a few more pieces of clothing for you to try on. The Dark Raider insisted that you choose what you prefer, and that I'm not to sway you in the least."

Shocked, for a moment, all I could do was stare at her. "*I'm to choose?*"

Her smile grew even broader. "Yes, my lady. Whatever you like is what you will get."

A small smile worked across my face when I stared at the selections in her hands, and for the first time that I could ever remember when visiting a clothing shop, a bolt of excitement ran through me.

CHAPTER 15

The sun had sunk below the horizon when we finally left the shop, and the three moons glowed in the sky. A few stars twinkled in the galaxy, and my stomach gave another huge growl, but I didn't care that I was ravenous.

A grin stretched across my face. I took long strides, the comfortable pants adorning my legs moving easily with me. The material was soft and supple, and it billowed in the hot breeze, allowing me to stay comfortably cool.

"I have to say, Elowen,"—Phillen stroked his chin through his mask—"pants suit you."

"I think so too." My smile grew even wider. My new loose-fitting cream-colored slacks didn't constrict my movements. Their simple design allowed me to walk quickly and easily without the hampering material of a heavy gown.

On my upper half, I wore a long-sleeved cottonum top of a rich dark-purple color. The shirt's collar dipped slightly but wasn't revealing, and while the material hugged my waist, it wasn't form fitting. It did match the gem in my collar, though, something the shopkeeper had been enthralled by.

But other than the choker encircling my neck, nothing about my attire was fitted or called attention to me. If anything, the slacks and top were so ordinary that they detracted attention, blending in with the other fae of this small town, which was just fine in my opinion. For once, I wasn't being stared at. I felt light and buoyant. I felt *free*.

But even though I wasn't being ogled, the six black-clad and masked males at my side were another story.

Everywhere we went, fae dipped their heads or bowed in respect. It was entirely different from the reaction they'd gotten in Faewood.

"Do you like the clothes?" Jax asked as we strode through the streets. Several bags of other items I'd chosen were being carried by Guardian Alleron.

I beamed at him. "I do. I've never been allowed to wear pants before, but I've always wanted to. Thank you," I added, suddenly feeling shy.

Jax canted his head. "You're welcome, and in that case, I should get you a dozen more outfits."

"A dozen?" My eyebrows shot up. "But surely the ones I have are enough."

He shrugged, and I couldn't tell from that gesture if he agreed with me or not.

We rounded a turn, and a male wildling rushed out from a

small home on the corner. I wasn't entirely certain of his subspecies since I'd never seen six horns or blue hair on a wildling before, but neither Jax nor the other males seemed surprised by his appearance.

"Dark Raider." The male bowed deeply and extended something covered in a thin cloth.

Jax's brow furrowed, and he stopped in the middle of the street. He lifted the cloth slightly, just enough to reveal what was underneath it—a small branch of pure-white bark. A single pale golden leaf sprouted from it.

My jaw dropped. For a moment, I just stared at it. *That can't be what I think it is.*

The male thrust it toward Jax. "I've been hoping you'd ride through again soon. I've been holding onto this in case I was lucky enough to find you."

Jax carefully fingered the leaf, and a brush of potent magic rose from it, but he replaced the cloth and shook his head. "This is entirely unnecessary . . . Malimus, was it?"

Malimus straightened, and a broad grin parted his pale lips, revealing large oblong teeth in his snout. "Yes, Dark Raider. I'm honored that you remember me."

Jax canted his head. "I do. And how's your daughter?"

Malimus's entire expression lit up. "She's fine, fully healed and back to her usual impish self." He took a step closer to Jax. "I have you to thank for that. If you hadn't found her when you did, she would have died at the bottom of that *bolum.*"

"Then it's a good thing we tracked her as quickly as we did."

He nodded vigorously. "My Valorus is everything to me. She's the light of my life." Malimus bowed again. "Please, accept my gift. It's the least I can repay you with."

But Jax held up his hands and shook his head. "I insist that you keep it. Please make good use of it."

Malimus's eyes widened. "But I traveled all of the way to Silventine Wood to get this for you."

Bowan let out a low whistle. "It takes balls to go in that Wood."

Trivan grunted. "Sure does."

Lars nodded as well but didn't say anything.

Jax also inclined his head in agreement. "Which is all the more reason you should keep it. If you were brave enough to venture into the Silventine Wood and come out alive and with *that*, then you deserve to be the bearer of its good fortune."

The wildling bowed again and then again. "Thank you, Dark Raider. Thank you. May the stars, moons, and galaxy bless you."

"And you."

Jax carried on, leaving the simpering wildling behind. Malimus continued to hold that priceless branch within his grasp while he watched the Dark Raider depart.

My jaw refused to stop resting on the ground. "But, he—" I shook my head. "Did you really just turn down a *goldling branch*?"

"I did."

I gaped at him, but he continued to walk casually through the streets as more fae called greetings to him or bowed reverently.

"But . . . *why?*" I shook my head in disbelief. Most fae would kill to possess one of those. "A single leaf can create ten gold bars from a simple brick or a dozen diamonds from a plain rock."

"That's right. Alchemy is possible with that leaf."

"Yet, you refused it." I shook my head again, and I didn't have to turn around to know that Guardian Alleron was likely salivating after that branch. "Why?"

"Because I don't need it."

I gazed up at him, but whatever I'd hoped to decipher from his expression was guarded by his mask. "Are you truly so wealthy that you'd turn down that kind of payment?"

"Not all wealth is measured in gems and metals, Elowen."

"No, but that leaf could buy someone a lifetime of independence." I worked a swallow. "What I wouldn't give for a gift like that."

His gaze cut to mine, his aura beginning to churn, before he glanced briefly at Guardian Alleron, who was still bound at the wrists with Bowan's magic. Several bags were draped over him from my shopping venture, however.

"Did he never give you fair payment for what you've done?" he asked in a low voice. "For all that you've sacrificed?"

I twisted my hands. "He gave me an allowance."

"How much?"

"Five rulibs per month." I made sure to keep my focus forward since I could feel Guardian Alleron glaring at me. "But he did other things too. He provided for me. He bought me gowns and jewels, fed me, housed me." I frowned. "But I never had many rulibs of my own." In fact, since purchasing that dillemsill, I had next to nothing now.

A low, discontented sound came from Jax, but several giggles and tittering calls shifted my attention forward.

At the doorstep to a home just ahead, three female siltenites stood on the porch. Each was dressed in a colorful yet simple gown that showed off her figure. And all of them gazed at Jax adoringly.

"Good day to you, Dark Raider!" one called. She angled herself, which showed off her svelte waist and long hair.

"It's always a good day when we see you," another called, bumping the other female aside, who I guessed was her sister since they shared similar features.

The first female stumbled on the step, then glared at the other one.

The third one draped her arms over the porch's railing, but instead of gazing at Jax, she eyed Phillen. "Plans for tonight?" she asked coyly.

Phillen grunted and ignored her.

"He might be busy, but I'm not!" Trivan called.

All three of them burst into excited giggles.

We passed the females, and it struck me again how differently everyone was acting toward Jax and his friends in this town.

My frown deepened. "What happened to Malimus's daughter?"

Jax turned another corner, and more homes appeared as the market fell behind us. "She ventured into the desert, a bit farther than she should have, and fell into a bolum. We were nearby, passing through when it happened, so we helped."

"What's a bolum?"

Bowan came up behind me and whispered into my ear, "It's the part of the Shadow Valley that gets hungry."

I sputtered a laugh. "Hungry? The *desert*?"

"The Shadow Valley isn't like other lands." Phillen swung his brawny arms and inclined his head. "Only those who've grown up in this region could survive a fall into a bolum, but sadly, most are never able to climb free."

"Okay, now I'm thoroughly confused."

Jax's eyes crinkled in the corners, and I knew he was either smiling or smirking beneath his mask. "Bolums are creatures that live within the desert. They're part animal, part land. Some days they're entirely immobile and more rock than alive. Other days they're quite alert and awake, and *those* are the days that you want to steer clear of them."

"Because otherwise they'll eat you?" I asked with a scrunched-up nose, nodding toward Bowan and his comment about it being hungry.

Lars snorted quietly at my expression.

"Precisely." Trivan thumped me on the back, and a lock of blond hair peeked out from under his bandana. "Death by bolum is entirely painful and a prolonged experience. Since they wax and wane between being alive and being sand and rock, they can take weeks to digest you. It's said that some fae are awake and conscious throughout the entire ordeal. I wouldn't wish it on my worst enemy. Well, except maybe that pirate arsehole we encountered last summer. I wouldn't mind throwing him into a bolum."

Bowan laughed, and I could have sworn Lander's mouth twisted in a sly smile from beneath his mask.

"And you all saved his daughter from that." It struck me again that these males might be feared and hunted by the most powerful fae on the continent, but here, they truly were saviors if they'd risked their lives to retrieve a young female wildling from certain death.

A thought struck me, and I cocked my head. "If those here love you so much and you needn't worry about them calling the kingsfae, then why the disguises? Why not remove your masks entirely?"

The laughter died in the group. But instead of answering, Jax nodded down another lane. "Come. We'll dine up here."

CHAPTER 16

We waited outside another inn with a salopas beneath it. Jax and Phillen had gone inside to secure rooms before we had supper, and the rest of us had chosen to wait on the street with its perpetual breeze versus the small, stuffy entryway.

Secretly, I thought Trivan opted to stay outside because he and Bowan could then strut and posture for the local females passing by.

Lander casually held onto the ropelike magic that bound Guardian Alleron, not seeming to think anything of the fact that he'd been dragging my former guardian around like a whipped dog all evening.

"What'd you do with your blue gown, Elowen?" Trivan asked distractedly when he watched a female with long brown hair and swaying hips saunter by.

She cast him a smile and winked.

"I asked the shopkeeper to throw it away." I darted

Guardian Alleron a quick look. I'd been careful to avoid his accusing stares, but his current demeanor was practically burning holes into my back. Probably because that blue gown had cost him over three hundred rulibs.

Nobody else seemed to care about that dress, though. Lars and Lander laughed, and Bowan appeared to be grinning, given the deep wrinkles around his eyes.

"Good call." Trivan nodded. "And what do you think of that, Alleron? Do you also agree that garish gown was best tossed in the rubbish bin?"

"I suppose," Guardian Alleron replied through gritted teeth.

I cast a wary look toward my former guardian. Since the shopkeeper had draped the sacks containing my new clothes over him, at Jax's insistence of course, he was not only being dragged around like a pet but also like an indentured domal.

I hadn't taken much from the shopkeeper, only three more pants and six additional tops, along with new undergarments, so it wasn't like the bags were heavy. But one would have never guessed it from the miserable frown Guardian Alleron wore. He'd walked the entire way here as though the bags had been packed with solid stone. And I had a feeling that if it wasn't for his fear of Jax, he would have been verbally lashing out at me and looking anything but humble.

I gave him my back again and played nervously with the hem of my new shirt. The feeling of betrayal still seared my insides, but unwanted nagging guilt had begun to creep in.

The sharpness of the previous night, when my guardian's full betrayal had been revealed, had begun to die. But that only left room for an aching sense of disbelief and searing hurt to move in.

Sighing, I tried to shove my pitiful emotions down. I wished I could be like Jax and feel nothing but contempt for my guardian, but . . . I couldn't. As hard as I tried to stop it, guilt kept biting me, and I still fiercely hoped that underneath my guardian's pile of lies and deception, a part of him truly did love me. Even if it was a small part.

Scents from inside the inn drifted into the street, and I inhaled sharply, using that to distract me. Hunger pains clenched my stomach anew. It wasn't helping that every time someone opened the front door, mouthwatering fragrances of grilled meats and herbs assaulted me.

My stomach let out another loud howl.

As though he'd heard it, Jax appeared in the doorway. His shoulders nearly brushed against the frame they were so broad.

My mouth went dry. He stood over me with his sapphire eyes glittering like gemstones, and I was once again struck by the sheer force of this male. His aura was pulsing, dominant in a way, and I knew all it would take was a whisper of his magic to rob me of sight and sound.

Yet, as before, even knowing that, I wasn't afraid. Instead, what I felt was something I'd never experienced before. My stomach did a little leap, my pulse turning thready. And my breathing . . . Goddess, it was hard to take a deep breath.

"They have enough rooms. We'll stay here for the night." His voice lowered, and a hint of amusement rolled into his tone. "And they have plenty of food, Little Lorafin. Best come in before that howling beast in your stomach wakes the dead."

SIMILAR TO THE inn in Lemos, a salopas filled the entire first floor of the inn. Although unlike during the time we'd stopped for a meal there, this salopas was crowded, loud, and the entertainment was in full swing.

A group of wildlings was on the small stage, *yewens* from the looks of it. They played music through their trunks, whacked drums with their three-fingered hands, and thumped their feet. It made for a lively, jovial sound. Already, my foot was tapping to it.

The other patrons seemed to be enjoying the music too. More than a few were dipping their heads in time with the beat or slapping their thighs. Half a dozen fae were also dancing.

"My kind of place," Trivan said with a grin.

Lars sighed. "A bit too loud for me."

Phillen elbowed the redhead good naturedly. "They're talented. Don't tell me you can't appreciate that?"

Lars shrugged. "Just noise, all of it."

My eyebrows shot up. "You can't be serious?" All yewens were naturally gifted with a musical aptitude, but this group seemed even more so, given the musical range their trunks produced. It reminded me of the instruments played at Faewood's court, when the trumpets and drums announced the king. Only here, it was actually entertaining.

Lander snorted. "Don't mind Lars. 'Tis just his opinion. He's always preferred the quiet of the Wood to any kind of city."

Trivan dipped down and said softly into my ear, "He's never liked crowds or cared for music either. He can be quite boring in that sense."

"I heard that," Lars replied in a dry tone.

Trivan chuckled, and Phillen replied, "I think that was the point."

I gave the redhead a tentative smile. "I can understand liking the quiet and solitude of the Wood. I grew up in it. I've always enjoyed it too."

Lars arched an eyebrow. "You do?"

I nodded. "I didn't always wear gowns and pay regular visits to the king. When I was a child, we traveled regularly. Oftentimes, we camped in the Wood, much as you've all been doing."

Jax's attention drifted to me. "I didn't know that you often camped, but I suppose that also explains why you've never complained about sleeping on the ground."

I raised my shoulders. "I don't mind that either, although I'd be lying if I said I didn't prefer a soft bed." I winked playfully.

The corners of Jax's eyes crinkled, and there was a smile in his voice when he replied, "I think I can safely say all of us prefer beds over the ground, but we make do with what we have."

Phillen grunted, then pointed toward a corner booth that fae were clearing out of. Once standing, they gestured toward the now-empty table. "Looks like they're giving you your favorite spot, Jax."

Jax brushed slightly against me, and a smattering of goosebumps worked up my arms. "Elowen? After you."

"I'll send a tray over in a minute, Dark Raider!" the bartender called from behind his workstation as the seven of us and Guardian Alleron skirted our way to the booth.

The bartender returned his attention to his work. He held the handles of three mugs in one hand and moved them beneath a stream of ale before slapping them onto an awaiting enchanted tray. The second the mugs were steady, the tray glided off to serve its patrons.

Floating trays drifted through the air, carrying pints of beer, wine, *leminai*, and a few other alcoholic beverages I wasn't familiar with. Just as many trays carried food. I sighed longingly when a tray filled with six plates of spiced meat and fluffy rice floated by.

Most of the fae and wildlings who were seated were drinking, talking, and enjoying the music, but all I cared about was the next tray that drifted past me carrying a plate of *ustorill* roast sitting on a bed of root vegetables with a side of steamed greens.

Jax put his hand on my lower back, and all thoughts of supper vanished when the heat from his palm warmed me. He weaved us through the crowd, but as soon as more of the patrons became aware of his presence, a path was cleared as dancers moved out of the way, and chairs scooted to the side.

The Dark Raider stopped at the booth in the corner. It struck me anew that each time he'd chosen a place to be seated, it was where he would have a clear view of the entire room, windows, and doors. Even here, in a village that revered him, he didn't seem to take his safety for granted.

I dropped onto the bench, scooting toward the center. Jax immediately slid in beside me.

His thigh bumped mine, his leg so hard it resembled steel. I froze. I couldn't remember the last time I'd been so aware of a male's every move, each dip of his head, brush of his fingers, sound of his laugh, warmth from his skin . . .

But with Jax, it was as though he'd enchanted me, even though the reality was he'd *abducted* me.

Stars, Elowen, what's the matter with you?

I was acting as idiotic as those females who'd been swooning after him on their porch step, and I really needed to stop.

Phillen slid onto the bench to sit on my other side, Lars beside him. On the opposite end, Lander, Trivan, and Bowan made themselves comfortable. Guardian Alleron, however, stood awkwardly to the side, still magically chained. Several fae gave him curious looks, but none commented, and I couldn't help but wonder if they were used to seeing the Dark Raider arrive with captives.

In minutes, we had mugs of ale and plates of food before us. Everyone dug in. Apparently, I wasn't the only one ravenous from the long day of traveling.

It wasn't until I'd cleaned the meat off the bones and spooned every last bite of the delicious sides into my mouth that I felt satiated. Sighing in contentment, I returned my attention to the music and was soon drinking the bottomless rounds of ale the bartender seemed intent on sending our way while the lively beat ignited my soul.

"I take it you like music?" Jax asked quietly, his words like a low rumble beneath the steady beat. Around us, Phillen and the other males had fallen into a lively discussion about the upcoming Centennial Matches and were placing bets on who would win what competition, but Jax hadn't joined in.

I trailed a hand through my hair, moving the long strands behind my back. "I do. I've always loved music."

"Do you play any instruments?"

"Only one, the piano."

"Is that so?"

I nodded. "It was part of my education growing up. What about you? Do you play anything?"

He scratched his chin through his mask. "The fiddle, but

very badly." I laughed lightly, and he inclined his head toward Guardian Alleron. "Did he teach you?"

"No, he hired a piano tutor for me when I was younger and we lived for two full seasons in Ironcrest Kingdom." I eyed Guardian Alleron. He still stood stiffly, his expression neutral, but I'd been with him long enough to notice the tightness around his jaw. For a moment, I worried he could hear us talking about him, but then I realized the music was too loud for words to carry. I could barely hear Jax, let alone someone as far away as my guardian.

Jax leaned in closer and whispered in my ear, "Maybe you can play for me sometime."

I whipped my head toward him. "Play for you?"

He shrugged. "I don't see why not."

"But that would require having a piano."

He shrugged. "True, which might prove tricky at the moment, but eventually we'll be near one."

I frowned, cocking my head. I took another drink of ale, letting the delicious frothy liquid fill my mouth before swallowing. "And where will that be? Is wherever we're going blessed with musical instruments?"

He chuckled at my wry tone and took a drink of his beverage, the mug disappearing beneath his mask. It was impossible to ignore how his throat worked and not glance at the corded muscles in his neck that moved with each swallow. There was so little of him that I could see, and I couldn't help but soak up what hints were visible.

When he finished, he set his mug back down. "There'll be a piano."

"Which is at . . ." I let my words hang and raised my eyebrows.

"What else did he teach you?" He inclined his head again toward Guardian Alleron. "Did he allow you to go to school?"

Sighing, I let it go that he was avoiding my questions. "No, I wasn't allowed to attend school, but like the piano, I had tutors. Many of them. My guardian thought I would be more appealing to lordlings if I was educated."

Jax's eyes hardened. "So that education wasn't to benefit *you* but rather to increase his profits?"

My lips parted. I'd never thought of it that way. I'd simply been grateful for the lessons that had broken up the monotony of my days. I hadn't been allowed to play with other siltenites, had never had another female or male siltenite to call a friend. The only friends I'd ever had were wildlings, and I'd always suspected that was only because Guardian Alleron didn't know I'd befriended any of them.

Usually, when I wandered around in the Wood, my guards followed far behind me. They were often bored out of their minds, so much so that they'd had no idea of the quiet conversations I'd struck up with nearby wildlings. And I suspected that was only because wildlings were so good at blending into the Wood. My guards probably hadn't even known they were there.

Looking down, I played with my fingers as those

confusing feelings within me rose again. "He took care of me, you know. I know that he enslaved me to him, and I now know that he killed my mother"—my throat rolled in a swallow—"but it could have been so much worse considering what I am. He provided food for me, clothing, shelter. Alone, I would have either died or killed many, many fae, and then I would have been executed because of it."

Jax made a low sound in his throat. "I can see he's fed you many beliefs over the seasons."

I looked up, my eyebrows pinching together. "Meaning that *everything* he told me was a lie?" I knew my guardian had indeed deceived me, but to think that every single thing he'd ever said to me had been fabricated and twisted to serve his own convoluted purposes was so evil that—

Pain fired through me, twisting my stomach and sinking my heart. I shook my head. I couldn't accept that. Guardian Alleron *did* care for me on some level. He had to. Surely, there was something worthy enough in me to love, even if he betrayed me.

Jax's eyes softened, and his tone gentled. "I'm just saying that what you're telling me doesn't entirely align with what I know of lorafins, but you're probably right that not everything he said was a complete lie."

I smoothed my hair again and cleared my throat. Even though my stomach was twisting, I shoved my reaction to what Jax was implying about my guardian down as far as it would go. Sitting a bit straighter, I asked, "And how do you know that your knowledge of my kind is correct?"

He shrugged. "I trust the scholars who educated me, and I certainly trust them more than I trust *him*."

"Do you know him?" I angled myself toward Jax more, and my arm brushed against his. An acute array of shivers blasted up my spine. "Sometimes the way you speak of Guardian Alleron, it's as though you've met him before."

He looked down at where we'd touched and then said gruffly, "No, I haven't met him, but I know an abuser when I see one. I've met plenty."

I took another drink. "Is there anyone in your life who's abused you?"

I could have sworn his jaw tightened. "Define abuse."

I ran a flustered hand through my hair once more, and Jax's attention followed the movement, his gaze straying over the long chestnut strands. "I don't know. Did anyone hit you? Or starve you? Or lash out at you verbally?"

"Yes, to all of those things."

My heart thumped. "*All* of them?"

He took another drink, and the aura around him pulsed like a growing orb of light. "There's a reason I became the Dark Raider, Elowen."

He said that so softly that it took a moment for me to comprehend his words. "You became what you are because you were the victim of the things you're trying to stop?"

He neither nodded nor shook his head. He just chuffed. "I

can't believe I'm telling you all of this." He took another drink, then faced me. His blue eyes flashed in the salopas's glittering lights, and his expression turned serious. A heartbeat of silence passed, but his gaze didn't waver. "There's something about you, Elowen. Something I recognize in you is in me too."

He waited, watching me, his look so intent, so full of . . . *something*. It was as though he expected me to say similar words in response. But I didn't even know what he meant by that.

My heart leaped, and that strange feeling flipped my stomach. It coiled around me, pulling me in and making me feel . . .

I struggled to put a word to it, but these feelings felt more like . . . *yearnings*. And nothing about them felt safe.

I faced the dancers, looking away from Jax entirely, and changed the subject completely. Anything to get away from whatever this emotion was clogging my chest.

"Now that we're in Stonewild, are you going to have me search for whomever it is you're seeking?" I cast him a brief side-eye, but he'd looked away, and his gaze was once again entirely veiled. Whatever that strange emotion was that I'd detected in him only seconds ago had vanished. "I know I said I would be able to soon, but it may take an extra day. And it sounds like we may be reaching wherever it is you had in mind tomorrow? This mysterious place with a piano?"

I could have sworn his lips twitched, but then he cocked his head. "How do you know that we'll be there tomorrow?"

"You told the shopkeeper we only have another day of travel, implying one day."

"Ah, I suppose I did say that."

"So you don't want to have me perform your calling here?"

He arched an eyebrow. "You want to do that *here*?"

I shrugged. "It would be no different from anywhere else, I suppose."

But he shook his head. "Not here. It's why we're traveling to the place I've chosen. It's secure there, and there won't be any distractions. From what I've been told, it's important for a lorafin to feel safe, rested, and mentally sharp when performing a calling. I don't think *here* is a wise place for that to occur, even if we're in Stonewild. So, no, we'll wait."

I released a breath. Those were the most details he'd ever revealed to me of what he planned. I took another drink of my ale to calm my nerves and then another.

A smile entered his voice when he added, "And perhaps being intoxicated while you perform a calling isn't the best idea either."

"What? I'm not drunk." A hiccup escaped me.

Another twitch came from under his mask. "Perhaps not drunk quite yet, but you certainly seem more talkative." His eyes glowed with mischief.

I scowled at him. "Okay, fine, Dark Raider. I may be slightly impaired and tired and—" One look at his mocking gaze, and I slugged him in the shoulder.

He laughed and rubbed his arm. "So violent."

"Compared to you? Hardly."

He shook his head, still chuckling.

"But back to what you were saying earlier. About where we're going tomorrow . . . That destination is *where*, exactly?"

"Our destination is somewhere that's not here."

I sighed dramatically. "Back to the cryptic answers, I see."

"You can hardly blame me."

"Actually, I can completely blame you. My life has been turned entirely upside down because of you. Not only do I have no idea where we're going, but in the span of three days, I've learned my guardian meant to enslave me forever, and this"—I pointed to my collar—"is never to come off."

He looked down at his drink and rubbed his finger along the wet ring it left on the table. "I've been thinking of that, and I think we should try what I suggested last night. I can command your former guardian to release your collar's hold on you and never restrain you again with it. The collar will still be on your neck. I won't be able to physically remove it, but at least its magical capabilities will lessen and possibly be removed entirely."

A sharp sense of hope filled me. Jax appeared to be trying, *truly* trying to find a way around the collar's restrictions. Maybe it was possible I would still be freed after all.

"I could command him to do it tonight," he added softly. "There's no reason we need to wait until after you do my calling to rid you of that collar's stifling hold. Would you like that?"

"Tonight?" My heart instantly leaped, and the thought of my lorafin magic being entirely free sent a bolt of panic through me. I fidgeted, running my fingers up and down my beverage. "No, not tonight. I'm not ready. I mean, I don't know . . . or rather, I'd have to prepare . . ." I hastily took another drink of ale. "No. Not tonight."

"Are you sure?"

A buzzing energy filled me. It was possible when my collar was loosened, that my magic would burst out of control, and the thought of hurting fae in this town or subjecting them to possible death . . .

My pulse fluttered. Schooling my expression, I replied, "I'm sure. Not tonight. But thank you."

A groove appeared between his eyes. "Is it me you don't trust or your guardian?"

My attention snapped to him, but his gaze was entirely veiled. "I suppose I don't know. So much has happened that I don't know what to believe or trust, but I'm not ready yet for my collar to be subdued. I need to prepare."

He inclined his head, his brow furrowing. He took another drink of his ale. "In that case, I'll wait until you're ready."

A flush of gratitude rushed through me that he wasn't pushing me, but I also knew that me being ready had a time limit. It wasn't like the Dark Raider was going to cart me around indefinitely. After his calling, I would be forced to allow him to command my guardian to remove the collar's suppressing magic, or I could kiss my chances at being free of its caging hold goodbye. Because once Jax's calling was over, we were parting ways.

But that also meant I had at least another day, possibly two, before that time came. It wasn't happening yet, but knowing it was coming and knowing consequences might arise because of it made unease slither through me.

After all, I'd always pictured that day coming on my thirtieth birthday. I'd imagined myself preparing beforehand for weeks, possibly months, for that event. I'd secretly hoped my guardian would employ a tutor to coach me or teach me about what to expect. I certainly hadn't thought it would be thrust upon me with no tutoring in sight and only one day of preparation.

Oh Goddess.

I chugged the remainder of my drink, the cool liquid flowing down my throat in anxious gulps.

Around us, the music grew louder, and my attention drifted to the fae who were dancing. I focused on them, welcoming that sliver of distraction. Even more were on the dance floor, and the wildling band was in full swing.

I listened to the music and began tapping my foot to the beat again. The other males were still talking about the Centennial Matches, their voices getting louder and rowdier as the drinks flowed, but Jax sat quietly.

He sipped his beverage, and it wasn't lost on me that he was still nursing his first one. The Dark Raider's energy remained subdued yet alert, and I couldn't help but wonder what he was thinking. He appeared lost in thought.

The band finished their song and shifted to a new one. Their trunks played louder, the tempo increasing. I swayed my upper body to the tune, and as each song passed, and the energy in the room grew, I began to wish I could join the dancers. Expelling my nervous energy on the dance floor seemed like the perfect way to deal with what was to come.

"Do you want to . . ." Jax gestured to the open floor.

"Dance?" I asked with a hopeful grin.

"If you'd like."

My eyebrows shot up, and my stomach flipped. "Are you inviting me to dance . . . with you?"

A ripple of energy shot through his aura, and I could have sworn his eyelids grew slightly hooded. "As tempting as that is, not with me. I'm not much of a dancer, but feel free if you'd like."

Another flip tumbled my stomach. *It was tempting to dance with me?* I didn't know how to interpret that, and a rush of relief flowed through me that he declined joining me. Dancing was always something I loved, but I'd never danced with another. And to think of Jax beside me, his hands on my waist, our bodies shifting as one . . . To feel a male like that, especially *him*, made a zing of electricity barrel through me, getting a vibration from my collar. Doing such a thing would completely contradict the point of why I wanted to dance. I was trying to expel nervous energy. Not acquire it.

Sweet Goddess.

"I won't be long." I barely waited for his affirmation to leave the group before elbowing Phillen to get out of the way. "Move, if you would, kind sir."

He snorted in amusement before he and Lars slid out of the booth.

Once free of the confining table, I stepped away from the corner, dancing along the way to the center of the room. I could feel Guardian Alleron's glare, but since I didn't care, I knew that I was indeed slightly drunk, if not completely intoxicated.

Candlelight flashed from the salopas's corners, and a fairy light glittered above the dance floor. That, along with the music, made for a hypnotic ambiance.

I closed my eyes and quickly got lost in the music.

I couldn't remember the last time I'd been given the luxury of something as simple as this. Occasionally, Guardian Alleron would allow me to leave whatever home we'd been staying in to attend a nearby ball or to join a village celebration. Sometimes I was allowed to dance, yet not often. It usually depended upon which guards he'd sent me with and how accommodating they were feeling.

But when the opportunity presented itself, I never turned it down.

I lifted my arms, letting my hair fall down my back. My new clothes made moving easy, and my limbs felt flexible and eager to be set free after so many days atop a stag.

I was soon shifting and swaying, dipping my hips, waving my arms, and fluttering my hands. My feet moved of their own accord, following the natural beat of the song as I twirled and flowed, getting lost in the rhythm. The dancers around me were doing the same, some dancing as couples, others dancing alone.

I danced and danced, joy spreading through my soul at this one simple freedom.

Sweat soon beaded down my back, and the longer the night went on, the more my muscles quivered, and my breaths quickened. Pants lifted my chest, but it felt so good to move, to feel this *alive*.

A few times, between songs, I glanced toward the booth, just to see if any of Jax's friends had joined the dance floor. A female fairy was entwined in Trivan's embrace on the floor, but the others were still talking to one another, although Bowan now had a female sitting on his lap. Only Jax sat quietly.

Every time my attention shifted his way, our gazes locked. The Dark Raider's eyes were hooded, his expression impossible to read with that damned mask on, but his attention seemed to be entirely focused on me.

The intensity of his stare sent a ripple of goosebumps skating over me. It felt as though I was the only thing in the realm when he looked at me like that.

Turning away, I carried on and soaked up every minute of the night that I could, but as the hour progressed, the dance floor began to clear out, and more locals came in. Many were already inebriated, and the atmosphere in the salopas began to change.

The band continued playing, the lively music never faltering. Bawdy laughter and whistles began, though, in addition to the beat. I slowly became more aware of my surroundings and realized an entire group of males I hadn't seen earlier were sitting around a table. All of them were watching me. Some weren't even trying to hide their lustful stares and suggestive smirks.

They were looks I was used to. As a lorafin, my magic had blessed me with physical beauty and a sultry physique. They certainly weren't the first males to ogle me, and they wouldn't be the last.

But I'd learned to ignore males like them, so I kept moving, heaving in breaths. My body felt blissfully alive, but I was also beginning to grow tired.

Slowly, I began to wind down, not moving quite as sharply and quickly as I'd been.

"Don't stop on account of us, beautiful!" one of them yelled over the music. "I was enjoying the show."

I took a step back and glared at him. "The show wasn't for you."

One of the males beside him laughed and slapped the other's back. "She must not be interested in you, you big oaf." He turned glittering eyes on me. "But what about me?"

Before I could respond, he prowled to his feet and closed the distance between us.

A sharp zing from my collar made my heart leap. The male towered over me. He was a siltenite with coarse ashen-colored hair and sharp brown irises. A glaze filled his eyes, telling me he'd had more than a few drinks.

A new song started up, and he slipped his arms around my waist, not even asking if I was okay with it.

My breath sucked in, but before I could push him off, he rammed his pelvis against mine. I was so speechless at the feel of him grinding against me that I momentarily froze.

But before I could blink, an avalanche of magic swelled around me.

The drunken male dipped unsteadily to the side to gaze at the male barreling toward us. A vicious snarl tore from Jax, and then in a flash of speed, he ripped the male off me.

The drunk went sprawling, sliding across the floor, his body squeaking along it the entire way.

My chest heaved, and I nearly yelped.

Jax stood over the male, murder shining in his eyes. "I don't believe my lady enjoys your touch."

The male scurried back on his elbows, and several of his friends stood from the booth, but in a flash, all of Jax's friends were surrounding us.

Violent energy swelled around them, and each and every one of them pulsed with magic.

"Best to sit this one out." Trivan patted one of the males

condescendingly on the shoulder as Jax arched an eyebrow at the male who groped me.

I could tell that Jax was waiting. Just waiting for the male to rise and fight. Malicious energy strummed around the Dark Raider.

"Sorry," the male mumbled quickly. "I'm very sorry," he added in a rush.

Jax leaned down, glaring at the male. "It's not *me* you need to apologize to."

The male's gaze cut to mine. Fear bled into his eyes. "I'm . . . I'm sorry, my lady."

The band kept playing, as though used to such occurrences during their riffs, but the bartender stood as tense as a board behind his bench. He didn't interfere, not even when the rest of the dancers moved farther away, but he called out, "That group isn't from around here. Apologies, Dark Raider."

The male's friends all sat back, panic growing on their expressions when they realized who they provoked.

Jax cast me a questioning look. "Elowen, do you accept this male's apology?"

I glanced between Jax and the male and wondered what Jax would do if I said *no*. I wasn't sure I wanted to find out. There'd been enough violence today.

Chest heaving, I nodded. "Yes."

Flickering candles and the glittering fairy lights continued to bathe the room in a myriad of changing colors, but I could barely breathe, and a warning rattle came from my collar.

Jax righted himself, but a barely leashed storm seemed to swell around him. The male who assaulted me still lay on the floor, staring up at the Dark Raider with terror in his eyes.

Jax paused, and I could have sworn that his jaw was pumping beneath his mask. His hands fisted, and pulsing malevolent energy grew around him. From the tense way he held himself, despite me telling him it was fine, he appeared on the brink of erupting.

But another moment passed, and the intensity of his aura dimmed.

Finally standing back, Jax growled, "You're lucky her heart is more forgiving than mine." He rounded on the other males sitting at the booth. "Anyone else care to touch her uninvited?" He arched an eyebrow, and for some inexplicable reason, I had a feeling he wanted one of the males to bait him, that he was spoiling for a fight.

But the remaining males didn't say a word. A few hastily shook their heads, and one even apologized.

Another tense moment passed, but when none of the males rose from their seats, Jax finally gave them his back. "Tie them up," he told his friends. "They stay bound until we leave tomorrow. We can't trust them if they're not local."

Magical ropes extended from Bowan's hands, unfurling from his palms, as he called upon whatever magic he'd mastered to conjure such restraints. The bands lashed around all of the males, tying them up completely.

Lars's eyes took on a manic glee as he moved around the males to help Bowan secure them to the booth.

"Elowen?" Jax stepped closer to me, moving like a predator. I barely heard the music, even though it still played despite the tense interruption. He lowered his voice and pressed a hand to my lower back. "Let's get you upstairs. No one else will hurt you tonight. You have my word."

My head snapped up, my attention fixating on him.

Bottomless, cobalt irises met mine, barely leashed fury still evident in them, yet instead of fear for the violent tendencies this male continually displayed time and time again, strangely, I felt nothing but safe.

CHAPTER 17

Jax led me up the stairs and pulled the keys from his pocket. Footsteps came from behind us, his friends following with Guardian Alleron in tow.

"Elowen?" Jax said softly when we reached the second floor. "I was planning to give you your own chambers to sleep in, but after that"—a grinding sound came from beneath his mask—"*incident* downstairs, I would rather you're not left alone tonight. Just in case anybody else gets any ideas. If it's all right with you."

"Will . . . we be sharing the bed?" My heart began to gallop when I thought of how we'd lain in the tent last night before Lordling Neeble attacked. Jax's arm had been slung around me, his heat pressed to my back.

The Dark Raider lifted a hand to his head, as though he was going to rake it through his hair, his movements agitated.

"No, of course not. I'll sleep on the floor, but I don't want you alone even if I lock and ward the room."

Music still carried up the stairwell, causing the floor beneath my shoes to hum, but it no longer called to me. The male's attack downstairs had seen to that.

I wrapped my arms around myself. A strange sense of comfort filled me at the thought of Jax being so close, even if he was on the floor. "Yes, I'd like that."

He gave a curt nod, then distributed the rest of the keys to the other males. "Lock him up." He inclined his head to my former guardian. "And then, everyone, get some sleep. We ride early."

THE SECOND I was alone in the chamber with the Dark Raider, I began to second-guess my decision.

Heightened, powerful magic swirled around him. He prowled around the room, checking all of the locks and doors. Following that, he searched for any hidden exits or entrances, trap doors, magically veiled chambers, and even peepholes. And considering how small the chamber was, there was no escaping Jax's ever-present aura.

And you thought you could sleep soundly with such a male near you?

When he finished his inspection, he placed his hands on

his hips. "It's safe." Moonlight spilled around him, highlighting his inky-dark eyebrows and crystalline blue eyes. "There's a washroom in the corner if you'd like to use it." He gestured to the door by the far wall, then took another step back until he was pressed to the wall.

I couldn't be certain, but he seemed to be making an effort to keep himself as far away from me as the room allowed.

I eyed the lone bed, then my bag on the floor that Phillen had handed to Jax before shuffling Guardian Alleron down the hall. Silverly light was the only thing that illuminated it since neither of us had bothered to ignite the fairy lights. "I just realized I don't have any sleeping attire. I forgot to buy that today, so there's really not much I need to do in the washroom."

Jax's eyebrows pinched together, and he cleared his throat. "Right. In that case, I can give you my shirt. It'll keep you fully covered and be more comfortable than your clothes."

My eyes rounded, but before I could protest, he was unbuckling his belt and lifting his tunic over his head, then the looser shirt beneath it. His broad, muscled, and very naked chest appeared in the moonlight. Several scars were carved into his flesh, dipping over his defined abs and planed back.

My breaths sped up, and I hastily gulped. The fact that I was twenty-eight summers old and had never been with a male in *that* way came roaring back to me. My virginity wasn't by choice, after all. My guardian was entirely controlling and had never allowed any male near me who hadn't paid for my lorafin services, so seeing Jax now . . . a male with a body like a god and a scent that went straight to my head . . .

My virgin body was practically salivating.

Goddess, don't embarrass yourself, Elowen.

Averting my eyes, I somehow managed to ask in a fairly normal-sounding voice, "What will you sleep in? Won't you be cold?"

He made a soft sound, like a laugh or scoff. I couldn't be certain because blood was thundering through my ears.

"I rarely get cold."

I gave him a side-eye, but I couldn't help my gaze from skating over him. The male was truly breathtakingly beautiful.

But then a barely perceptible scar, right below his breast-bone, flashed in the moonlight. It was brighter pink than the others, still somewhat fresh looking, and my eyes widened when it hit me that it was the only remaining evidence of Lordling Neeble's attack.

And here I was ogling him after he nearly died last night.

For all the shame, Elowen.

Jax held out his big, loose shirt. I snatched it, then hurried to the washroom, berating myself the entire way. It was silly, my reaction to him. I'd seen males without their shirts on before. The guards at Emerson Estate trained that way regularly. That was nothing new.

Yet this felt new.

I was no longer under Guardian Alleron's care. I was no

longer subject to his rules, and something told me if I chose to bed a male, Jax wouldn't stop me or try to control me.

And knowing that, I couldn't help but want to stare at him. I didn't want to be a virgin. I wanted to learn every dip and turn of a male's flesh and the rise of his muscles. And Jax was a gorgeous male. Anyone attracted to his gender would notice that.

I argued internally as I passed him, that it was only natural to be having illicit fantasies about how his body would feel atop mine.

A sharp inhale came from Jax when I brushed by him, but I didn't slow my steps. I would likely embarrass myself if I did.

It was only when I was safely locked within the washroom that I allowed myself a moment to breathe. Yet an ache filled my belly, a wildly delicious ache that I'd never had the pleasure of a male satisfying before.

Stars and galaxy.

I sagged against the wall, gripping his clothing to my chest as I tried to ignore the tantalizing scent of pine and spice rising from it.

I was truly losing my mind if I wanted nothing more than to give my virginity to the Dark Raider.

TRUE TO HIS WORD, Jax slept on the floor. He settled as far

away from me as the chamber would allow him to, which wasn't that far.

Consequently, it took much longer than usual to fall asleep, even though the least of my worries was some male breaking into my room and harming me.

I was acutely aware of every breath Jax took, and I was painfully aware of every rustle of the blanket that I'd insisted he take from the bed. Other than those small sounds, it was quiet.

Silence filled the room, the wildling band in the salopas below now quiet.

Yet, never had the silence felt so . . . loud.

I finally fell asleep sometime in the early hours of the morning when one of the moons had set, and the stars were most alive. Yet, it wasn't a restful sleep. Dreams plagued me. Intense dreams. Indecent dreams.

Each time I awoke, I was certain that I'd find Jax beside me with his fingers fiddling the sensitive bud between my female flesh. Or that my hands would be upon his chest as I memorized and marveled at the leashed strength harbored in his muscles. My body felt as taut as a bow string. I was that aroused, that needy.

But every time my eyes fluttered open, it was only to me alone on the mattress with that aching desire pounding through me.

The only other sound in the room was Jax's breathing.

Sometimes it was steady and deep. Other times it was so quiet that I couldn't help but wonder if he was awake too.

Yet, I was too afraid to call out to him, too embarrassed to reveal just how inexperienced I was.

So I turned on my side and gazed out the window, my body humming with awareness for the male across the room who had entirely turned my realm upside down.

BY THE TIME MORNING CAME, even though I'd only had a few hours of restful sleep, I didn't feel tired. I felt alive, and, *Goddess,* did I need release.

I wasn't new to such an experience. I'd pleasured myself in the privacy of my chambers many times over the seasons— since it was all I'd ever been allowed to do. But despite that, it'd still never fully quenched the lust in me. But it would have to do. The last thing I wanted was to beg the Dark Raider to finally rid me of my unwanted virginity.

Goddess, talk about mortifying.

Sighing, I opened my eyes to find that Jax was already awake, and—

I gulped.

He was watching me.

The Dark Raider lay on his side, his half-hooded eyes locked on me. Mussed hair covered his head, and the blanket was bunched around his toned waist. In the early morning daylight, his chest looked smooth despite the myriad of scars.

Eyes widening, my attention drifted to his head. His scarf had fallen off sometime in the night, and I greedily soaked up his appearance.

As if only becoming aware of that, Jax's hand flew to the bandana lying on the floor.

"Fuck," he whispered beneath his breath.

Unfortunately, his mask was still in place, so only his eyes were visible, but his hair was just as black as I knew it would be. He wore it short, yet his locks had a slight wave to them. Several strands curled around his forehead, but before I could look more, he secured his bandana and then stood.

"I should go." His aura pounded from him, filling the room in a heavy magical cloud. He held his pillow over his groin, even though he was dressed from the waist down. Also strange, he seemed to be breathing through his mouth, given the puffs coming from his mask.

"Okay," I managed to reply, but I couldn't stop *looking*.

Morning sunlight dipped over his broad chest. It was much easier to see him in this light. He only wore pants, his upper body bare, and *stars and galaxy*. The male was entirely carved of sculpted flesh and defined muscle. Sinewy forearms gripped the pillow he held over himself, and his biceps and shoulders flexed involuntarily.

"I'll, uh, give you some privacy so you can get dressed." He strode across the room before I could blink, pillow still in place. It was only when he was out of the room, with the door locked behind him, that I finally breathed again.

A pulse pounded in my most intimate area, and when I glanced down, my jaw dropped.

Jax's shirt was hanging off one of my shoulders. It was so low that one of my breasts was nearly exposed, and from the feel of my hair, it was the epitome of bedhead. On top of that, after all of the indecent dreams I had during the night, my body *ached* for a male.

I could only imagine what I'd just looked like.

Elowen, what in all the realms?

Inside, my prickly conscience admonished me, but the need in my belly grew too great, and my growing attraction to Jax wasn't helping.

I lay back on the bed and let my fingers wander south. The second I touched myself, my body arched.

I knew it was insane, that my actions bordered on crazy. I was fantasizing about the Dark Raider and what it would feel like to have his hard length slide inside me.

The thought of him pounding me, claiming me, owning me . . .

Stars, I wanted to know what that would feel like.

I came almost instantly and had to turn my head into the pillow to muffle my cry. But a part of me still felt unsated. A part of me still *burned*.

But I wasn't about to humiliate myself by asking Jax if he'd mind tending to my salacious needs while I was his captive. I'd seen enough to know that Jax might have respect for me, and he might strive to provide protection to all females, but that didn't mean he desired me.

"Elowen, are you dressed, lovely?" Phillen's booming voice carried into my chambers through the door not long later.

"Coming!" I called.

My cheeks still burned from what I'd done the second Jax had left the room, but it wasn't like he had any idea that his corded muscles had taken center stage in my fantasies.

I smoothed the black slacks and ebony top I wore. A quick glance in the mirror revealed my chestnut hair swaying down my back in gentle waves. My bright-green eyes were still alive with evidence of desire, but other than that, I looked normal. With any luck, my outfit choice today would take all their attention away from any lingering traces of my arousal.

When I reached the door, I unlocked it. With a frown, I realized Jax hadn't spelled it on his way out, since it'd just unlocked like any other door. Even though he knew I could eventually undo his spells with a counterspell, he hadn't even tried to keep me caged. *Weird.* It was almost as if he'd been in a hurry to leave and had forgotten.

I opened the door with a flourish and flashed Phillen a wide smile.

The large, brawny male took one look at me and burst out

laughing, his mask puffing from his face with each exhale. "Are you taking the piss, lovely?"

I glanced down innocently at my black leggings, black tunic, and then smoothed the black bandana that concealed the top of my head and was tied with a knot at the nape of my neck—all newly acquired clothing thanks to the shopkeeper yesterday.

A spark of glee ran through me. Indeed, with this outfit, nobody would question what I'd been doing in the privacy of these chambers. They would be too busy laughing or shaking their head at my style choice.

But even though the bandana hid the top of my head, my hair was still mostly visible, and I wasn't wearing a mask so my identity wasn't concealed like Jax and his friends. Still, I definitely looked like one of them now.

I couldn't help my playful response. "What makes you say that?"

He chuckled. "So you have a sense of humor, do you, Newole? I knew I liked you." He gestured down the hall. "If you're ready, we're heading out."

I started at the sound of his new nickname for me. *Newole?* It was a strange thing to call me, but despite wondering how he'd come up with that, a smile spread across my lips. I'd never had a nickname before.

Phillen lumbered ahead. He didn't check to see if I was following him, so I figured he either trusted me to do so, or his stag shifter magic allowed him to hear my footsteps even though they were nearly silent.

I hitched my bag over my shoulder and kept pace behind him. We hopped down the stairs and passed through the salopas until we stood outside under a blazing morning sky. Dusty wind flew around us. In the distance, beige clouds swirled that were growing darker with every second that passed.

"Is that a storm?" I shaded my eyes, trying to see better.

"Dust cloud's coming. We best be far from here when that arrives." Lander waved toward it, his voice its usual monotone.

Lars dipped his head in agreement but didn't say anything.

Jax stood by the door, his arms flexing. Piercing blue eyes found mine, and a flash of heat consumed me. A sharp inhale came from him, then his gaze raked over me, but instead of showing amusement or appreciation, he sharply looked away.

A moment of disappointment hit me, but the other males began to laugh and pat me on the shoulder, all of them either smirking or trying not to smile, given the twitching movements beneath their masks.

My tensed shoulders relaxed, even more so when Trivan whistled and said, "Goddess, Elowen . . . these outfits look better on you than they do on us."

"I was thinking the same," Bowan agreed, not even trying to hide his ogling.

I arched an eyebrow at all of them. Their tunics and leggings did little to hide their powerful physiques. "That's debatable."

Bowan chuckled, and Lander made a noise that sounded suspiciously like a snicker.

But Guardian Alleron was a different story. His spiteful stare hit me. He was still bound, dried blood visible beneath the bands restraining him, and his glare told me how much he hated all of this.

I glanced away, anything to avoid my former guardian's accusing glowers, and in doing so, I became aware of the other activity in the street.

Shopkeepers and local fae were busy securing outdoor items with ropes or magic bands. Shutters were getting locked over windows, and dozens of fae were casting spells over doors and window frames.

"What are they doing?"

Jax nodded toward the clouds in the distance. "Sealing the crevices to keep that storm out. When that dust begins to fly, it's toxic."

My eyes bulged. "And we're leaving when it's about to hit?"

"We can outrun it if we leave now." Lander jerked his thumb toward the other males, and in a flash of magic, four of them shifted.

Lander grabbed Guardian Alleron and secured him to Lars while Jax leaped atop Phillen, then held out his arm to me. "Ready to get on?"

I couldn't be sure, but his words sounded slightly irritated.

But why is he angry with me? Stomach tumbling, I nodded.

Lander grasped me around the waist and lifted me as though I were as light as a feather. He draped me across the stag, right in front of Jax, and when Jax's arm slid around me, every indecent thought I'd had about the Dark Raider came roaring back.

My pulse thumped. "Where are we going?"

"North." Jax's clipped comment met my ear.

I squirmed. "Um, *where* in the north?"

"Somewhere safe." In a flash, he shot back when my rump met his groin, his entire body tensing.

I stilled, stopping my fidgeting completely just as humiliation hit me. Oh Goddess. He *knew*. Jax knew that I'd been aroused by him. It was why he was suddenly acting so distant.

Never had he been so stiff and formal with me, and never had he made certain that not even an inch of our bodies touched. It was becoming entirely apparent that the Dark Raider knew of my lust this morning, and he was telling me quite clearly—no words needed—that he wasn't interested.

Shame cascaded through me. Thank the Goddess I hadn't acted on my desire to lose my virginity. I could only imagine how awkward that rejection would have been.

Phillen leaped forward just as a bolt of lightning flashed in the distance. The rest of the stags followed and collectively picked up speed. But it wasn't until we reached the end of the town and all of the fae were out of the way that they really let loose.

Jax's arm tightened, holding me in place as energy

pounded around him. In a blink, a cloud of his magic surrounded us, cutting through the wind even though it began to howl.

As before, the realm turned into a blur of colorless sound the second they fully exacted their magic, and in a blink, Fosterton and the impending storm disappeared behind us.

Everywhere I looked was a void. A large, suffocating, never-ending span of nothingness.

And the only fairy I had for company for the rest of the day was the Dark Raider.

CHAPTER 18

"Goddess," I sighed. "What's a female to do?"

"What's that?" Jax replied, a frown in his voice.

"Ah . . ." I snapped my spine upright. "Did I say that out loud?"

We hadn't even been riding ten minutes, and already I was aware of every single breath Jax took. It seemed even my humiliation couldn't stop the fact that I desired this male. And I had no clue how to stop it.

"You did," he replied, and if I didn't know better, a smile had slid into his voice. "Care to share why?"

"Not really," I replied too quickly.

"Are you sure?"

I huffed a laugh, thankful that he was beginning to sound more like he had previously and was no longer irritable, but I still changed subjects. "So where is it we're going? And please don't say north again."

He took a long, deep breath. The blurred void around us continued, and it felt as though we were the only fae in the realm. "To the capital."

My eyes bulged. "Stonewild Kingdom's capital? As in Jaggedston? But why there?" It didn't seem like a safe place to venture. So many fae lived there, and the kingsfae were strong in their numbers, making it seem like a place Jax would avoid.

Another heartbeat of silence passed. "Because that's where I live."

My breath stopped. Stunned, I couldn't reply.

"And I'm assuming you know that's not information I generally share freely," he added.

My insides curled. Of course it wasn't something he would share easily. I was certain his enemies would kill for that information. But he'd told me.

Warmth spread through me, and it hit me that even though he didn't desire me, we'd still called a truce between us. I could even consider him a friend, because despite the fact that he'd abducted me, he was going to free me to the best of his ability. If that didn't deserve a tentative friendship, I didn't know what did.

I sat up straighter. "As your lorafin, I take the responsibility of guarding that knowledge very seriously."

His fingers played with the hem of my shirt, his movements quick and agitated. "You're not my lorafin, Elowen," he said softly.

"I'm not?"

"No, you're your own. Nobody owns you. Not unless you willingly give yourself to someone." He added the last bit so quietly I strained to decipher it.

I ran my fingers along my collar. My pulse spiked, but not from its magic. "This would speak otherwise. Only someone who's owned would wear something like this."

"Stars Above. I hate that thing." He cursed softly under his breath.

I angled my head up to see him better, and my pulse leaped. He was so close I could see the individual stubble hairs on the underside of his jaw, barely visible beneath his mask.

My entire body thrummed, and I wondered how I was going to go an entire day like this. It felt as if every second that passed, my awareness of him increased. His scent, his feel, his voice . . . For one crazy moment, I considered asking him to rob me of my senses just so my mind could realign, and I could force my budding attraction into submission. Just so my stupid virgin body would stop wondering what it would be like for this male to take me.

But I couldn't, not without raising questions from him and thoroughly embarrassing myself in the process, so to distract myself, I launched into a discussion about books, the places I'd traveled with Guardian Alleron, and the wildlings I'd met over the seasons.

Jax listened attentively, asking questions as well, as though he truly was interested to learn all of those mundane details. Or perhaps he was just being polite.

But surprisingly, when I asked questions of him—his favorite hobbies, favorite foods, favorite entertainment venues —he answered, but more evasively, so I couldn't know *where* he enjoyed those things, just that he did.

Still, I had a feeling that what he revealed to me wasn't how he usually interacted with captives. He had told me where he lived after all. The actual city, nonetheless.

But at least my plan worked. As the hours wore on, and my chattering continued, I wasn't completely aware of his every movement.

Just mostly aware.

WE TRAVELED through the morning and into the afternoon, and I perpetually wondered when we would reach Jaggedston. Jax had us stop once, to give everyone a chance to drink and grab something to eat. Supplies were low, so it was only dried meat and a few apples, but I didn't complain. Come tomorrow, I would perform Jax's calling, and then . . . he would free me to the best of his ability.

Each time that thought struck me, my internal magic warmed, heating and igniting as though knowing that it was the last time I would ever have to perform a calling outside of my own choosing. And that warmth infused life into me, especially since the temperature had cooled as the terrain around us turned into rolling hills with vast mountainous peaks looming on the horizon.

And as the day wore on, the scent of the sea grew in the air. Salt kissed my senses, and I tried to remember what I'd learned of Stonewild Kingdom's capital. It sat near the sea on the northeast side of our continent. Like all of the continent's kingdoms, ten noble Houses ruled the land, yet the king was the supreme ruler of them all. It was also the largest city in the north, over two million fae calling it home.

Beyond that, there wasn't much I knew, but in a population that big, it would be easy to blend in. Perhaps that was why Jax had chosen to call the capital his home despite the numerous kingsfae who heralded there as well.

"Did you grow up in Jaggedston?" I asked, the land once again a blur around us as Phillen ran at his full pace.

"I did," Jax replied.

I perked up. So he hadn't chosen the city. The city had chosen *him*. "Do you have family there?"

He stiffened. "I do."

"Tell me about them and about how you ended up being the Dark Raider." The bold statement left my lips, like a whisper on the breeze, but his comments from last night still sat with me, the hints he'd given about also being abused. And since he'd answered some of my questions today about his hobbies and favorite foods, I figured he might answer more.

Jax's hand shifted, his fingers curling around the hem of my shirt. "There's not much to tell."

"We both know that's a lie."

He inhaled, and his fingers rubbed my shirt more. "I've been the Dark Raider for more summers than I can remember."

"Did someone teach you how to do what you do?"

He smirked, the telltale sound of his scoff giving that gesture away. "No, Little Lorafin, nobody taught me."

"But you obviously learned how to fight. Someone must have taught you that."

"You're right in that aspect. I've been trained in combat since I was young. It was expected of me."

"Expected? By who?"

"My father."

My heart jolted. "Your father? Is he still alive?"

A grinding noise came, and I knew he was clenching his jaw. "He is."

"Oh, I see." I didn't press him for more information about his family. The aura strumming off Jax increased, and I had a feeling it was a sensitive subject, so instead I asked, "What ultimately made you decide to be the Dark Raider? You mentioned last night it was because of things you also suffered, but did something specific happen?"

He shifted again, and his throat rolled in a swallow. "There was something that set it off, but it was also an accumulation of things. Too many injustices were happening in our realm, and not enough was being done about it, so I decided to take matters into my own hands."

My fingers entwined through Phillen's mane more. "Have you ever come close to being caught?"

"Come close?" He chuckled. "I *have* been caught."

It felt as if my heart stopped. "You were? When?"

"When I first created this role. I wasn't as practiced in evading the kingsfae then."

"How did you get away?"

He leaned closer, and a smile entered his voice. "Haven't you learned a thing or two about my magic, Little Lorafin? I can be rather *persuasive*."

My eyes bulged when his meaning hit me. "You commanded them to free you?"

"I did, but in the process I also revealed that about myself. Most of the kingsfae now think I herald from Mistvale, so most of their efforts to find me are focused there, which has actually been a blessing. But, because of what I revealed, they also know what I'm capable of. I've heard they wear devices in their ears now to resist a Mistvale fairy's influence."

"Even though most fae from Mistvale aren't strong enough to command as you do?"

"Yes, even though most fae can't do what I can, they still wear them, so if I'm caught again, I may not be as lucky to escape twice."

Fingers tangling more in Phillen's mane, I tried to ignore the turning of my stomach that thought provoked. "Do they not know that you command magic from all of the kingdoms?"

"No, they don't. They believe I only hold Mistvale magic."

"Then how come I know that?"

For a heartbeat, he was quiet, and his fingers rubbed on my shirt again. "I don't know, Elowen. I normally don't reveal as much with captives as I have with you, so . . ." His fingers fiddled with my shirt more. "I don't know."

WHEN LATE AFTERNOON ARRIVED, the stags slowed to a canter, moving at a natural pace. My head spun at the abrupt shift in speed, but Jax held me steady.

I sniffed. The scent of thick salt filled the breeze, and when we crested a large hill, the outskirts of a huge city waited just across the valley, and the rolling waves of the sea waited just beyond.

I gasped. "Is that Jaggedston?"

"It is."

Crashing waves from the Adriastic Sea curled like white blankets along the cliff's shore as the capital glimmered just west of the vast ocean. Soaring buildings made of stone, brick, and steel stretched for miles, and the Wildland Mountains rose in the distance like sharp sentries just north of it.

"It's so big," I murmured. "And beautiful."

Hundreds of zigzagging streets could be seen from this high up, and at the top of the highest hill, stood the palace. Black stone walls and an onyx roof held true to the whisperings I'd heard throughout the kingdoms about the Stonewild royal's residence. It looked dark. Sinister. But captivating too.

Beyond the capital, the jagged peaks of the Wildland Mountains gave a hint to what had inspired the capital's name. Their frosty tips, still covered in snow despite it being end of summer, promised to chill one's skin. North of those peaks lay Silventine Wood, one of the deadliest forests on the continent, yet I wasn't able to see a single tree given the height of the mountain peaks.

And that was when it fully hit me—that my former life was forever behind me. Fosterton was so many miles south, Faewood Kingdom even farther. And seeing Jaggedston now reminded me of how far we'd come. I was well and truly a captive of Stonewild Kingdom until Jax said otherwise.

"As you can see . . . we're here," Jax said softly, his chest pressed to my back.

"Are we going to your home now?" I asked warily. No fae were about, but there were small houses ahead. They dotted the valley and rolling hills that led up to the capital.

"We are."

"Will I be staying in your home for the calling you want me to do tonight?"

"You will be."

"And tomorrow, when I'm free, will you show me the city?" I knew it was a long shot. While a part of me had begun to hope for friendship with the Dark Raider, the other part of me knew that Jax had a life outside of me. He likely

KINGDOM OF FAEWOOD

had little time for someone like myself after he took what he needed.

Tensing, I waited, hoping he would prove me wrong, but all he said was, "No more questions, Little Lorafin."

A stinging pain clenched my heart. Perhaps hoping for friendship from anyone who wasn't paid to be in my company was asking too much. Dipping my chin, I did my best to ignore how much his reply had hurt and instead continued to gaze at our surroundings as Phillen broke into a canter.

Picking up his pace, Phillen galloped down the steep hill, the other stags keeping pace behind him. The closer we got to the capital, the more Jax's aura grew. With every step, his aura pulsed and swirled around me, like a magical cloak settling over my skin, and I was reminded of the epic power he wielded.

But when the homes I'd seen from afar grew closer, the stags abruptly slowed and stepped off the road before dipping into a patch of trees. Bird song trilled in the air, and the breeze was even thicker with salt, but despite being closer to the capital, I still hadn't seen a single fairy anywhere.

"What are we doing?" I asked Jax when Phillen ground to a halt.

Jax's arm tightened around my waist. Blazing sapphire eyes met mine when I glanced up questionably at him.

"I'm sorry, but I have to do this. Forgive me, Elowen."

Just as his words registered, the realm around me plunged into darkness. I swallowed a scream. *Nothing.* I could see absolutely *nothing*. Blackness, as dark as the semelees themselves, coated my vision. Behind me, Guardian Alleron let out a sound of fury, and I could only guess his sight had been taken too.

"Jax?" I gripped for him, but his touch disappeared along with his presence behind me, and then the sound of boots hitting the ground came.

A cold breeze billowed against my back, and it hit me how cold I would have been during this journey without Jax's warmth pressed into me.

"Jax?" I said again, my voice rising. I hated the fear that shook it, but I couldn't stop it.

"Just sit quietly, Elowen. All will be well."

The sound of fabric being shifted and rustling sounds came. Before I could cry out again, Jax swung back onto Phillen again, and his solid chest pressed against my back once more.

I trembled, my breaths speeding up. "What's happening? Why did you take my sight? And why did you get off Phillen?"

"I'm sorry," he said so quietly it was a whisper against my ear. "But blinding you is necessary."

"Why?" I demanded. Terror had darkness stirring within me, and my collar released a sting in warning.

"I must keep my identity a secret. This is safer for you." His voice ached, and some foolish part of me thought blinding me had actually pained him.

But if it did, he wouldn't have done it.

My hands flew upward. I would stab his eyeballs, take away his sight too, just so he could know how absolutely terrifying this was, but the second my hands reached his face, I stopped.

His mask was gone.

He truly was exposed, and perhaps he *was* hiding his true identity from me. My fingers encountered stubbly cheeks, firm lips, and—

He growled and forced my hands down. "Don't, Elowen."

"Where's your mask? Why did you take it off? And why is everyone else allowed to see you but not me?" Sooner or later, fae would be on this road. They would see Jax, but he didn't want me to.

Instead of replying, Phillen trotted forward, and we were moving again.

Jax's arm locked around my waist to keep me in place, but I rubbed against him, something, anything to give me a clue as to what was happening.

And the second I came in contact with his clothing, I felt the difference.

The smooth dark shirt he'd been wearing since we'd met was gone. In its place was something thicker and rougher.

"You've changed your clothes too."

"Elowen," he said in a low warning tone.

Something in me snapped. Any hope that had been building within me that the Dark Raider actually cared for me and perhaps wouldn't deceive me broke. *Lies.* Everything with him had been a lie. He was hiding things from me. Possibly many things. And to think I'd desired this male and had even hoped of possibly being considered his friend.

Stupid, so stupid, Elowen. Did you actually think he cared for you? Nobody cares for you. He's just using you like every other male, and you fell for it.

"Elowen," he said more quietly as we rode on. His tone turned lower, rougher. "It's not what you're thinking."

"Then what is it?" I hated that my voice broke.

"Please, just trust me on this. You can't see or—" His throat bobbed in a swallow. I could feel it since he was sitting so close. "Or hear when we get closer to the capital."

"You're going to take away my hearing too?" Panic tightened my throat.

"Only for a short while."

A moment of silence passed, and the only sound that carried on the breeze was the clopping of the stags' hooves. Everywhere I looked was darkness so black that terror tightened my chest anew.

The age-old feeling of betrayal and knowing that there was *nobody* in this realm who I could trust or count on sank in.

"Why, Jax?" my voice sounded broken, pleading. "Why are you doing this to me?"

His breath caught, and his arm tightened even more at my waist. "I'm sorry, Elowen. It's truly necessary. Please forgive me."

CHAPTER 19

I sat in a realm of black silence. It felt like time took on no meaning in this bottomless void I'd been plunged into. As promised, as soon as the sounds of the city grew near, Jax had muttered another apology, and then he'd robbed me of hearing too.

With only my sense of touch, scent, and taste left, I clung to them, desperately soaking up every detail that I could decipher.

Phillen, in his stag form, continued to shift beneath me. Each time he moved, my legs tightened in worry that I'd fall off despite Jax's steady grip.

Scents of a crowded city eventually came. I could tell when we passed a salopas—the aroma of wheat brewed in the air. And I knew when we passed a shop that sold leather products due to the rich fragrance of tanned hide swirling around us.

Other sensory clues came as well. The feel of Jax's breathing. The pounding of his heart. The steady way he held me, or how his body turned tenser and more rigid with every step we took.

I had no idea where Jax was taking me or why it was clouded in mystery, but I clung to his promise that this was temporary and that he wouldn't leave me in this state, even if I was a fool to believe that too.

I had no idea how long it'd been since he deprived me of sight and sound, but it felt like hours even though I guessed it wasn't.

Still, I wasn't ready for the feel of my hearing to return. Out of nowhere, sound came flooding back.

I gasped, and Jax's arm held me steady, then the press of his lips came to my ear. "We're here."

I trembled in his arms. My sight was still gone, and I struggled to understand this clandestine arrival or why he would allow me hearing but not eyesight.

"Now what's happening?" I *hated* that my voice shook. *You're weak, Elowen, so weak.*

"We're going inside."

"Inside *where*, Jax?"

"Shh, please keep your voice down."

It was on the tip of my tongue to do the exact opposite, but his arm tightened around my stomach. "Elowen, I can only allow your voice if you stay quiet."

My lip curled in a sneer. "You're going to take that too?"

"Please don't make me."

His low warning had me snapping my mouth closed. It was quickly becoming apparent to me that here in Stonewild's capital, Jax feared something or someone—so much so that he didn't want me to potentially alert his presence to any fae passing by. And maybe it was in my best interest to also heed that plea. For all I knew, if the kingsfae found us, they would shoot their deadly arrows first and ask questions second. I could be dead before I knew it.

"Do I have your word you'll stay quiet?"

My nostrils flared, but I gave a sharp nod.

He swung off Phillen, then helped me dismount. From the sounds of it, someone was helping Guardian Alleron down too.

Distant sounds of a street made my head cock. We weren't far from the city's bustle, and a soft breeze flew across my cheeks. I knew we were still in the capital. The city's scents hadn't abated even once.

"You need to follow me, but stay quiet. If you don't, I'll be forced to—"

"I know." I bristled at his promised threat, yet a part of me ached at what his warning implied. Gone was the Jax I'd been traveling with during the past few days. The one who protected me, spoken with me, *slept beside me.*

This Jax was entirely guarded and cold, but perhaps this was the real Jax, and the one I'd been journeying with had been a figment of my imagination.

The Dark Raider clasped my hand, his large palm closing

over mine. The sound of a door opening came next, and then he led me down a dank stone walkway.

I knew it was stone from the instant humidity and coolness that pressed around me. Sure enough, several times I reached out, and my fingers met cold rock.

The sounds of the city fell away. Footsteps, from who I assumed were his friends and Guardian Alleron, came from behind us. We were in a tunnel, moving underground. Dank air swirled around us. Musty scents of water and mold flooded my senses. Without my sight, I tried as hard as I could to decipher where we were and what Jax had planned, but I couldn't.

His hand squeezed mine. "Not much farther."

My feet shuffled along the rough path, then we were moving upward, my breaths becoming winded as the climb grew steeper.

"There are steps here."

My shin knocked into the first one, and I cursed.

A hiss came from Jax. "On second thought, I'll carry you."

Before I could respond, Jax swung me up in his arms. His spicy scent flooded my senses more potently than it ever had before.

And then we were flying.

His shifter magic gave him superior strength and speed, making us move faster than a normal fairy. Wind flowed over my cheeks, and I clung to him, desperately clinging to his solid form as the dark realm turned around me.

"Jax?" That stupid fear was still in my voice, but I desperately needed answers.

"Almost there."

We reached the top of the stairwell, the only clue to it being his abrupt stop. He shifted, his arm moving from beneath me. Another door creaked open, and a strong wash of magic prickled my skin when we stepped over a warded barrier, but after we passed through it, the dank humidity fell behind us. Rustling sounds came again, and then we were walking.

Jax turned and turned again. He did it all so fast that I couldn't tell if we were in another tunnel or hall or if he was purposefully moving in a way as to disorient me.

Another door opened and closed, and with a start, I realized that Lander, Bowan, and the other males' footsteps had disappeared.

"Are we alone?" I whispered.

"We are." Finally, Jax set me on my feet. "You're going to stay here for now."

"Where's here?"

"You'll see in a minute."

Uneasiness crept through me, and I wrapped my arms around myself. "What is this place, Jax? What's going on?"

Sorrow filled his tone when he replied, "It's a bedroom chambers. It's safe for you. You'll stay here until I can meet with you and Guardian Alleron again. Once you locate who I'm seeking, I'll let you go and command your former guardian to permanently relieve you of that collar to the best of his ability. I promise."

But for the first time, his words didn't ring true. I wrapped my arms even tighter around myself. "What aren't you telling me, Jax? Why are you hiding everything from me? *Why* are you doing this to me?"

His voice turned grim. "I'll be back soon."

The sound of a door came, and I swirled around. In a whisper of magic, my sight returned.

I started. Everything was suddenly as clear as day. Jax had lifted his magic in a heartbeat, and he'd done it after he left because I was alone.

I swung in a circle, taking in the bedroom chambers. Large windows soared to the ceiling on one side of the room, allowing sunlight to stream in, but the glass was foggy and distorted. Even though light bled through it, I couldn't see out.

And nobody could see in.

A large bed stood to the side of me, its frame ornate, the bedding plush and soft. It reeked of wealth. Across the room, through a large arched doorway, was a sitting area filled with couches and chairs. Other doors were also in the room that led to who knew where.

I nearly stumbled as I searched for where Jax had gone.

I raced to the door nearest me and yanked on the handle.

Locked.

I whispered an unlocking spell and then another and another. The lock didn't budge.

Pulse quickening, I raced to the next door and yanked on that one too. It opened, and I nearly stumbled since I'd pulled so hard. But it was only a massive wardrobe, empty of clothes or shoes. I flew to the next one. An elegant bathing chamber in pristine whites and soft blues stood before me. A clawed foot bathtub sat in front of another foggy window.

Shaking, I went back into the bed chamber, then the sitting area. I explored every area, learned every turn, studied every detail, and it soon became apparent I was in a suite. A large, grand suite, but no matter how hard I tried to find a way out, I couldn't. The two doors that I suspected would lead me to another part of this house were both locked, and no locking spell I tried undid them, not even the more complex ones I'd been taught.

It seemed Jax had learned a thing or two about my magic since my escape in Lemos.

Staggering, I turned away from the door in the sitting area, finally giving up on my unlocking spells. I pitched forward and nearly vomited at the panic that was consuming me.

The Dark Raider took one's senses so easily, as easy as a thought on the breeze. His magic was that strong. That powerful. And he'd just locked me in this chamber as though I was his captured lorafin after all.

Worst of all, he'd made no mention of when he was coming back.

CHAPTER 20

Bright morning sunlight streamed into my chambers. My eyes opened slowly, only to see the light coming through that dreaded frosted glass. Jax had never returned the previous evening. I'd thought he wanted me to do his calling, but since he hadn't made an appearance, I was beginning to wonder if I'd been put in this plush, gilded cage because he intended to keep me after all.

Stomach churning anew, I stretched and sat up. "At least, I slept," I muttered to myself. The soft mattress and plump pillows could probably be thanked for that. Still, it was a miracle I'd slept at all, considering my current circumstances.

Whatever the case, I didn't want to be found in my under-things, so I hurriedly got up and made quick work in the bathing chamber, washing myself and brushing my teeth in the traditional manner before dressing in another new outfit from Fosterton—a cozy emerald sweater and tan breeches—but when scents of food tickled my nose, I stopped mid-brush from tending to my hair.

I peeked out of the chamber, and my jaw dropped when I spotted an entire tray of food on a table in the sitting area. I approached it warily, gaze darting about as I searched for whomever had brought it in.

The scent called to my howling stomach, but anxious nerves turned it just as fast. Despite the mouthwatering array of eggs, breakfast meats, fresh fruit, flaky pastries, and a pot of fresh tea, I didn't reach for any of it.

Instead, I searched for signs of who crept in here while I'd been bathing.

But nobody was about.

Somebody must have snuck in here and then out.

Realizing that nearly made my heart stop, and considering this new discovery made my stomach turbulent, I wasn't able to eat.

I was standing near the window an hour later, desperately trying to see some kind of detail through its thick fog, when a soft knock came on the door.

I jumped, just as an unlocking spell followed, and given the aura wafting under the door, I knew who it was.

Tensing, I watched as the Dark Raider opened the door and stepped into the room. He did it so fast that I couldn't see any details of the hall behind him, but I did see enough to know it was a hallway, not another stone tunnel, but as soon as that detail revealed itself, it disappeared.

For a moment, we both stared at one another. Once again, Jax wore a mask and a bandana, but his clothes were different. Instead of leggings he wore black slacks. And in place of a tunic, he wore a thin gray sweater.

I could tell even from the distance that the material was finely woven. Jax hadn't been kidding when he'd said he had rulibs. Apparently, he was as wealthy as Guardian Alleron.

Our gazes stayed locked, and my heart beat even faster as cold fury began to consume me. My collar rattled violently against my throat, but I didn't even try to stop it.

"You've returned." My comment came out as frosty as the window behind me.

His throat bobbed in a swallow. "Good morning," he offered.

I curled my hands into fists.

He took a step toward me, but an air of hesitance billowed around him, and I couldn't help but wonder if he was feeling guilty for what he'd done to me, or perhaps he was feeling guilty for whatever he was about to demand.

Of course, I had no way of knowing. As always, his features were hidden behind that damned mask.

"Back to hiding then?" I asked in a sardonic tone as I arched an eyebrow. "You certainly had no problems *not* wearing that mask yesterday when we arrived."

"It's a necessity."

I scoffed. "Of course it is."

The mysteriousness of him only added to his commanding presence. I was itching to know what he looked like, but I figured at this point the likelihood of that happening was as promising as me traveling to planet Jeulic.

He walked slowly toward me, each step silent on the thick carpet, until he stood only a foot away.

"How did you sleep?" The muted sunlight hit his eyes, and his irises became a dazzling display of blues and navy.

"Oh, just fine, thank you. And how about you, Dark Raider?"

My syrupy tone had him huffing, but instead of replying, his finger began to tap against his thigh. He gestured toward the food tray on the table in the attached sitting room. "Did you eat?"

"No."

The tapping increased. "Would you like breakfast first? Before the calling?"

My lips thinned. So that was why he was here. *Right down to business then*. I didn't know if I should be offended or relieved.

Shrugging, I replied, "It honestly doesn't matter. If you're eager to get started, we can begin."

Hesitantly, his hand drifted forward until it brushed against mine. In my next breath, he clasped ahold of me. My chest tightened at the feel of his hard callouses. Eyes sparkling like sapphires, he squeezed me gently.

"Thank you. After this, I'll release you, ensuring your freedom from that collar to the best of my ability, and I'll be sure you have enough rulibs to start whatever life you'd like."

Hope surged within me. Stupid, *stupid*, hope. *When will you ever learn, Elowen, that you can trust no one?*

"I'll believe that when I see it."

A flash of raw emotion streaked across his eyes. It almost looked like pain or perhaps disappointment. But he veiled it too quickly for me to fully grasp whatever it was, but one thing I'd learned since being locked in here, I was a fool to fall for anything he said or did.

But despite knowing Jax could very well be deceiving me now, I didn't yank my hand back. Instead, I tried to quell my growing desire to do whatever he wanted just so I could potentially gain my freedom. A true family was never in the cards for me now, thanks to my guardian's betrayal, but perhaps at least I could be the maker of my own destiny, no longer a slave if the supernatural courts deemed me safe.

You're an idiot, Elowen.

But I couldn't completely ignore the singular goal that was now staring me smack in the face. My entire life I'd been working toward this moment. Autonomy. Independence. Perhaps Jax would keep his promise, and the entire past four days would end up being one long nightmare that I could hopefully forget one day. Perhaps . . . but I supposed only time would tell.

Jax dipped his head. "Ready?"

I pulled my hand free of his. "Yes."

In a few strides, Jax was at the door again. My nostrils flared when the door opened readily for him.

"Phillen?" he called down the hallway. "Bring him in."

I tried to see into the hall again, but he'd barely opened the door enough to call to his friend. In less than a minute, Guardian Alleron was in the room with Phillen right behind him. The rest of Jax's friends filed into the chamber too, slipping through the door so quickly that my head spun.

All of them were masked, bandanas in place, yet that was where the similarities ended. Trivan, Lander, and Bowan wore clothing as fine as Jax, but Phillen and Lars wore uniforms of forest green, gold, and sapphire blue—Stonewild Kingdom colors.

But uniforms for what?

Before I could ponder that, Jax was in my space again with Guardian Alleron right behind him. At least, I wasn't the only one afraid. Given my guardian's terrified expression, I couldn't help but wonder if Jax had robbed him of his senses the entire night and had only just released them.

Jax handed the adaptor to Guardian Alleron, then turned his azure eyes on me. "Elowen? Shall we begin?"

I walked stiffly to the bed, and my collar vibrated as

emotions roiled within me. I took deep, steadying breaths, but it did little to calm my nerves.

This could potentially be my last demanded calling ever. Tomorrow, I could be free. *Or not.* This could all be a ploy to trick me.

I lay on the bed, placed my arms at my sides, and waited. But nobody moved.

Guardian Alleron raised his eyebrows at the Dark Raider. "Are you going to touch her?"

Jax's brow furrowed, and he growled, "Why would I touch her?"

I flinched, unable to help it, even though a part of me knew that Jax thought Guardian Alleron was inviting him to touch me indecently, as Lordling Neeble had, yet it still hurt. Jax had rejected me very clearly yesterday morning, so maybe he truly thought I was hideous, and his touches earlier had been out of necessity, not choice.

I fought the urge to rub my temples. Confusion filled me at Jax's waxing and waning actions. He couldn't very well rob me of my senses and lock me up, then feign irritation at Guardian Alleron inviting him to touch or harm me. Stealing my senses and holding me captive *was* harming me.

Guardian Alleron's nostrils flared. "She needs to access your magic to perform your calling. In order to do that, she needs to be touching you."

The Dark Raider's eyebrows slanted sharply together. "That isn't how I was told callings worked."

My ears pricked. It wasn't the first time Jax had implied he knew about lorafins, and I couldn't help but wonder if what he knew was true and where he'd acquired his information.

Guardian Alleron sighed again, and subtle sarcasm dripped from his tone when he replied, "By all means, if you know more about Elowen and her callings than me, do whatever you prefer."

Jax and I regarded one another. His shoulders tensed, and his hands fisted.

Sighing, I gave up on trying to understand any of this. I just wanted his calling over and done with.

I raised my arm, holding out an outstretched palm to him. "If you want someone or something found, and I want to be free, this is the only way. Take my hand."

The adaptor flashed in Guardian Alleron's palm. A jolt skated down my spine from the collar, and I yelped.

My former guardian gave Jax a mock frown. "Sorry, my finger twitched."

Jax scowled, and his aura abruptly pounded through the room. Out of nowhere, Guardian Alleron cried out in pain, his face contorting, the muscles in his neck flexing.

Just as soon as it started, though, it stopped.

"Sorry," Jax said sarcastically, then prowled closer to Guardian Alleron. "My mind twitched."

My guardian leaped back, and Jax stopped just short of him.

"You do that to her again, and then pretend that it *wasn't* intentional, and I'll make the next time I hurt you a hundred times more painful. Do you understand?"

Guardian Alleron cowered. "Yeee . . . yes, Dark Raider."

The rest of the males watched on, not interfering, but tension strummed from them, and I swallowed the fear rising inside me. Jax was ruthless, truly *ruthless*. I'd been a fool to think I could ever trust him.

Bottom line, Jax had no qualms about hurting others. He'd likely eventually hurt me too, even if I'd thought he would never hurt a female. I just hadn't provoked him enough yet.

I need to get out of here.

Guardian Alleron bobbed his head. "I sincerely apologize. I'll ensure her collar isn't triggered again."

Jax placed his hands on his hips. "Will this calling hurt her?"

Guardian Alleron's lips thinned. "It's nothing she can't handle."

"That isn't what I asked," Jax growled.

"I'll be fine," I called. "Come, let's get this over with."

The Dark Raider searched my guardian's face one last time before stepping to my side. He hovered his hand over mine. "Is here okay?" he asked gruffly.

My entire body locked up, but I nodded. "There's fine."

His hand gently entwined with mine, and a current ran up my arm that had nothing to do with the adaptor or my collar. *Stupid, Elowen, so stupid. You're seriously still attracted to him?* I wanted to hang myself.

"When you're ready, Elowen." Guardian Alleron pressed the gem on his adaptor in a series of specific taps, and a rush of magic washed around my throat.

The collar loosened its vise-like hold on my power, slowly falling away until it no longer felt like a constant pressure around my magic. But it was still there, still monitoring me. If the collar sensed that I was becoming too free of its grip, it would strengthen once more and rein me in.

I closed my eyes and opened my senses just as Jax's abilities spiraled into me.

CHAPTER 21

A slam of power skated over me, stabbing and firing just beneath my skin. The force of it was like a living dragon, roaring its might on a tight leash. My breath caught. Power, *so much* power. Jax had more magic than any fairy I'd ever encountered.

Trembling, I forced myself to concentrate even though I dreaded what was to come.

Best not to think about that. Just get this over with so you can get out of here and away from the Dark Raider and away from these illicit feelings he's born in you.

Breathing deeply, I fell inward, following the pull of the darkness inside me. I dove down, down, to the center of where my powers lay.

My magic's enchanting coldness swirled around me, and I cradled the darkness that flowed through my veins and commanded my essence.

Take me away.

My magic heeded my call and flowed out of me, detaching my soul from my body and venturing me to the Veiled Between—the realm between realms, the plane that existed between life and death.

I shot through the galaxy, traveling instantaneously with my lorafin magic until I drifted in nothingness, and the Veil appeared.

A wispy fog parted the darkness, and I reached for it until my phantom fingertips met cool mist. I parted the Veiled Between and shifted through it.

The semelees on the Veil's other side stirred and writhed, sensing my growing presence.

Hello, my beautiful creatures, I crooned to them.

A large one drifted forward, and its inky blackness swirled around me. Teeth gnashed in its black jaws, venom dripping from its fangs. I ran a hand along its cool back, my fingers trailing over its frigid skin.

More semelees appeared, swirling and dipping around me, roiling me in shadows as their whispers began.

She's come to us, Daughter of Darkness, Commander of Shadows. What do you seek, Lorafin?

My soul tugged on Jax's magic, calling it forth until images came to me.

The picture of a young male appeared in my mind. A half-breed.

I cocked my head. *How curious.*

Antlers sprouted from the male's head, and eyes so blue they resembled the Adriastic Sea regarded me from a rugged siltenite face. Dark-blond hair. Sharp features. Wide nostrils. An eagerness filled his eyes that reminded me of prideful youth.

Brow furrowing, I studied the male.

This was who Jax sought.

I had no idea who he was since Jax had refused to tell me, but considering the lengths the Dark Raider had gone to in order to find him, he had to be somebody important.

I showed the image to the semelees. *Find him,* I commanded. *Tell me where he is or if he's passed to the afterlife.*

The semelees crooned and swirled more. They spun around me, touching, caressing, and reveling in my presence. Bewitching images of me locked within their embrace came from them. Feathered touches and swirling darkness called to the shadows inside me. I could have that for eternity if I succumbed to them.

A vibration along my throat jolted me, and I wrenched back.

Find him, I instructed in a firmer tone and forced myself to ignore how they begged me to fall deeper into their realm.

They sped away, and I floated in the darkness again, letting my fingers slide through the shadows. Minutes passed. Maybe hours. Perhaps days. I floated and existed, staying in the Veiled Between for longer than seemed normal.

What's taking so long? I finally called into the void as I forced myself from the enchanting mist.

A semelee slithered forward. *The male you seek, we've found him, we think, but . . . something's not right.*

What do you mean 'something's not right'? Find him!

Yes, Princess of Darkness. The semelee swirled away again, its tail flickering in the shadows.

I floated again, and a sense of this plane's otherness began to overtake me once more, but I forced myself to concentrate. I'd never had a semelee unable to locate someone or answer a question. They were all-knowing beings. I'd had siltenites commission me, with seemingly impossible questions to answer, yet the semelees had always known.

And they'd always been right.

Inky power swirled in my soul, and magic crackled around me as another thought struck me. *Are they toying with me? Perhaps hoping to trick me into staying too long and becoming imprisoned in their embrace?*

That thought jerked me to the core.

Well? I snapped at them, calling in the distance. *Where is he?*

Another appeared in the shadows. *It's him. We're certain now.*

Why did you hesitate before?

His feel in the fae lands at this moment in time, and the feel from the image you showed us, are different, which is why we took a closer look, but it's him, and he's alive. Although, he's not right.

Not right? My brow puckered. *Explain.*

The semelee showed me an image. The Wood. The male Jax sought, standing despondent with several other half-breeds. But the male who Jax was looking for was there. It was clearly him. He matched the picture Jax had mentally shown me completely.

That's him, I said.

Yes, but even though his image matches, the feel *of him is different. It is why we wanted to assess him more, but now we are certain.*

I had no idea what was going on, so I studied again what the semelees revealed. A grand arena was behind the male and the other half-breeds. Flags in the colors of turquoise, white, and dark brown waved in the wind. Faewood Kingdom colors.

I studied it more. The image spanned out. Wildlings worked around an arena. Construction was underway every-where I looked, and when the image grew to an even larger area, I saw the palace. With a sharp intake of breath, I realized where the male was.

The Centennial Matches.

The semelee seemed to sense when full understanding hit me. Its cold, shadowy claws dug into my torso, holding me in its embrace as it dragged me deeper into the Veiled Between.

Too far, I called to it.

Come with us, Commander of Darkness, Princess of Fate. This is where you belong.

My concentration faltered at that last title. To command the fates was the ultimate power of a lorafin. I'd never been able to grasp it. Only a queen could do that, and the semelees had told me countless times that I was still a princess.

But the thought of controlling that much power, even if only a fool would do such a thing . . . It called to something deep inside me. Something my birthright demanded I heed.

No, I pulled back, forcing the semelee to relax its hold. *I have what I want. You need to let me go.*

But the semelee hissed, embracing me in its coldness as more joined in. They swirled around me. Inky blackness, scaled backs, venomous bites. As more semelees writhed together, they pulled me farther into the Veiled Between.

No! I struggled and fought against them, but they were sluggish to respond.

If only I was stronger, they would yield to me more. A true lorafin could command them completely, not only partially as I could.

Come, Princess of Darkness.

They sucked me under, pulling me down, down . . . deeper, farther.

Oh Goddess! They were pulling me under. *Jax!* I screamed his name, yet no sound came out.

A powerful zap abruptly came from my collar, then another and another. My soul convulsed. My spirit ignited.

Another electrifying jolt enflamed my limbs, and then I was falling.

Falling.

Falling.

Pain erupted along my skin. Darkness. Silence. Eternal flames. A void.

Agony ripped through me, searing through my soul and electrifying my nerves. I screamed, anything to hear my own voice and know that I still lived, and that this pain was a figment of my imagination.

But . . . nothing. No sound came.

And then the pain *exploded*. Searing, burning fire erupted across my limbs, and the reality of what was occurring hit me.

Oh Goddess, I've been lost.

CHAPTER 22

I writhed and bellowed. I was burning, being eaten alive, my skin being flayed. All of my existence echoed around the pure torture someone was delivering upon me.

"Elowen?" A male's voice echoed from far away. He sounded urgent. Panicked. But so very quiet and so very, very distant.

"By all the gods and goddesses. Help her!" the male growled so savagely that, for the briefest moment, it cut through the haze.

"I can't. This is part of a calling. She suffers the effects of a fairy's magic when she awakens." Whoever had just spoken sounded almost smug. *Guardian Alleron.* "For someone who claims to know so much about lorafins, I'm surprised you're ignorant of this."

"But she's covered in bruises!"

"She is. You can thank your magic for that."

Jax snarled. "Stop this!"

"I can't."

I screamed again when another stabbing sensation ripped through me, but I could have sworn no sound came from my lips.

Somehow, I managed to register what was happening. I hadn't been lost. I'd been frozen in Jax's magic. His power had robbed me of sight, sound, touch, taste, and smell. That was the terrifying void I'd experienced. It wasn't because I'd been lost in the Veiled Between. It was because of the side effects, and it was only now starting to wear off.

But the strength of Jax's internal pain-inducing psychic power was pure agony. His magic barreled through me unchecked, tearing, beating, and burning everything inside me. My organs, my veins, my very essence. Not one part of me was left unscathed.

And there was nothing I could do to stop it.

"I'm sorry. Stars, Elowen, I'm *so* sorry."

I tried to rouse more from the agonizing void. My heart beat at a furious pace. Another burst of sizzling flames sped through my innards. *Galaxy Above, make it stop!*

"I should cut off your fucking head for this!"

"I apologize, Dark Raider, but this is what you . . . you wanted," Guardian Alleron stammered. "This is the price of a calling."

"How much longer until she's conscious?" Jax demanded.

"That would depend upon the strength of your magic, but

since she's twitching now and making those mewling sounds, I would imagine fairly soon."

"But it's already been an entire day."

A day? Stars Above, I've never been under that long.

"True, which would imply you're quite powerful." Guardian Alleron's reply sounded uneasy, as if he was reminded once again of the magic harbored within the Dark Raider. "But her own magic will soon rise and suppress yours. Usually, at this stage, she begins to regain control."

And some part of my mind knew I was close to coming out of this, so I fought against Jax's magic and struggled to regain all of my senses. I did my best to quell the burning and beating pain barreling unchecked through my body. The darkness within me flared, my magic rising even though the collar hummed. I ignored the painful zaps that followed and consciously began to douse Jax's crackling power.

A moan came, a loud one. *My* moan. My voice was back.

"Elowen!" Jax called. "Can you hear me?"

My eyes opened to slits. Dim sunshine greeted me. Slowly, so slowly, Jax's magic receded more as my darkness cooled his monumental power.

One last flash of shadows crept through me, the collar tingling along my throat again, but in a whisper, my magic calmed everything completely. My eyelids fell limp again as the remains of his magic at last, blessedly receded.

The calling was done. *Finally.* But Goddess, I hurt *every-*

where. It felt as though a herd of domals had stampeded over me after my skin had been flayed.

I whimpered despite trying not to, but the aftermath of Jax's calling was *brutal.*

"Damn all of this!" Jax snarled. "Elowen?"

It took me a minute to realize that my hand was clasped in his. Hard callouses rubbed my skin, and with each touch of his palm, my senses grew more alive. A soft bed was beneath me, and the aroma of spice and pine hovered in the air.

"Her bruises are starting to fade," Phillen said gruffly, and I vaguely registered that all of Jax's friends were present as well.

"Ah, she's beginning to fully wake," Guardian Alleron said matter-of-factly. "The Dark Raider's magic should no longer be affecting her."

"Elowen?" Jax called again.

"Jax?" My voice sounded parched. Hoarse. I was thirsty. So very thirsty. But at least the torture was over.

"Are you okay?" he whispered.

"She'll be fine," Guardian Alleron replied for me. I cracked my eyes open again just in time to see him wave dismissively. "After she comes to, the magic that hur—I mean—suppressed her always wears off."

"And the bruises?"

"Will likely be fully gone within the hour," my former guardian replied. "She heals quickly."

Another low growl came from Jax.

I opened my eyes wider and shifted slightly on the bed. I

was in the same position I'd been in when the calling had begun. Jax's bloodshot eyes met mine, and I stared at him in confusion, remembering what he'd snarled at Guardian Alleron.

"Was I really under for a day?" I rasped.

Through his mask, his jaw clenched. "Yes," he replied hoarsely.

Goddess, I've never been under that long. I tried to sit up, but my muscles screamed in protest. Wincing, I settled back down but slowly raised an arm. The long-sleeved emerald-green sweater I wore had been pulled up to the elbows. Bruises littered my forearms. Tentatively, I lifted the hem to reveal my stomach.

Jax's breath sucked in when the black and yellow splotches covering my abdomen were revealed.

"By the galaxy and stars," I whispered. I pulled the hem back down, then tugged on my sleeves so my arms were covered too. I didn't have to look at my legs to know they were beaten as well.

I couldn't remember ever having been this affected by a calling before. A shudder ran through me. Jax's calling was by far the worst one I'd ever experienced, thanks to his horrifically powerful magic.

"Water?" I croaked.

"Lars!" Jax boomed.

A minute later, the redhead was at my side, handing a cup to Jax. The Dark Raider cradled my head, his strong fingers sliding through my hair. He massaged my neck briefly, soothing my aching muscles before he helped me up, then held the cup to my lips.

"Drink."

The smooth, cool water rolled down my throat, and I greedily consumed all of it. "Goddess, that's good," I said with a sigh when I finished.

"Lars, get another one," Jax snapped.

Lars disappeared from the room and returned with an entire jug of crystal-clear water. I eagerly drank another full glass. When finished, I didn't sound quite as hoarse. "You're probably wanting to know what I saw and what the semelees told me."

I could have sworn Jax scowled in response. "That can wait. Phillen?" he called over his shoulder. "Have a bath readied for Elowen and summon food."

Phillen gave a curt nod and strode into the bathing chamber. The sound of running water came next.

I eyed his other friends. Lander, Trivan, and Bowan remained. All of them stood stoically, and they all wore the same clothes yet were still masked. But if they'd also remained the entire time I'd been under, that meant they'd *all* stayed up through the night, and nobody had slept.

"You must all be exhausted."

Jax's eyebrows slanted together. *"That's* what you're worried about?"

"May I be excused now?" Guardian Alleron asked stiffly from behind him. "Now that my work is done here?"

Jax cut him a glare, then snatched the adaptor from his hand before signaling Bowan over. "Take him back to his chamber and secure him."

"Gladly." Bowan's earring winked in the morning light as he clasped Guardian Alleron by the elbow and hauled him from the room.

"The rest of you are also dismissed," Jax called to his other friends.

They nodded and filed out the door. A few minutes later, the bath water stopped, and Phillen also exited the room. It struck me how readily and easily Jax issued orders to his friends. Strangely, they never seemed to mind.

It was on the tip of my tongue to ask him why that was, but the scent of food abruptly filled the air.

Frowning, I peered around Jax to see a tray of food sitting on a table near the end of the bed. Steam rose from it, and fragrant aromas followed. But nobody had come in the room carrying it.

My eyes bulged. "Where did that come from?"

"This chamber's enchanted. All you have to do is call to the magic, and what you need appears."

My jaw dropped. "That's how the food got in here before? But I never wished for it."

"No, you didn't, but I did."

How Jax had known that a hot bath and food were all that

I craved right now, I didn't know, but given how tired I felt, I wasn't going to ask.

I managed to wrestle myself upright into a sitting position. Jax immediately reached for me, but I brushed him off. "I'm okay."

His hands balled, but he relented.

Fragrant scents continued to rise from the food. Jax retrieved the tray and set it gently on my lap. My mouth watered, and I spooned the thick stew, grateful for the tender meat and vegetables because my jaw was still sore from the calling. *Goddess, even my mouth hurts.*

I ate slowly and carefully, my stomach rumbling in contentment after a day with nothing.

Jax's intent attention never left me, not even when he pulled the chair by the foggy window to sit at my bedside.

"Did none of you leave throughout the calling?" I spooned another bite of stew.

He shook his head.

"Not even when Guardian Alleron informed you we no longer needed to remain in contact?"

"I removed my hand at that point, but—" Again, he shook his head. Leaning forward, he placed his elbows on his knees and clasped his hands. He looked . . . defeated.

Cobalt irises shifted, his attention drifting over me. I was still entirely covered in the sweater and breeches I'd put on yesterday, but the backs of my hands were visible, and splotchy bruises still covered them even though a few had faded.

"Does this happen often?" he asked quietly.

I followed his line of sight. He was staring at my hands. "Bruising? Not necessarily. It depends what the magic is of the fairy I'm performing a calling for."

"Meaning . . ."

I finished the last bite of my stew and pushed the tray away. Jax immediately whisked it from my lap and set it on the table. He grabbed the pot of tea that he'd also summoned and poured me a cup.

Once I was sipping the hot brew, he returned to his hunched position in the chair, watching me and waiting for me to continue.

"Meaning that whatever adverse effects one can suffer from another's magic are what I experience," I explained.

His eyes narrowed. "So all of your senses were gone during the last twenty-four hours?"

"Yes."

"And the bruising and I'm assuming burning"—he raised his eyebrows, at which I nodded in confirmation, causing a snap of his jaw—"is because of my ability to cause pain in others?"

"Yes."

"You felt the *worst* of my magic?"

I took another sip and nodded. "All of it."

He sat back, his aura rising. "Is it always the most painful aspect of a fairy's magic that you suffer from?"

"Usually. Just count yourself lucky that I didn't shift into a stag." When my attempt at humor failed to elicit any crinkling around his eyes, I cleared my throat and took another drink of tea.

"Why didn't you shift?"

I shrugged. "Shifter magic has never affected me during callings. I think it's because our intrinsic magic can't affect another fae, only our extrinsic magic."

He rubbed his chin through his mask. "In other words, because I can't make other fae shift into a stag, but I can rob their senses and cause them pain, that's what you experienced."

"Exactly."

"But you didn't experience any of the elements?"

"I felt your fire, but blessedly, your water, earth, and air stayed at bay." I forced a smile. "So it could have been worse."

He leaned back. "That's probably because fire is my strongest element. Goddess Above."

Steam from the bathing chamber wafted into the room, and I itched to sink into the bath that was waiting for me. I felt marginally better after the food and drink, but the beckoning heat from the tub was deliciously inviting, considering how much my muscles ached. "Would you rather I tell you now what the semelees revealed, or would you prefer I . . ." I gestured toward the bathing room.

Jax pushed to standing. Energy pulsed around him. "No, you bathe first."

My eyebrows shot up. "But you abducted me for this one purpose. To know what's become of him."

His jaw locked, and before I could say more, he was at my side, his arms going around me. The feel of him made my heart stop.

"It can wait." In one large sweep, he'd cradled me in his embrace and was striding across the room.

"Jax, what are you—"

"I'm helping you," he cut in gruffly.

My cheeks reddened.

He strode into the elegant bathing chamber. White floors and white wallpaper flecked with light blue flowers greeted me. Someone had also put a bouquet of freshly cut blue roses on the counter.

"Where did those come from?"

Jax averted his gaze. "I summoned them. I thought the roses might smell good and provide a more . . . relaxing environment."

"Oh." His thoughtfulness pierced my heart, and I was reminded of the oscillating feelings he'd elicited in me before the calling.

He slowed when he neared the tub, then stopped at its edge. Floral hints rose from the water, and the pale pink color alerted me to the elixir the enchantment had added. A fresh stack of white towels also sat on a small stool beside the tub. Next to that waited soap and products for my hair.

"Impressive. Your enchanted room missed nothing."

He made a noncommittal sound. "It's pretty attentive to details." He set me down and waited until I was steady before removing his hands. "Do you . . . need help undressing?"

My eyebrows shot up. The other morning, when I'd been so aroused following our night together at the inn, I probably would have taken him up on that offer, but now . . .

"Is this how you attempt to get a female's clothes off? You abduct her, then use her until she's black and blue before offering your services?" I asked mockingly.

His brows slanted together so sharply that I knew my verbal dagger had hit its mark.

Before he could say anything further, I shook my head. "No, I'll manage."

His harsh expression smoothed, yet his voice was stiff when he said, "Thank you for what you did." His throat bobbed. "Saying thanks doesn't seem like nearly enough considering what my magic did to you, but *thank you* for asking the semelees." Before I could reply, he swung away. "I'll be in the hall if you need anything."

He disappeared out the door, leaving me reeling following his heartfelt words, but then the lock falling into place rang through the chambers.

I was once again all alone . . . and caged.

I shook my head and peeled my clothes carefully off me. And with each garment that fell, my suspicions were confirmed. Not one inch of me was left unmarked, but at least the bruises were already fading.

I stepped over the tub's tall rim and eased myself into the hot water. Candles abruptly appeared on the counter by the roses. They flickered and only added to the atmosphere, making it entirely soothing and tranquil. Apparently, Jax wasn't done perfecting the ambiance.

Too tired to contemplate that, I sank more into the hot water and sighed in relief when it began to soothe my battered muscles.

"You're very good at this," I said to the chamber, which I knew was silly, but perhaps the enchantment would understand.

A shimmer of magic appeared around the tub, and with a small smile, I realized the tub had just been spelled. I had a feeling the water wouldn't cool as long as I remained in it.

Settling back more, I closed my eyes, and even though I'd been unconscious for the better part of a day, fatigue hit me. I rested my head back, and my mind began to drift. My thoughts scattered, and then the allure of sleep pulled me under.

CHAPTER 23

"Elowen?" a male's voice called from the distance.

I murmured something in response but was enjoying the warm lake I was floating in too much to heed his call. It was peaceful here. Serene. An alien violet sky arched above me, and foreign birds flocking nearby on the shore's trees cawed.

Hands fluttering, I drifted on the water.

"Elowen!" the male bellowed.

Something banged, startling the flock of birds, and the next thing I knew, a pulse of magic rippled over the lake.

Hands abruptly gripped my shoulders. Very *real* hands.

The dream disappeared, and my eyes flashed open to see two dazzling sapphire irises. Wildness filled them, and with a groggy start, I realized I still lay in the enchanted bath. I must have fallen asleep.

And I was entirely naked.

"Jax!" I wrenched from his grip and sat up. "What in the realm!"

Droplets of water cascaded down my arms, around my breasts, and disappeared back into the hot bathwater. But my bruises were gone. My magic had healed that in the time I'd been sleeping.

The Dark Raider tore his gaze to the side. "I'm sorry. I thought—" He ran a hand over his scarfed head. "You've been in here so long, not making a sound, and when you wouldn't reply to my knocks and calls, I . . ." He let out an aggrieved sigh. "I thought the worst. I'm sorry."

My chest heaved, and a glance at the foggy window showed bright afternoon sunlight. "How long was I asleep?"

"Two hours, maybe longer."

My jaw dropped. "And you've been waiting in the hallway that entire time?"

He gave a curt nod, still looking to the side.

I sighed, and some of my embarrassment faded, but I crossed my arms over my breasts and pulled my knees up. It was still obvious I was naked, but at least I wasn't on full display.

His throat rolled in a swallow. "I'll, uh . . . leave you to it." He moved to the door.

Shaking from my abrupt awakening, I reached for the soap but hissed when a slice of pain worked up my arm from the movement. *Okay, I guess I'm not fully healed.*

Jax stilled at the bathing chamber's threshold, his back still to me. "Elowen? Are you all right?"

"I'm fine, just stiff and sore."

He growled softly. Facing me again, he kept his gaze above my head. "I can help."

My cheeks heated. "You don't need to. I'll—"

He growled louder. "Let me help you. *Please.* It's the least I can do, considering I put you in this state." But even though authority rang in his tone, he didn't move closer to me. Instead, he stood there. Waiting for my approval. Waiting for my consent. And his line of sight never strayed below my chin.

My heart began to pound, and soft feelings again flowed through me. *Damn him. Damn him for making me second-guess if he truly is a ruthless bastard who can't be trusted.* In this moment, he reminded me of the Jax I'd spent the past few days with. The Jax I'd begun to feel things for.

I tried grabbing the soap again, but another spiral of blistering pain shot up my arm.

"Elowen," he growled.

"Okay, fine. But no looking."

He returned to the bath to kneel beside me, and his gaze stayed carefully upward, never dipping to my exposed flesh.

A moment of awkwardness made me want to renege my agreement. Jax was literally kneeling at my side as I sat naked, inches away from him, but before I could say *never mind*, he grabbed the soap and cloth and dipped them into the water.

"Lean forward if you would."

For a moment, I couldn't speak. "You're really going to wash me?"

"If you'll let me."

Embarrassment flushed across my neck, and I reminded myself that plenty of males had seen me exposed. But something about this felt different. It felt . . . intimate.

Only Jax's eyes were visible with his mask on, but the intensity of his gaze didn't lessen as he worked the soap through the washcloth until suds covered it.

I didn't know if he could feel my hesitance or know that I'd never been in a position like this with anyone, but he said softly, "I would never hurt you." His throat worked. "Not intentionally at least."

A stifled breath lifted my chest. For some inexplicable reason, I believed him. Once again, stupid me, I believed him. *Him*, the Dark Raider, the male feared by all in the kingdoms was strangely who I felt safest with. Yet he'd kidnapped me, stole my senses, locked me in this chamber, and had done it all to use my lorafin skills to his advantage.

The conundrum of skewing emotions he brought out in me again took hold, like a clamping fist around my heart. Yet I leaned forward anyway and wrapped my arms around my legs. And as I settled in the soothing, hot water, the full meaning of his words hit me.

Not intentionally at least.

Once again, my heart wanted to believe those words to be true. That Jax had never *wanted* to hurt me. I thought back to how he'd taken lengths to explain things to me when we arrived in Jaggedston, when he *had* hurt me, but he'd seemed so remorseful, as though hurting me hurt him too.

Frowning, I let that truth sink in, and then I whispered, "I know you wouldn't." And somehow, the belief that he never wanted to cause me pain dug deep.

He exhaled a breath and raised the washcloth to my back. Fragrant scents of wildflowers rose from it. He ran the soft cloth across my skin, massaging it in circular motions. He touched me carefully to avoid any lingering bruises.

It felt so good that I closed my eyes. Never, in all of my memories, could I recall anyone ever caring for me like this. Not after a calling. Not as a child. Never.

Of course, as fae, we didn't actually need to bathe. We could use our magic to self-cleanse, but soap always smelled fragrant and left my skin more moisturized than cleansing magic did. Taking baths was one of the few luxuries I truly enjoyed in my caged life, especially after callings.

"Does any of this hurt?" he asked quietly.

I shook my head. "No. It feels nice."

"Good." When he reached my neck, he did the same, except he used his hands to soothe my aching muscles after rubbing more soap all over me.

A low moan escaped me when his fingers worked deep into my stiff shoulders. He paused momentarily, his aura pulsing, but then he continued and took his time, thoroughly cleaning each area and massaging all of the hurt away.

He washed me everywhere, my back and each arm, and then he asked me to settle back in the tub so he could wash my legs.

Complying, I did as he asked even though all of me was visible when I lay supine. But even when I was naked before him, he kept his gaze firmly on safe areas only. It would have been so easy for him to ogle my breasts or leer at my female flesh, but he didn't.

And I knew he truly wasn't looking when the washcloth traveled over the mark on my lower stomach, the mark that signaled that I was a lorafin, and he didn't so much as pause.

Instead, every movement Jax made was gentle, each touch reverent, and his gaze never strayed anywhere it shouldn't.

From how serious his demeanor was, I wondered if only I was being affected by this strange encounter. Similar to the morning I'd woken in Fosterton, a heat began to rise inside me.

With each swipe of his hand running up my thighs, a clench of need tightened my belly. And with each caress of his fingers along my arms or the deep rub of his hands when he massaged my feet, a smattering of nerves tightened my core. I had to bite my lip to stop from moaning a few times.

It was embarrassing, this response he elicited in me so easily. Even though all of his touches were respectful, my starved body wanted more. I wanted *him*. Wanted him to touch me in the ways I'd never been touched. I wanted his fingers to slide inside me, his mouth to kiss my skin, his tongue to devour my breasts. Once again, I wanted to give him my virginity, and I was so aroused by the time he finished, I was nearly panting.

"Did you enjoy that?" he asked in a low raspy tone.

I dipped under the water to rinse all of the soap away. I ached fiercely, and I wanted nothing more than to let his fingers stray south to rub the small nub that would offer me release.

I resurfaced and nodded quickly. "I did. Thank you."

His gaze locked onto mine, and his aura swelled. For a moment, we both stared at one another.

Not moving, my heart began to pound, and my breaths came faster until the need in me soared to a staggering height.

"I'll get you a towel," he said in a gruff voice.

Before I could respond, he strode to the counter even though towels waited on the stool right beside me. When he reached it, he placed his palms on the counter's smooth stone. For a moment he just stood there, his shoulders tense, his backside taut, his chest rising with deep breaths.

The power of his aura strummed through the room, but with a sharp inhale, he straightened and grabbed a towel off the shelf near the frosted window.

Turning back around, he approached the tub, but he was careful to keep his gaze averted. At the tub's side, he snapped open the towel and gazed entirely upward, his chin tilting back until he stared at the ceiling.

The need inside me spiraled to an entirely new level as I gazed at his broad chest, strong throat, and square jaw, which he probably hadn't even realized he'd just revealed in that movement. Since he'd spent so long massaging me, my muscles no longer ached, and the only thing that pulsed now was my female flesh.

Standing, I forced myself to breathe deeply and ignore the curling inside me. Water dripped down my limbs, trailing over my scorched skin.

Jax's breath sucked in when my fingers brushed his as I grasped the towel.

I hastily wrapped it around myself. He didn't move. He still stood tense, his body looking entirely on edge.

I was so tempted to glance down and see if there was evidence of his arousal. It would be so easy. One tiny look south of his waistband would confirm if he was as turned on as me. Despite his new, fancy clothes, his slacks wouldn't hide an erection completely.

But as soon as that thought came to me, it fled. Jax had been nothing but respectful and courteous to me in the time since he'd entered this bathing chamber, and I couldn't bring myself to do anything but show him the same respect in return.

"Thank you." I knotted the towel at my front.

He backed up and gave a curt nod. "I'll leave you to get dressed, if you're all right?"

I nodded hastily. "I am. Again, thank you."

He walked stiffly to the door, and even though I couldn't see his face, I did hear him inhale. His jaw snapped before he strode away, and it struck me that with his sensory magic, it was possible he could detect heightened scents, which meant it was possible he could smell how incredibly aroused I was now.

And had been in Fosterton.

But if he was aware, he didn't comment. The sound of the door opening and closing came next, and then a fierce emptiness consumed me.

Out of the tub, I sank to the bathing chamber's floor as conflicting emotions rose within me again and again, pummeling my conscience and making me second-guess and rethink everything.

Because I'd just experienced the most erotic encounter I'd ever had with a male, and it was with a male who was as elusive to me as our distant stars.

CHAPTER 24

Jax returned an hour later, all of his friends in tow. Their masks were in place, their bandanas secured. They all wore the same clothes and uniforms as before, but now that I wasn't so distracted, I had a moment to study them.

Again, it struck me that Phillen's and Lars's uniforms appeared to be what guards would wear.

But guards for what? Perhaps hired hands? Regardless of their status, that had to mean Jax was somebody important if he had official guards under his command. He had to be as rich as Guardian Alleron. Or perhaps he was even a ruler of one of the ten Stonewild Houses. It would certainly explain this chamber's wealth.

But I didn't have time to contemplate that further before Jax joined me in the sitting area. The other five spanned out around us.

The Dark Raider's piercing blue eyes once again were

reminiscent of the dazzling Adriastic Sea. An intensity illuminated them that reminded me of lightning striking water, and I knew immediately why he was here.

The time had come for him to demand answers and for me to reveal what I'd seen in the Veiled Between. The entire reason he'd taken me had been leading up to this one moment.

Dipping my chin, I looked away, but it didn't stop a flush from working up my neck. He might be here to demand answers, yet all of my attention still focused on memories of what it felt like to have his hands on me. Images assaulted my mind of his strong fingers trailing up my legs and along my back. They wouldn't stop.

But they had to.

This was why I was here, and this one act would finally set me free.

I took a deep breath. "You're probably wanting to know about the male you seek?"

He gave a curt nod. Every part of Jax exuded nervous energy, but despite that, he fell into a relaxed posture on the couch, much like he had this morning when I'd been bedridden. He leaned forward, resting his elbows on his knees, and then clasped his hands.

"Very much." His voice was hoarse, and the aura around him pounded through the room even though he tried to appear nonchalant.

My throat bobbed in a swallow when his anxiety hit me. He'd been waiting for *hours* to learn the fate of whomever the male was he'd lost, and it was someone he obviously cared for deeply. Yet he'd allowed me time to eat, sleep, bathe, and dress. Nobody had ever awarded me that courtesy before following a calling.

My stomach twisted at the news I had to deliver. "He's alive."

A collective intake of breaths went around the room, then a few cheers and pats on one another's backs came from Jax's friends.

"I knew it." Trivan placed his hands on his hips. "I just knew he was still alive."

"Where is he?" Jax demanded.

I clenched my hands and looked down. "Faewood Kingdom. The Centennial Matches."

"*What?*"

I shrugged at his soft growl. "I can't tell you why. I wasn't able to get those answers, but he's there, and he's alive." I curled my fingers into my palm. "But, the semelees said something isn't right with him. He doesn't *feel* as what you showed me."

"What does that mean?" Phillen pushed away from the wall, his brow furrowing.

"Your guess is as good as mine. I've never had a response from them like that before, and I'm sorry, but I didn't push them for an answer." Memories of them pulling me deeper into their realm surfaced, and I shuddered. I hadn't been strong enough to demand more.

"But he's alive?" Jax pushed to standing and began to pace.

"Yes."

"Is he imprisoned?"

I frowned, shaking my head. "No. He's free."

Jax shared a look with his friends. It was obvious, even with the masks hiding their features, that this news perplexed them.

"Why hasn't he contacted you then?" Lars said under his breath, but I still heard it.

Eyebrows slashing together, Jax shook his head, then returned his attention to me. "What else can you tell me about what the semelees revealed?"

"Not much, unfortunately. They showed me where he is." I went on to describe the arena and construction and the identifying details I'd seen. "I saw those images myself, in real life, just last week. It's the construction around Faewood's palace for the Centennial Matches."

"And he was there, with other half-breeds?"

"He was, and they all looked as despondent as him."

Jax's breath hitched, and he shared another conspiratorial look with his friends before asking me, "Can you tell me anything else?"

I described the other structures I'd seen, giving him as much detail as I was able, but even I knew the information I'd garnered wasn't much to go on. But I'd done as he'd asked. I'd traveled to the Veiled Between and located who he sought.

When finished, I fingered my collar. It'd been calm most of

the morning, on account of my sleeping and relaxed state. But now, a shiver ran through it when my nerves pulsed with worry. "As for our deal now being complete . . ." I said tentatively.

The intensity of his eyes burned. "You're ready to be free."

I took a deep breath. I still didn't know if I was ready, if I would ever be considering what could happen with my collar becoming loosened, but it was now or never. And I chose now. I chose freedom.

"Yes."

A heartbeat of silence passed. Jax continued to watch me. Silent. Intent. An emotion blazed in his eyes. It was raw. Wild. And it swirled with so much regret that I sucked in a breath.

But in a blink, it was gone.

"Of course. You deserve nothing less than complete freedom and happiness, Elowen." Absolute sincerity rang in his tone. "You deserve the realm. And I'll do everything I can to ensure you get that."

My lips parted. His heartfelt words pierced my soul, but before I could even contemplate a response, he signaled Lars over.

The guard hefted a huge sack of coin that I hadn't realized he'd been holding and gave it to Jax.

The Dark Raider deposited it at the end of my bed. His throat rolled in a swallow. He wouldn't look at me, but I could have sworn that something hovered over him. Something that was on the tip of his tongue, that he wanted to say, but . . .

He released the sack and stepped back. "Rulibs, as promised, to begin your new life."

The full sack dipped the mattress toward it. Heavy coins within it clinked together.

For a moment, I was speechless, then I managed to sputter, "That's all . . . *mine?*"

Jax nodded. "It's enough to buy a nice property and whatever else you'll need to get started. As for leaving this chamber and relaxing the hold your collar has on you, I'll return with your guardian shortly." His throat rolled again in another swallow. "And I wish I could help you more, that I could help ensure your freedom is guaranteed"—a swell of power pulsed in his aura—"but it'll be up to you to venture to the supernatural courts and plead your case for true freedom." He didn't elaborate further and instead turned stiffly, then signaled his friends with a nod.

But even though he hadn't spelled it out for me, I knew what he meant. It was up to me to convince the courts, because we wouldn't be staying in touch. He wouldn't help me with the authorities, because Jax and I weren't actually friends. We wouldn't stay in one another's lives. After today, I would never see him again.

I was on my own. And he would be someone I'd known briefly in my life, someone who had come into it as violent as a thunderbolt yet had left me as silently as soft rain.

And realizing that, knowing that he would now only be a memory . . . Something inside me threatened to shatter.

At the door, Jax glanced at me one last time. I could have sworn that he was trying to control his aura, but pulses from it pounded through the room.

A flash of wildness shone in his eyes anew when our gazes locked, but as before, he snapped his attention away the second we made eye contact.

With stiff movements, he left the room, and all of his friends departed behind him just as quickly.

Alone, the quiet of the extravagant chambers threatened to suffocate me. I sat there, stunned and confused. My heart cracked, and I had no idea why I felt like crying.

A huge bag of rulibs was now mine. Jax would be returning soon with my guardian to release my collar to the extent of his ability. And then he would let me go.

Almost everything I'd ever hoped for was coming true.

So why do I feel so empty?

Hours passed. Hours and hours of pacing and waiting, and pacing some more. The sunlight through the foggy windows grew less intense. Evening had come, yet Jax hadn't returned, and neither had any of his friends. My *soon*-to-be release had come and gone.

I paced faster in my gilded cage. The earlier raw emotions that had nearly cleaved me in two had morphed into feelings of impatience and uneasiness.

I thought surely Jax would have returned by now. That, by this time, I would be walking the streets of Jaggedston on my way to the courts, with my loosened collar hopefully under my control.

But he hadn't come back.

Evening eventually bled into night and then night into morning. I slept fitfully, waking at every little sound, hoping against hope that the ring of the key in the lock would jar me awake. Nothing greeted me but the sound of my breathing, the bells in the capital beginning to toll, and the pounding of my heart that wouldn't stop its erratic beat.

Yet Jax still didn't come.

When the sun was fully risen, my pacing continued. Up and down. Up and down. I walked across the chambers back and forth in hurried strides, eating up the carpet like a ravenous beast.

But no matter how fast I walked, no matter how hard I wished for Jax to come back—he didn't.

And then one day turned into two. And two days turned into three.

Yet Jax still didn't come.

ON THE AFTERNOON of the third day, I thought for certain I was going to jump out of my skin. The waiting was suffocating. Debilitating. And the terror in me grew that I'd been tricked and left to rot, or simply made to wait until the Dark Raider needed another calling.

Because, as the days passed, my belief that I was Jax's prisoner grew. Jax had lied to me and deceived me completely, even though I thought we'd made a truce and had agreed upon a deal.

But I knew now he was never going to let me go.

The enchanted room seemed to sense my soul-lashing anxiety. Each morning, soft music would abruptly start playing. Flickering candles would appear hovering in mid-air. Fragrant scents of new bouquets of flowers would tickle my nose.

But no matter what calming and soothing ideas the enchantment thought up next, it did nothing to relieve my anxiety.

Three days had passed with nothing but the enchantment to keep me company with its trays of food and vases of perfumed flowers. Yet I couldn't eat. Could barely sleep. Could hardly function.

Yet Jax still didn't come.

By the time evening rolled around, the bells chiming five rings strong, I'd bitten my nails to the quick, a habit I'd had as a child when Guardian Alleron had pushed me too vigorously to learn my lorafin magic. There'd been so many times when I'd never been able to please him, and I'd taken out that anxiety on myself. I thought I'd beaten that habit, but with the promise of a fourth day coming, I'd bitten my nails down to nothing.

Yet Jax still didn't come.

Nostrils flaring, I went to the door for what felt like the hundredth time. Of course, it didn't budge when I tried to unlock it. I tried again, using one unlocking spell after another, calling upon the most intricate spells I'd ever learned, but as before, the lock stayed engaged.

"Stars and galaxy!" I howled and kicked the door. "Let me out of here!"

I spun and pressed my back to the solid frame, then lowered myself to the floor. A sob shook my chest. A giant fist squeezed my heart.

There was no way for me to escape. Not until Jax chose to free me, which he apparently was never going to do.

Shivers raced down my spine, dancing across my skin like icy fingers.

I need to get out of here.

And when the bells in the capital chimed six, an idea came to me like a flash of lightning. I bolted upright, my heart leaping into my throat.

There potentially *was* a way for me to unlock this door.

If I was willing to pay the price.

CHAPTER 25

I twisted my hands, thinking of what would come if I did this, but if Jax had tricked me, if he had no intentions of letting me go, and I just sat here naïvely believing he would eventually free me, it would be better if I took matters into my own hands and escaped when he least expected it.

Besides, I had rulibs. I had enough coin to start my own life. But the collar was still entirely in place. However, if I escaped now, and neither Guardian Alleron nor Jax knew where I went, I could truly start anew. They would never find me. And with the collar in place, I truly wouldn't be a danger to others. Then, the supernatural courts would definitely deem me worthy of being free.

My heart raced, and hope began to spread through me again. Blessed, beautiful, courageous *hope*.

Nobody knew me in Jaggedston. I could escape into the masses and actually stay living in society since the collar meant

I wouldn't have to flee to the Wood. I could do my best to lead a normal, low-key life. It wasn't what I wanted for myself, but in my current circumstances, it was probably the best outcome I could hope for.

A sharp pain of regret hit me that I would never know true freedom, but what Guardian Alleron had confirmed in the Ustilly Mountains remained. I would never be free of the collar. It *couldn't* come off. I would have to make the best of it, and since I already knew my mother was dead, did I even need to do my own calling anymore?

Magic rattled inside me when my mind was finally made up.

I raced to the bag that contained the clothes I'd gotten in Fosterton and quickly hefted the sack of rulibs into it. That, along with my meager pile of clothes, was all I had, but it was plenty to get me started.

I strapped the heavy bag to my back and returned to the door. This was it. This was the moment I'd spent my entire life waiting for.

A shallow breath lifted my chest, but I closed my eyes and delved down into the darkness inside me. My collar vibrated, warning me at the abrupt shift in power, but I was careful. If I ventured to the Veiled Between as I had when I'd been trying to delay Jax on our trip to Stonewild, I could end up in a perilous state, entirely broken and unconscious.

But if I did it slowly and withdrew the second I got what I needed . . .

❧ 346 ❧

Concentrating, I dove to that place within me, to the center of where my powers lay, and latched onto the darkness, demanding that it heed my call and venture me to the Veiled Between.

My collar jolted me with electricity, warning me, but I didn't stop.

Weightlessness drifted around me, and the collar zapped me again, but I sped through the galaxy until the Veil appeared, then punched through its mist.

A bone snapped.

White-hot agony seared along my corporeal limb. I screamed, instinctively cradling the injury as my soul remained unattached from my body. My physical hand was cradling my wrist, and I could feel enough of my body to understand what was happening. The collar had broken one of my bones. *So be it.* I could still walk with that injury.

Wincing against the suffocating pain, I returned my attention to the Veiled Between but stayed on the edge, hovering at the entrance. Despite my care, another zing shot from my collar, burning my throat.

Panting, I called into the darkness. *Come to me. Quickly!*

A semelee drifted forward just as another zap electrified me, an even bigger one than before. A tendon severed in my hand.

I screamed anew.

What do you seek, Princess of Shadows? the semelee crooned.

Breathing heavily, I called to it. *I need your power.*

Lightheadedness consumed me when another blazing blast from the collar electrified my nerves, but I managed to stay conscious as the semelee curled around me and offered me its monumental strength.

I pulled on its magic, mixing it with my own. Breathing through the pain, I whispered the unlocking spell again.

In the fae lands, the door's lock clicked open.

Triumph skated through me just as another bone snapped, this one at my elbow. I cried out again and hurriedly let the semelee go. *Thank you.*

Breathing hard, I immediately calmed my lorafin magic and barreled back into my body before my collar could punish me more.

Panting, I came awake and became aware of my surroundings, only to find my arm hanging at an odd angle at my elbow. My wrist throbbed, and my fingers hung limply. I was relieved to see it was all on the same side, though. I wouldn't be able to use that arm or wrist until everything healed—several hours at least—but my other arm was still workable.

I cradled my injury, and mind-numbing pain blazed through me, but panting, I quietly opened the door and peered into the hallway.

Nobody lay about.

Being careful to keep my footsteps quiet, I ducked into the corridor, the heavy coins in my bag jingling slightly, and I wondered which way to go. Searing pain cut through me again, and I clung to consciousness, sagging against a wall. The pain was *agonizing*, but I needed to keep my wits about me.

Which way? Through a haze of pain, I was able to make out the wide hall that was extravagantly decorated. It was just as decadent as the suite I'd been in—Jax was obviously extremely wealthy—but the door to where I'd been lay at the hall's end.

Only one way to go. Evening light streamed in through windows ahead, and the hallway intersected with another not far away.

I blinked and shook my head slightly to stay focused. Once certain I wouldn't fall over from the throbbing in my limb, I picked up a run, keeping my footsteps light and quick.

When I reached the windows, I almost stopped. They were clear, and I could easily see the blazing city of Jaggedston spilling out before me. Wherever I was, it was high up, giving a clear view of the city and the stunning Adriastic Sea just behind it, but I didn't slow. I couldn't.

Not stopping to contemplate just how grand Jax's residence was, I carried on. A stairwell appeared to the left, and I took the stairs down as fast as my feet could carry me under the bag's strain.

I'd managed to travel down two flights, my vision only going black once, as the monstrosity of Jax's home baffled me anew. *He has to be a lordling of one of the ten Houses.*

At the bottom of the second flight, voices drifted to my ears. *Female voices.*

I came to a careening stop and ducked behind a window's long curtain just as two wildlings walked by. Thankfully, the jingling coins quieted just in time, and I made sure to keep my injured arm still. If I jarred it, I didn't know if I would be able to stop from crying out.

I froze, not moving a muscle even though it nearly killed me to quiet my breathing.

"He's in a right tizzy tonight," one of them said quietly to the other. "Best to steer clear of the ballroom if you can manage."

"Stars Above," the second replied. "He punished poor Willowman this afternoon when all he was doing was dusting the chandelier in preparation of their arrival now that they're all back in residence, but I guess Willowman's odor offended the king. It must be because of that emergent meeting that House Graniteer called. The king's been positively dreadful."

The king? House Graniteer? It felt as though my heart stopped, and for a moment, my disbelief cut through the pain. I couldn't be where it sounded like I was. *No.* That wasn't possible.

The other one *tsked* and said something more, but they'd grown too far away for me to hear any of their conversation.

Chest heaving, I stepped out from behind the curtain and peered cautiously down the hall. The females were gone.

I paused to study more of the details of wherever I was. Forest green, gold, and sapphire blue colors were everywhere.

With a sickening sense of dread, I held my arm carefully and bolted.

I flew down the remaining stairs as fast as I could. Panic began to consume me, making my movements louder, but if I was where I suspected . . .

I yelped when I hit the bottom floor too fast and jarred my arm.

Cradling it more, I searched for a way out. A wide hallway spread out before me, but pain was clouding my vision again. Blinking, I tried to see straight. Through a fog, I could barely make out two large doors ahead. The city was visible through them, and its meaning was clear.

An exit.

Relief hit me. Panting anew, I leaped off the last stair and plunged right through an invisible ward.

My body seized, the ward's grip holding me briefly before releasing me.

Once on the other side, I didn't pause to contemplate why a ward had been surrounding where I'd been kept. Instead, I ran, surging toward the exit.

A clatter came from the side, then someone boomed, "You there! Who are you?"

My collar rattled violently at my throat, and my arm throbbed with every beat of my feet, but the doors promised freedom. If I could just reach them.

My uninjured hand clasped the door handle and yanked on it.

Fresh air swirled into the entryway. *I made it!*

I leaped out of the door, but just as my feet were about to touch the stones outside, someone clamped onto my shoulder.

I screamed and tried to jerk away, but whoever grabbed me was strong. He wrestled me back inside, then slammed the door and spun me to face him. The spin threw me off kilter, and my broken arm collided with the closed door. Blazing white-hot pain sizzled along my nerves, blacking out my vision.

"Who are you?" the male demanded.

My vision cleared just enough to gaze up at a wildling. He wore serving garb, very similar to what the staff wore in Faewood Kingdom's court.

A sickening sense of dread filled me all the way to my toes. "I'm no one."

He harrumphed and hauled me roughly toward him, his eyes widening when the rulibs clinked together in my bag. "What have you got in there? Coin, eh? Are you stealing from the king?"

Oh Goddess. I fought him, tried to get free of him, but when he knocked into my injured arm again, blackness coated my vision.

"What's going on out here?" another male called, running into the room.

"I found this female fleeing the west tower, then trying to escape. She's a thief. Got a bag full of rulibs from the sounds of it."

The wildling thrust me forward, and I nearly collapsed from the pain.

The second male frowned, also a wildling and also a servant considering his attire. "It looks like she's injured. Was that your doing?" he asked the first one.

The large wildling who had grabbed me huffed. "It most certainly wasn't. I found her like this, trying to exit the serving fae doors. Perhaps she broke her arm when she was running through the palace, or she injured it when she broke in here."

The second male sighed and grabbed a hold of my uninjured wrist just as more voices came from farther away in this monstrous castle. "I'll take it from here. I'll bring her to the Master of Arms. He'll know what to do with her."

Panic nearly closed my throat, but I managed to beg, "No, *please*. Let me go."

"None of that. Thieves are always punished. Come with me."

"But I didn't steal anything! Please!"

But he dragged me down the hall, and my hope of escape was fading as fast as my vision. He pulled me around the corner, and a sharp intake of breath met my ears.

"What in the realm?" a male growled.

I gazed up at a male dressed in black slacks and a cobalt sweater. Black shoes covered his feet, and two guards marched behind him. One was tall, brawny, and had auburn hair, the other a flaming redhead. None of them wore masks.

And all three of their eyes widened.

My stomach bottomed out as I stared up at Jax.

I knew it was him. I would know those eyes anywhere.

Dazzling blue irises, which were a mixture of swirling azure and navy, filled with shock. My attention traveled swiftly over the rest of him. A strong nose, defined lips, a ruggedly handsome masculine face. Stars and galaxy, he was . . . *beautiful*.

The two guards behind him—no doubt Phillen and Lars—wore the same uniforms they'd been in the other day, that I now realized were probably what all royal guards wore at Stonewild's palace.

Slack-jawed, they stared at me, and I had a feeling they felt as flabbergasted as I did.

"I apologize, Prince Adarian." The servant bowed.

Oh Gods, he's the prince.

The wildling's hold on me tightened, forcing me to stay in place despite my pathetic attempts at inching away. His rough treatment made a shock of pain zing up my arm, and I cried out again.

Jax snarled at the servant, and he made a move toward him, but at the last moment he pulled himself up short.

"I found this female running through the halls stealing rulibs," the wildling added. "I'm not sure how she got in, but I'll take her to the Master of Arms to be dealt with."

Dizziness made my vision swim. The pain was so blinding now that I was close to passing out.

"Did you harm her?" Jax's nostrils flared, his aura beginning to pulse.

The servant gasped. "Of course not, Your Highness. I found her in this state."

"Release her," Jax snapped.

The wildling's fingers immediately relaxed. "I'm sorry, my prince." The wildling bowed again and stepped away from me. "I was simply detaining her."

"This female is my guest," Jax replied, his tone sharp. The Dark Raider, or rather Prince Adarian, or Jax, or whatever other name he went by, assessed me again. His gaze shot to my injury, his eyes hard, and the intensity of his aura made me want to flinch.

The servant's eyes popped wide. "Oh, my prince, I do sincerely apologize. I didn't realize she was authorized to be here. Please, Your Highness, accept my apol—"

Jax waved his hand. "It's fine. I brought her here the other day, but given the emergent meeting that came up that required all of us to leave quite suddenly, I wasn't able to tell her I would be gone. No matter. I'll take her from here." Ice filled his eyes, his expression so cold I shivered.

The servant inclined his head and scurried off, rounding the corner and disappearing back into the monstrous palace.

I struggled for words, struggled to comprehend what I'd just uncovered.

Jax signaled Phillen with a twitch of his fingers. "Nellip, find an empty chamber. Now."

Nellip?

"Yes, Your Highness." Phillen, or perhaps Nellip was his real name, bowed, but his eyes burned with worry, and he quickly moved to the nearest door and opened it before peering inside. "No one's in this one."

Jax ushered me forward, his movements careful to avoid jarring my injury further, and we entered a drawing room of some kind. It was small, with several couches, an unlit fireplace, and no lights. The crown prince closed the door and locked it.

The second we were hidden inside, he rounded on me. "You're hurt."

But I flinched away. "*Don't* touch me."

He pulled back as if I'd slapped him, but then his nostrils flared. "And not only are you injured, but you escaped from the suite. Dammit, Elowen. Do you know what this means?" He raked both hands through his hair, his fingers tangling in thick dark locks. "You probably thought I wasn't returning. Is that why you escaped?" But he didn't wait for me to reply and instead hissed. "Fuck! I knew I should have asked for Saramel's help. I should have told her to tell you we'd been called away."

My gaze darted between the three of them. "That's why you never came back?" I swayed, his reason hitting me like a steel drum. But my abrupt movement jarred my injury, and I inhaled sharply through the pain.

He immediately stepped closer to me, a heavy frown

descending upon his features. "Elowen . . ." His frown increased, renewed concern overlapping his anger. "You need a healer. Fuck, let me help you."

But I whipped my head back and forth. "No, I don't need a healer, but . . ." I struggled to comprehend the last three days of never-ending anxiety. "I *didn't* think you'd be returning. You're right. That's why I escaped. Because for three days I waited for you to free me, but you never came, even though you promised to return, but . . . you didn't." To my absolute mortification, tears filled my eyes.

His face fell, his expression so crestfallen that for a moment I couldn't breathe. "You thought I left you. You truly thought I would do that to you." His attention dipped to my arm again, and a look of such regret passed over his features that for a moment, I physically *felt* the weight of his despair. It pounded through his aura in steady, throbbing waves. "I should have told you. I should have found a way to explain what was happening. I'm sorry. I'm so *fucking* sorry, Elowen."

He sounded so aggrieved, and it struck me that if he'd been called away to an emergent meeting with the ten Houses, then he likely hadn't been searching for the half-breed he sought.

My heart twisted at that realization. I wasn't the only one who'd been caught up in anxiety. Jax likely had been as well, not just because of me, but because who was to say where that half-breed was now.

I cradled my injured arm more. My heart was pounding so wildly it felt like a caged bird beating its wings against a wall, but at least my vision wasn't fading as much anymore. Standing still helped, and despite the commotion, I was slowly healing.

"What do we do now?" Phillen asked Jax, the worry on his face not lessening.

The prince raked a hand through his midnight hair again. Wavy, thick strands poked up between his fingers. "I don't know."

"Well, I do," I countered. "What you need to do is let me go, because that's what you promised to do three days ago."

Phillen let out an irritated sigh. "My prince, she can't . . ." He fiddled with the sword on his belt, and Lars did the same. Both looked entirely agitated. "She can't be allowed to leave now. She knows too much."

Lars nodded in agreement. "Nellip's right."

My stomach sank. "What? Why? I won't tell anyone what I know or what I've seen. I won't reveal your identities."

Phillen glared at me. "Even so, and even if we could trust you, the risk is too great."

Stomach sinking to the bottom of my toes, I turned pleading eyes on the prince. "But you can command me, right? You could command me to forget everything with your Mistvale magic, and all of this will be fine. I won't tell anyone your secrets, Jax. I promise. I won't tell a single soul you're the Dark Raider or who your raider friends are."

Lars's head whipped to the door, his eyes widening. "Keep

your voice down," he hissed even though we were still alone in the room.

"I've already cast a silencing Shield," Jax replied just as fast. "No one can hear us."

My head whipped to the side. *Silencing Shield?* But I didn't see anything. Turning my attention back to him, I practically begged, "Please, release me. Command me. Do whatever you need to do to feel safe so you can free me. Please, Jax. You promised."

Jax placed his hands on his hips, his fingers tapping them repeatedly. "My psychic magic doesn't work like that. I can command you not to speak of it, but I can't command you to forget."

"Then command me not to speak. I'll never tell anyone, and it doesn't matter if I remember. Your secret's safe with me. *Please,* just let me go!" I grabbed his sweater with my uninjured hand, my fingers digging into him like claws. I was met with firm muscle underneath that jumped at the contact.

He stared at my hand, and the muscle in his jaw pumped. A fleeting emotion washed over his face. Longing. Regret. Or perhaps despair. I couldn't tell because it passed so quickly.

Fingers covering mine, his expression filled with sorrow. "Elowen . . . I want to—"

"She knows too much, Jax," Phillen interrupted on a low growl. "We're *all* at risk if the truth comes to light. You know what that means, and you know what you promised all of us when we went down this road with you." He raised his eyebrows, and a silent exchange took place between them. "I have a family, Jax." His face burned with meaning.

"But *command* me not to tell anyone," I tried again. "Even if you can't make me forget, that'll fix that I've discovered your true identity. Right?"

Jax tore both hands through his hair simultaneously again before shaking his head. "No, it won't. If another fairy with magic like mine commanded you to tell the truth, if his or her magic was superior, it would overpower mine. You would be forced to speak of what you know, and it would implicate all of us."

My fingers gripped his sweater more. "Then we can do a fairy bargain that promises I won't be able to tell anyone!"

He slowly shook his head. "A fairy bargain only ensures you're punished if you speak. It can't stop you from talking if a Mistvale fairy commands you."

I released his sweater and threw my hand up. "But what are the chances of that happening? I'll stay away from Mistvale. I'll never speak to anyone from there who may have the power to do that. I promise. Please, Jax. *Please.*"

But Phillen's glare on Jax held firm, and Lars leaned closer to Jax and whispered, "Phillen's right. We can't take that chance, no matter how small. You promised us, Jax."

Prince Adarian's jaw locked, and his attention collided with mine. Another flash of raw emotion flitted through his eyes. Aching regret meshed with a flash of . . . fear.

My head snapped back as I struggled to understand that, but then he uttered, "I'm sorry, Elowen. I'm so sorry."

And I *knew*. I knew to the bottom of my heart that any chance of a new life, freedom, and independence had just disappeared from my grasp like mist on the wind.

And with a crashing realization, understanding dawned on me.

My freedom was entirely lost.

Because I'd uncovered the identity of the Dark Raider, I was now a liability to them all. And one look at Jax's intent expression told me that despite our deal, he wasn't going to let me go.

"You're not going to free me, are you?" I choked.

Jax's eyes dimmed, and slowly, he shook his head. He reached for me, tried to touch me, but I whipped back.

"No, you *never* touch me again!"

His eyes shuttered, and his jaw locked, but I held my ground as my shoulders heaved in a quiet sob.

Jax wouldn't release me now. And given all that I knew, any hope I'd once had of being free of my caged life disappeared like a dream. A coveted, hopeful, *stupid* dream.

I was so foolish to think my life would ever be anything else, because the crown prince of Stonewild Kingdom was now my new guardian. Forever, Jax would have to keep me close. Confined. Watched. *Owned*.

And I would never be allowed to escape or be free.

My collar rattled violently at my throat as hatred for him

instantly ignited inside me. Dark, burning hatred at what he was forcing on me erupted like a volcano within.

And when I seethed and cast my rage toward the prince, that fleeting flash of fear I'd witnessed earlier vanished, and in its place, the heir to the throne emerged.

An icy mask descended over his features. The prince's shoulders straightened, and his aura swelled. And his next words confirmed all that I feared.

"Nellip, escort Elowen back to her chambers. She's not to leave there again until I command it."

DON'T MISS BOOK TWO IN
FAE OF WOODLANDS & WILD

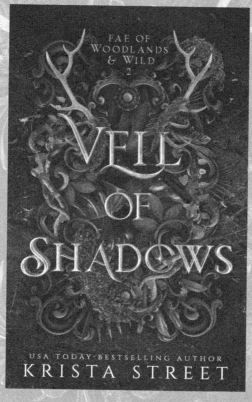

FAE OF
WOODLANDS
& WILD
2

VEIL
OF
SHADOWS

USA TODAY BESTSELLING AUTHOR
KRISTA STREET

After being locked away by the ruthless Dark Raider,
Elowen's fate lies in the hands of her captor, so she
must choose: fight him at every turn or accept that
life as she knew it has irrevocably changed.

ABOUT THE AUTHOR

Krista Street loves writing in multiple genres: fantasy, sci-fi, romance, and dystopian. Her books are cross-genre and often feature complex characters, plenty of supernatural twists, and romance in every story. She loves writing about coming-of-age characters who fight to find their place in this world while also finding their one true mate.

Krista Street is a Minnesota native but has lived throughout the U.S. and in another country or two. She loves to travel, read, and spend time in the great outdoors. When not writing, Krista is either chasing her children, spending time with her husband and friends, sipping a cup of tea, or enjoying the hidden gems of beauty that Minnesota has to offer.

THANK YOU

Thank you for reading *Kingdom of Faewood,* book one, in the *Fae of Woodlands & Wild* trilogy.

To learn more about Krista's other books and series, visit her website. Links to all of her books, along with links to her social media platforms, are available on every page.

www.kristastreet.com

Made in United States
Orlando, FL
29 May 2025

61690983R00225